THE SCREAMING MIMI

FREDRIC BROWN

THE SCREAMING MIMI
FREDRIC BROWN

FIRST PUBLISHED 1949

BLACKMASK.COM EDITION 2004
REVISED, MARCH 2005

ISBN: 1-59654-033-8

BLACKMASK ONLINE IS A DIVISION OF DISRUPTIVE PUBLISHING, INC.

CONTENTS

CHAPTER 1

YOU CAN never tell what a drunken Irishman will do. You can make a flying guess; you can make a lot of flying guesses.

You can list them in the order of their probability. The likely ones are easy: He might go after another drink, start a fight, make a speech, take a train . . . You can work down the list of possibilities; he might buy some green paint, chop down a maple tree, do a fan dance, sing "God Save the King," steal an "oboe . . . You can work on down and down to things that get less and less likely, and eventually you might hit the rock bottom of improbability: He might make a resolution and stick to it.

I know that that's incredible, but it happened. A guy named Sweeney did it, once, in Chicago. He made a resolution, and he had to wade through blood and black coffee to keep it, but he kept it. Maybe, by most people's standards, it wasn't a good resolution, but that's aside from the point. The point is that it really happened.

Now we'll have to hedge a bit, for truth is an elusive thing. It never quite fits a pattern. Like—well, "a drunken Irishman named Sweeney"; that's a pattern, if anything is. But truth is seldom that simple.

His name really was Sweeney, but he was only five-eighths Irish and he was only three-quarters drunk. But that's about as near as truth ever approximates a pattern, and if you won't settle for that, you'd better quit reading. If you don't, maybe you'll be sorry, for it isn't a nice story. It's got murder in it, and women and liquor and gambling and even prevarication. There's murder before the story proper starts, and murder after it ends; the actual story begins with a naked woman and ends with one, which is a good opening and a good ending, but everything between isn't nice. Don't say I didn't warn you. But if you're still with me, let's get back to Sweeney.

Sweeney sat on a park bench, that summer night, next to God. Sweeney rather liked God, although not many people did. God was a tallish, scrawny old man with a short but tangled beard, stained with nicotine. His full name was Godfrey; I say his full name advisedly, for no one, not even Sweeney, knew whether it was his first name or his last. He was a little cracked, but not much. No more, perhaps, than the average for his age of the bums who live on the near north side of Chicago and hang out, when the weather is good, in Bughouse Square. Bughouse Square has another name, but the other name is much less appropriate. It is between Clark and Dear-bore Streets, just south of the Newberry Library; that's its horizontal location. Vertically speaking, it's quite a bit nearer hell than heaven. I mean, it's bright with lights but dark with the shadows of the defeated men who sit on the benches, all night long.

Two o'clock of a summer night, and Bughouse Square had quieted down. The soapbox speakers were gone, and the summer night crowds of strollers who were not habitues of the square were long in bed. On the grass and on the benches, men slept. Their shoelaces were tied in hard knots so their shoes would not be stolen in the night. The theft of money from their pockets was the least of their worries; there was no money there to steal. That was why they slept.

"God," said Sweeney, "I wish I had another drink." He shoved his disreputable hat an inch farther back upon his disreputable head.

"And I," said God. "But not bad enough."

"*That* stuff again," Sweeney said.

God grinned a little. He said, "It's true, Sweeney. You know it is." He pulled a crumpled package of cigarettes from his pocket, gave one to Sweeney, and lighted one himself.

Sweeney dragged deeply at the fag. He stared at the sleeping figure on the bench across from him, then lifted his eyes a little to the lights of Clark Street beyond. His eyes were a bit blurry from the drink; the lights looked haloed, but he knew they weren't. There wasn't a breath of breeze. He felt hot and sweaty, like the park, like the city. He took his hat off and fanned himself with it. Then some three-quarter drunken impulse made him hold the hat still and stare at it. It had been a new hat three weeks ago; he'd bought it while he was still working at the *Blade*. Now it looked like nothing on earth; it had been run over by an auto, it had rolled in a muddy gutter, it had been sat on and stepped on. It looked like Sweeney felt.

He said, "God," and he wasn't talking to Godfrey. Neither, for that matter, was he talking to anyone else. He put the hat back on his head.

He said, "I wish I could sleep." He stood up. "Going to walk a few blocks. Come along?"

"And lose the bench?" God wanted to know. "Naw. I guess I'll go to sleep, Sweeney. See you around." God eased himself over sidewise onto the bench, resting his head in the curve of his arm.

Sweeney grunted and walked out the path to Clark Street. He swayed a little, but not much. He walked across the night, south on Clark Street, past Chicago Avenue. He passed taverns, and wished he had the price of a drink. A cop, coming toward him, said, "Hi, Sweeney," and Sweeney said, "Hi, Pete," but kept on walking. And he thought about one of Godfrey's pet theories and he thought, the old bastard's right; you can get anything you want if you want it badly enough. He could easily have hit Pete for half a check or even a buck—if he'd wanted a drink that bad. Maybe tomorrow he'd want one that bad.

Not yet, although he felt like a violin's E-string that was tuned too tight. Damn it, why *hadn't* he stopped Pete? He needed a drink; he needed about six more shots, or say half a pint, and that would put him over the hump and he could sleep. When had he slept last? He tried to think back, but things were foggy. It had been in an areaway on Huron over near the El, and it had been night, but had it been last night or the night before or the night before that? What had he done yesterday?

He passed Huron, Erie. He thought maybe if he walked on down to the *Loop,* some of the boys from the *Blade* would be hanging out in the place on Randolph and he could borrow something there. Had he-been there yet this time, this drunk? Damn the fog in his brain. And how far gone was he now? Did he still look all right to go into the place on Randolph?

He-watched along the windows for a mirrored one, and found it. He looked at himself and decided he didn't look too bad, too far gone. His hat was out of shape and he didn't have a necktie and his suit was baggy, naturally, but—Then he stepped closer and wished he hadn't because that was too close and he really saw himself. Bleary red eyes, a beard that must be at least three days, maybe four, and the horrible dirtiness of his shirt collar. It had been a white shirt a week ago. And he saw the stains on his suit.

He looked away arid started walking again. He knew now he couldn't look up any of the boys from the paper, not at this stage. Earlier on a drunk, yes, when he still looked all right. Or maybe later, when he didn't care how he looked. And, with the realization that he inevitably *would* do just that a few days from now, he started swearing to himself as he walked, hating himself, hating everything and everybody because he hated himself.

He walked across Ontario Street, across the night. He was swearing aloud as he walked, but didn't know he was doing it. He thought, The Great Sweeney Walking Across the Night, and tried to throw his thoughts out of perspective, but they wouldn't throw. Looking into the mirror had been bad. But, worse than that, now that he was thinking about himself, he could smell himself—the stale sweat of his body. He hadn't been out of the clothes he was wearing since—how long ago was it his landlady had refused to give him the key to his room? Ohio Street. Damn it, he'd better quit walking south or he would find himself in the Loop, so he turned east. Where *was* he going? What did it matter? Maybe if he walked long enough he'd get so damned tired he could sleep. Only he'd better stay within easy distance of the square so he'd have a place to flop if he felt ready.

Hell, he'd do anything for a drink—except, the way he looked and felt tonight, look up anybody he knew.

Someone was coming toward him on the sidewalk. A pretty boy in a bright checked sport jacket. Sweeney's fists clenched. What would be his chances if he slugged the fairy, grabbed his wallet and ran into the alley? But he hadn't ever done that before and his reactions were too slow. Much too slow. The fairy, edging to the outside of the sidewalk, was past him before Sweeney could make up his mind.

A sedan went by, slowly, and Sweeney saw that it was a squad car with two big coppers in it, and he went a little weak at the narrowness of his escape. He concentrated on walking straight and looking sober and realized that he was still swearing to himself and stopped. It would be hell on wheels to be pinched right now and face a drinkless tomorrow. The squad car cruised on without slowing down.

He hesitated at the corner of Dearborn and decided to walk back north on State Street, so he went another block east. A streetcar rolled by on flat wheels, sounding like the end of the world. An empty taxi cruised by, heading south, and for a minute Sweeney considered hailing it and going down to Randolph, telling the driver to wait until he went inside and got some money. But, hell, the taxi probably wouldn't stop for him if he hailed it, the way he looked. And anyway it was past now.

He turned north on State Street. Past Erie, Huron. He was feeling a little better now. Not much, but a little. Superior Street. Superior Sweeney, he thought. Sweeney Walking Across the Night, Across Time—

And then, quite suddenly, he was aware of the crowd standing around the entrance door of the apartment building a quarter of a block ahead of him.

It wasn't much of a crowd. Just a dozen or so queerly assorted people-1— the odd random dozen that would collect first on North State Street at two-thirty in the morning, standing there looking through the glass doors into the hallway of the building. And there seemed to be a funny noise that Sweeney couldn't quite place. It sounded almost like an animal growling.

Sweeney didn't hasten his steps. Probably, he realized, just a drunk that had had a fall or been sapped, lying unconscious or dead—in there until the ambulance came and collected him. Probably lying in a pool of blood; not as many as a dozen people would be standing there looking at him if he was just out cold. Common drunks are all too common *in* that part of Chicago. And the thought of blood didn't fascinate Sweeney. In his days as a legman, he'd seen enough blood to last him. Like the tune he was right after the cops going into the pool hall on Townsend Street where the four hop heads had had the razor party—

He started but around the people standing there without even turning to look over their shoulders. He almost got past, before three things stopped him; two of them were sounds and the third was a silence.

The silence was the silence of the crowd—if you can call a dozen people a crowd, and I guess you can if they're pressed two deep around a six-foot wide double doorway. One of the sounds was the siren of an approaching police car, less than a block away, just slowing down on Chicago Avenue to the north, getting ready to swing the corner into State Street. Maybe, Sweeney realized, what was in the hallway of the building was a corpus delicti. And if it was, with the cops coming, it wasn't smart to be seen head-ing *away* from the scene of a crime. The cops grabbed you to ask questions. If you were standing there gawking instead they'd shove you away and tell you to move on, and then you could move on. The other sound was a rep-etition of the one he'd heard first and he heard it clearly now, over the silence of the crowd and under the wail of the siren; it *was* the growling of an animal.

Add up all those reasons, and you can't blame him, can you? Not even after everything it led to. Sweeney turned and looked. . He couldn't see anything, of course, except the backs of a dozen miscellaneous people. He couldn't hear anything except the growling of an animal in front of him and the wail of a police siren behind him. The car was swinging in to the curb.

Maybe it was the sound of the car, maybe it was the sound of the animal, but some of the people in the middle of the group started backing away from the glass double door of the apartment building. And Sweeney saw the glass doors, and—through them. Not very clearly, because there wasn't any light on inside the hallway. Just the light that came in from the street lamps illuminated the scene within.

He saw the dog first, because the dog was nearest the glass, looking out through it. Dog? It *must* be a dog, here in Chicago; if you'd seen it out in the woods, you'd have taken it for a wolf, and a particularly large and menacing wolf at that. It was standing stiff-legged about four feet back from the glass doors; the hairs on the back of its neck were raised and its lips were drawn back in a tight snarl that showed teeth that looked an inch long. Its eyes glowed yellow.

Sweeney shivered a little as his eyes met those yellow ones. And they *did* seem to meet Sweeney's; naked yellow savagery boring into red, bleary weariness.

It almost sobered him, and it made him look away, uneasily, at what lay on the floor of the hallway beside, and slightly behind, the dog. It was the figure of a woman, lying face down on the carpeting.

The word *figure* is not lightly used. Her white shoulders gleamed, even in that dim light, above a strapless white silk evening gown that molded every beautiful contour of her body —at least those contours visible when a woman is lying face downward—and Sweeney caught his alcoholic breath at the sight of her.

He couldn't see her face, for the top of her page-boy-bobbed blonde head was toward bun, but he know that her face would be beautiful. It would *have* to be; women don't come with bodies as beautiful as that without faces to match.

He thought she moved a little. The dog growled again, a low-pitched sound under the high-pitched squeal of brakes as the police car stopped at the curb. Without turning to look behind him, Sweeney heard the doors of the car open, and the heavy sound of footsteps. A hand on Sweeney's shoulder pushed him aside, not too gently, and a voice that meant business asked, "What's wrong? Who phoned?" But the voice wasn't talking to Sweeney particularly, and he didn't answer it, nor turn.

Nobody answered.

Sweeney teetered a little from the push, and then recovered his balance. He could still see into the hallway.

There was a flashlight in the hand of the blue-serged man beside him, and with a click it shot a beam of bright white light into the dun hallway beyond the glass doors. It caught the yellow glow of the dog's savage eyes and the yellow glow of the bobbed blonde hair of the woman; it caught the white gleam of her shoulders and the white gleam of her dress-.

The man holding the flashlight pulled in his breath in a soft little whistle and didn't ask any more questions. He took a step forward and reached for the knob of the door.

The dog quit growling and crouched to spring. The silence was worse than the growl. The man in blue serge took his hand off the knob as though he'd found it red hot.

"The hell," he said. He put a hand inside the left lapel of his coat, but didn't draw the gun. Instead, he addressed the little knot of people again. "What goes on here? Who phoned? Is the dame in there sick or drunk or what?"

Nobody answered. He asked, "Is that *her* dog?"

Nobody answered. A man in a gray suit was beside the man in blue serge. He said, "Take it easy, Dave. We don't want to shoot the pooch if we don't have to."

"Okay," said Blue Serge. "So you open the door and pet the dog while I take care of the dame. That ain't no dog anyway; it's a wolf or a devil."

"Well—" Gray Suit reached a hand for the door, and pulled it back as the dog crouched again and bared its fangs.

Blue Serge snickered. He asked, "What way the call? You took it."

"Just said a woman lying passed out in the hallway. Didn't mention the dog. Guy put in the call from tavern on the corner north; gave his name."

"Gave a name," said Blue Serge, cynically. "Look, if I was sure the dame was just passed-out drunk, we could phone the humane society to pull off the pooch. They could handle it. I *like* dogs; but I don't want to shoot that one. Probably belongs to the dame and thinks he's protecting her."

"Thinks hell," said Gray Suit. "He damn well is. I like dogs, too. But I wouldn't swear that thing's a dog. Well—"

Gray Suit started peeling off his suit coat. He said, "So okay, I'll wrap this around my arm and you open the door and when the dog jumps me, I'll clip him with the butt of—"

"Lookit—the dame's moving!"

The dame *was* moving. She was lifting her head. She pushed up a little with her hands—Sweeney noticed now that she wore long white cloth gloves that came halfway to her elbows, and lifted her head so her eyes stared full into the bright spotlight of the flashlight's beam.

Her face *was* beautiful. Her eyes looked dazed, unseeing.

"Drunk as hell," Blue Serge said. "Look, Harry, you might kill the dog, even if you clip it with the butt of your gun, and somebody'd raise hell. The dame would raise hell when she sobers up. I'll wait here and keep watch and you get the station on the two-way and tell 'em to send the humane guys here with a net or whatever they use and—"

There was a gasp from several throats that shut Blue Serge up as suddenly as though a hand had been clapped across his mouth.

Somebody said "Blood," almost inaudibly.

Weakly, as in a daze, the woman was trying to get up. She got her knees under her body and had pushed herself up until her arms were straight. The dog beside her moved quickly, and Blue Serge swore and yanked at his shoulder-bolstered gun as the dog's muzzle went toward the woman's face. But before the gun was out, the dog had licked the woman's face once with a long red tongue, whimpering.

And then, as both detectives made a quick move toward the door, the dog crouched again and growled.

But the woman was still getting up. Everyone could see the blood now, an oblong stain of it on the front of her white evening dress, over the abdomen. And—*in* the bright spotlight that made the thing seem like an act on a stage or something seen in the glass screen of a televised horror show—they could see the five-inch-long cut in the white cloth in the center of the oblong stain.

Gray Suit said, "Jesus, a shiv. The Ripper."

Sweeney got shoved farther-to one side as the two detectives pushed closer. He stepped around behind them, watching over their shoulders; he'd forgotten all about his idea of getting away as soon as he could. He could have walked away now and nobody would have noticed. But he didn't.

Gray Suit was standing with his coat half on and half off, frozen in the act of removing it. He jerked it back on now, and his shoulder jarred Sweeney's chin.

He barked, "Phone on the two-way for an ambulance and homicide, Dave. I'll try to crease the dog."

His shoulder hit Sweeney's chin again as he, too, pulled a gun from his shoulder holster. His voice got calm suddenly, as the gun was in his hand. He said, "Reach for the knob, Dave. The dog'll freeze to jump you and I'll have a clear shot. I think I can crease him."

But he didn't raise the gun, and Dave didn't move to reach for the knob. For the incredible thing was happening, the thing that Sweeney wasn't ever going to forget—and that, probably, no one of the fifteen or twenty people who, by now, were \ in front of the doorway was ever going to forget.

The woman in the hallway had one hand on the wall now, beside the row of mailboxes and buzzer buttons. She was struggling to a standing position now, her body erect, but still resting on one knee. The bright white light of the flash framed her like a spotlight on a stage, the whiteness of her dress and gloves and skin and the redness of that oblong patch of blood. Her eyes were still dazed. It must have been shock, Sweeney realized, for that knife wound couldn't have been deep or serious or it would have bled much, much more. She closed her eyes now as, swaying a little, she got up off the Other knee and stood straight.

And the incredible thing happened.

The dog padded back and reared up behind her, on his hind feet but without pushing his forepaws against her. His teeth went to the back of the white dress, the strapless evening gown, caught something, and pulled out and down. And the something—they found out later—was a white silk tab attached to a long zipper.

Gently the dress fell off and became a white silken circle around her feet. She had worn nothing under the dress, nothing at all.

For what seemed like minutes, but was probably about ten seconds, nobody moved, nothing moved. Nothing happened, except that the flashlight shook just a little in Blue Serge's hand.

Then the woman's knees began to bend under her and she went down slowly—not falling, just sinking down like someone who is too weary to stand any longer—on top of the white circle of silk in which she had stood.

Then a lot of things happened at once. Sweeney breathed again, for one thing. And Blue Serge sighted his gun very carefully toward the dog and pulled the trigger. The dog fell and lay in the hallway and Blue Serge went through the door and called back over his shoulder to Gray Suit, "Get the ambulance, Harry. Then tie that damn dog's legs; I don't think I killed him. I just creased bun."

And Sweeney backed away and nobody paid any attention to him as he walked north to Delaware and then turned west to Bughouse Square.

Godfrey wasn't on the bench, but he couldn't have been gone long, for the bench was still empty and benches don't stay empty long on a summer night. Sweeney sat down and waited till the old man came back.

"Hi, Sweeney," God said. He sat down beside Sweeney. "Got a pint," he said. "Want a slug?"

It had been a silly question and Sweeney didn't bother to answer it; he held out his hand. And God hadn't expected an answer; he was holding out the bottle. Sweeney took a long pull.

"Thanks," he said. "Listen, she was beautiful, God. She was the most beautiful dame—" He took another, shorter pull at the bottle and handed it back. He said, "I'd give my right arm."

"Who?" God asked.

"The dame. I was walking north on State Street and—" He stopped, realizing he couldn't tell about it. He said, "Skip it. How'd you get the likker?"

"Stemmed a couple blocks." God sighed. "I told you I could get a drink if I wanted it bad enough; I just didn't want it bad enough before. A guy can get anything he wants, if he wants it bad enough."

"Nuts," Sweeney said automatically. Then, suddenly, he laughed. *"Anything?"*

"Anything you want," said God, dogmatically. "It's the easiest thing in the world, Sweeney. Take rich men. Easiest thing in the world; anybody can get rich. All you got to do is want money so bad it means more to you than anything else. Concentrate on money and you get it. If you want other things worse, you don't."

Sweeney chuckled. He was feeling swell now; that long drink had been just what he needed. He'd kid the old man by getting him to argue his favorite subject.

"How about women?" he said.

"What do you mean, how about women?" God's eyes looked a little foggy; he was getting drunker. And a touch of Bostonian broad *a* was coming back into his speech, as it always did when he was really drunk. "You mean could you get any particular woman you wanted?"

"Yeah," said Sweeney. "Suppose there's a particular dame, for instance, I'd like to spend a night with. Could I do that?"

"'If you wanted to bad enough, of course you could, Sweeney. If you concentrated all your efforts, direct and indirect, to that one objective, sure. Why not?"

Sweeney laughed again.

He leaned his head back, looking up into the dark green leaves of the trees. The laugh subsided to a chuckle and he took off his hat and fanned himself with it. Then he stared at the hat as though he had never seen it before, and began to dust it off carefully with the sleeve of his coat to reshape it so it looked more like a hat. He worked with the absorbed concentration of a child threading a needle.

God had to ask him a second time before he heard the question. Not that it hadn't been a foolish question to begin with; God hadn't expected an answer, verbally. He was holding out the bottle.

Sweeney didn't take it. He put his hat back on and stood up. He winked at God and said, "No, thanks, pal. I got a date."

CHAPTER 2

DAWN was different. Dawn's always different.

Sweeney opened his eyes and it was dawn, a hot, gray, still dawn. Leaves hung listlessly on the trees over his head and the ground was hard under him. All his body ached. His mouth felt and tasted as though the inside of it was caked with something unmentionable—unmentionable here, that is, not to Sweeney. He mentioned it to himself and ran his tongue across his lips to moisten them. He swallowed a few times and got the inside of his mouth moist.

He rubbed his eyes with the hairy backs of dirty hands and swore at a bird that was making a hell of a racket in a nearby tree. He sat up and leaned forward, his face in his hands, the bristle of his beard coarse against the palms of them. A streetcar went by on Clark Street and it didn't sound any louder than an earthquake or the crack of doom. Not much louder, anyway.

Awakening is never a good thing; sometimes it can be a horrible thing. With the cumulative hangover of two weeks of drinking, it *is* a horrible thing.

But the thing to do, Sweeney knew, is to get moving, not to sit there and suffer, not to lie back down on the hard ground and try to go back to sleep, because you can't ever go back to sleep when it's like that. It's hell on wheels, till you orient yourself; get wide awake and oriented and it's merely hell, one dull aching hell until you get a few drinks under your belt Then it's all right. Or is it?

Sweeney pushed the ground away from him and stood up. His legs worked. They carried him off the grass to the cement and along the walk to the bench where Godfrey lay still asleep and snoring gently. On the bench next to him lay the bottle, empty.

Sweeney pushed God's feet back and sat down gingerly on the edge of the bench. He put his rough chin in his filthy hands and rested his elbows on his knees, but he didn't close his eyes. He kept them open.

Had he finally gone over the edge, he wondered. The dame and the dog. He'd never hallucinated before. The dame and the dog.

He didn't believe it. It was one of the few things that couldn't have happened. So it hadn't happened. That was logic.

He held his hand out in front of him and it was shaking, plenty, but no worse than it had before at times like this. He put it back down on the bench and used it and his other hand to push himself up. His legs still worked. They carried him across the square to Dearborn and south on Dearborn—a walking ache rather than a man—to Chicago Avenue. Brakes squealed as a taxi swerved to avoid hitting him as he crossed Chicago Avenue diagonally, without looking to either side. The taxi driver yelled something at him. Sweeney walked along the south side of Chicago Avenue to State Street and turned south.

He walked three-quarters of a block and there was the Door. He stopped and stared at it, and after a while he went close to it and looked through the glass. It was dim inside, but he could see through the hallway to the door at the back.

A newsboy came along, a bag of papers slung over his shoulder. He stopped beside Sweeney. He said, "Jeeze, that's where it happened, ain't it?"

"Yeah," said Sweeney.

"I *know* the broad," said the newsboy. "I leave her a paper." He reached past Sweeney for the knob of the door. "Gotta get in to leave some papers." Sweeney stepped aside to let him past.

When the newsboy came out, Sweeney went in. He walked back a few steps beside the mailboxes. This, where—he was standing, was where she'd fallen. He looked down, then stooped to look closer; there were a few little dark dots on the floor.

Sweeney stood up again and walked to the back. He opened the door there and looked through it. There was a cement walk that led back to the alley. That was all. He closed the door and nicked the light switch to the left of it, at the foot of the stairs leading upward. Two bulbs went on, one overhead at the foot of the stairs, the other overhead up front, by the mailboxes. The yellow light was sickly in the gray morning. He flicked it off again, then—as he noticed something on the wooden panel of the door—back on again. There were long closely-spaced vertical scratches on the wood. They looked fresh, and they looked like the claw-marks of a dog. They looked as though a dog had lunged against that door and then tried to claw his way through it.

Sweeney turned off the light again and went out, taking with him one of the papers the newsboy had left in clips under several of the mailboxes. He walked past the next corner before he sat down on a step and unfolded the paper.

It was a three-column splash, with two pix, one of the girl and one of the dog. The heading was:

RIPPER ATTACKS
DANCER; SAVED BY
HER FAITHFUL DOG
Fiend Makes Escape;
"Can't Identify," Victim Says

Sweeney studied the two pictures, read the article through, and studied the pictures again. Both were posed, obviously publicity stills. "Devil" was the caption under the picture of the dog, and he looked it. In a newspaper pic, you couldn't see that yellow balefulness in his eyes, but he still didn't look like anything you'd want to meet in an alley. He still looked, Sweeney thought, more like a wolf than a dog, and a bad wolf at that.

But his eyes went back to the woman's picture. The caption, "Yolanda Lang," made Sweeney wonder what her real name was. But—looking at that picture of her—you wouldn't care what her name was. The picture, unfortunately, didn't show as much of her as Sweeney had seen last night It was a waist-up shot, and Yolanda Lang wore a strapless evening gown moulded to show off her outstanding features—which Sweeney well knew to be genuine and not padding—and her soft blonde hair tumbled to her softer white shoulders. Her face was beautiful, too. Sweeney hadn't much noticed her face last night. You couldn't blame him for that.

But it was worth noticing, now that there was less distraction to keep his eyes away from it. It was a face that was sweetly grave and gravely sweet. Except something about the eyes. But on an eighty-line screen newsprint picture you couldn't be sure about that.

Sweeney carefully folded the newspaper and put it down on the step beside him. There was a crooked grin on his face. He got up and trudged back to Bughouse Square. God was still snoring on the bench. Sweeney shook him and God opened his eyes. He stared up blearily at Sweeney and said, "Go away."

Sweeney said, "I am. That's what I came to tell you. Look, I meant it."
"Meant what?"
"What I said last night," Sweeney said. "You're crazy," God said.

That lopsided grin came back to Sweeney's face. He said, "You didn't see her. You weren't there. So long."

He cut across the grass to Clark Street and stood there a minute. He had a, dull headache now, and he wanted a drink damned bad. He held out his hand and watched it shake, and then put it in his pocket so he wouldn't have to think about it. He started walking south on Clark. The sun was up now, slanting down the east-west streets. The traffic was getting heavy, and noisy.

He thought, Sweeney Walking Across the Day. He was sweating, and it wasn't only from the heat. He smelled, too, and he knew it. His feet hurt. He was a hell of a mess, an aching mess, top and bottom and inside and out Sweeney Walking Across the Day.

And across the Loop, and on south to Roosevelt Road. He didn't dare stop. He turned the corner east on Roosevelt Road, kept on going on a block and a half, and turned into the entrance of an apartment building.

He rang a buzzer and stood waiting till the latch on the door clicked. He opened it and trudged up stairs to the third floor. A door at the front was ajar and a bald head stuck through it. The face under the bald head looked at Sweeney, approaching, and a disgusted look came over it.

The door slammed.

Sweeney put a dirty hand on the wall to steady himself and kept on coming. He started to knock on the door, loudly. He knocked a full minute and then put a hand to his forehead to hold it a while, maybe half a minute. He leaned against the wall.

He straightened up and started knocking again, louder.

He heard footsteps shuffle to the door. "Get the hell away or I'll call copper."

Sweeney knocked again. He said, "Call copper then, pally. We'll both go down to the jug and explain."

"What the hell do you want?"

Sweeney said, "Open up." He started knocking again, loud-er. A door down the hall opened and a woman's frightened face looked out.

Sweeney knocked some more. The voice inside said, "All right, *all right*. Just a second." The footsteps shuffled away and back again and the key turned.

The door opened and the bald man stepped back from it. He wore a shapeless bathrobe and scuffed slippers, and apparently nothing else. He was a little smaller than Sweeney, but he had his right hand in the pocket of the bathrobe and the pocket bulged.

Sweeney walked on in and kicked the door shut beside bun. He walked to the middle of the cluttered room. He turned around and said, "Hi, Goetz," mildly.

The bald man was still beside the door.

He said, "What the hell do you want?"

"A double saw," Sweeney said. "You know what for. Or shall I tell you in words of one syllable?"

"Like hell I'll give you a double saw. If you're still harping back to that Goddam horse, I told you I didn't shove the bet. I gave you your fin back. You took it."

"I took it on account," Sweeney said. "I didn't need the money bad enough then to get tough about it. Now I do. So okay, let's review the bidding. You touted me on that oat-burner. It was *your* idea. So I gave you a fin to bet, and the horse came in at five for one, and you tell me you didn't get the bet down for me."

"God damn it, I didn't. The heat was on. Mike's was closed and—"

"You didn't even try Mike's. You just held the bet. If the horse had lost—like you expected—you'd have kept my fin. So whether you got the bet down or not you owe me twenty."

"The hell I do. Get out."

The bald man took his hand out of the bathrobe pocket and there was a little twenty-five calibre automatic in if.

Sweeney shook his head sadly. He said, "If it was twenty grand, I'd be afraid of that thing—maybe. For twenty bucks you wouldn't put a shooting on your record. For a lousy double saw you wouldn't have the cops up here snooping around. Anyway, I don't think you would. I'll gamble on it."

He looked around the room until he saw a pair of pants hanging over the back of the chair. He started for the pants.

The bald man snicked the safety off the little automatic. He said, "You son of a bitch—"

Sweeney picked up the pants by the cuffs and started shaking them. Keys and change hit the carpet and he kept on shaking. He said, "Someday, Goetz, you'll call a man a son of a bitch who *is* a son of a bitch, and he'll take you apart."

A wallet from the hip pocket of the trousers hit the carpet, and Sweeney picked it up. He flipped it open, and grunted. There was only a ten and a five in the wallet.

He took the ten out and put it in his own pocket and tossed the wallet toward the dresser. He said. "What's the matter with the pool ticket racket, Goetz? *That* bad?"

The bald man's face wasn't pretty. He said, "I told you; the heat's on. You got your money. Now get out."

"I got ten," Sweeney said. "I wouldn't take a man's last fin, pally. I'll take the other ten in trade. A bath and a shave and a shirt and socks."

Sweeney peeled off his coat and stepped out of his trousers. He sat down on the edge of the mussed-up bed and took off his shoes. He went into the bathroom and turned on the water to run in the tub.

He came out stark naked, holding a wadded-up ball that had been his shirt, socks and underwear and put it in the wastebasket.

The bald man was still standing by the door, but he'd put the little automatic back into the pocket of the bathrobe.

Sweeney grinned at him. Over the roar of water running into the tub, he said, "Don't call copper now, Goetz. With me dressed this way, they might get the wrong idea."

He went into the bathroom and shut the door.

He soaked a long time in the tub, and then shaved leisurely with Goetz's razor—providentially an electric one. Sweeney's hands were still shaking.

When he came out, the bald man was back in bed, his back to the room.

"Asleep, darling?" Sweeney asked.

There wasn't any answer.

Sweeney opened a drawer of the dresser and chose a white sport shut with a soft collar. It was tight across the shoulders and the collar wouldn't button, but it was a shirt and it was clean and white. A pair of Goetz's socks proved a bit small, but they went on.

He eyed his own shoes and suit with disgust, but they'd have to do. Goetz's wouldn't fit. Sweeney did the best he could with a shoebrush and a clothes brush. He made sure the ten-dollar bill was still in the pocket of his trousers when he put them on.

He brushed his hat and put that on, and then stopped at the door.

He said, "Nighty-night, pally, and thanks for everything. We're even now." He closed the door quietly and went downstairs and outside into the hot sunlight. He walked north on Dearborn, past the Dearborn Station. In a little restaurant opposite the front of it, he had three cups of black coffee and managed to eat one doughnut of two he ordered. It tasted like library paste, but he got it down.

Under the shadow of the El, two blocks north, he got his shoes shined and then waited, snaking a little, in a tiny cubbyhole in the back of the shop while his suit was sponged and pressed. It needed more than sponging, but it didn't look too bad when he put it back on.

He took a look at himself in the long mirror and decided he looked fair enough by now. There were circles under his eyes and the eyes themselves—well, he wasn't a thing of beauty and a joy forever, and he had to remember to keep his hands in his pockets until he got over the trembling, but he looked human.

He spread the collar of the white sport shirt on the outside of the collar of his coat, and that looked better, too.

He kept to the shady side of the street, walking north across the Loop. He was starting to sweat again, and felt duly already. He had a hunch he'd feel dirty for a long time, no matter how many baths he took. Why did anyone in his right mind live in Chicago in a summer heat wave? Why did anyone live in Chicago at all? Why, for that matter, did anyone live?

Sweeney's headache had quit being dull, now. It was a rhythmic, persistent throbbing in his forehead and behind his eyeballs. And the palms of his hands were wet and felt clammy! despite how hot the rest of him was; and no matter how often he wiped them on the side of his trousers, they were wet and clammy again immediately.

Sweeney Walking Across the Loop. At Lake Street, under the El again, he stopped in at a drugstore for a double bromo and another cup of coffee. He felt like a coiled spring that was tied down too tightly; he felt like a claustrophobic locked in a tiny room; he felt lousy. The coffee seemed to be swishing around in his guts like bilgewater inside a leaky ship—tepid, brackish bilgewater filled with little green algae, if algae are green. Sweeney's were, and they wriggled, too.

He crossed Wacker Drive, hoping that a car would hit him, but none did; he walked across the bridge in the bright hot glare of sunshine and he lifted one foot and put it down and lifted the other and put that down, for six blocks to Erie Street; he walked east past Rush and then—not daring to stop —he put his clammy hands into his pockets and went into the areaway between two buildings and through an open doorway.

This was home, if it still was. This was the biggest hurdle, for today. He took his right hand out of a pocket and rapped gently on a door off the downstairs hallway. He put his hand back quickly.

Heavy footsteps came slowly, and the door opened.

Sweeney said, "Hello, Mrs. Randall. Uh—"

Her sniff cut off whatever he'd been going to say. She said, "No, Mr. Sweeney."

"Uh—you mean you've rented my room?"

"I mean—no, you can't get in it to get something to hock to keep on drinking. I told you that last week, twice."

"Did you?" asked Sweeney vaguely. He didn't remember, or did he? Now that she spoke of it, one of the two times came back to him dimly. "Guess I was pretty drunk." He took a deep breath. "But it's over now. I'm sober."

She sniffed again. "How about the three weeks you owe me? Thirty-six dollars."

Sweeney fumbled out the bills in his pockets, a five and three singles. "All I got," he said. "I can give you eight dollars on account."

The landlady looked from the bills up to Sweeney's face. "I guess you're on the level, Sweeney, about sobering up. If you've *got* money, you aren't after stuff to hock. You could do a lot of drinking on eight dollars."

"Yes," Sweeney said.

She stepped back from the door. "Come on in." And, after he had followed her in: "Sit down. Put your money back in your pocket. You'll need it worse than I do, till you get started again. How long'll that be?"

Sweeney sat down. "A few days," he said. "I can raise some money, when I'm okay again."

He put his hands, and the bills, back in his pocket. "Uh—I'm afraid I lost my key. Do you have—"

"You didn't lose it. I took it away from you a week ago Friday. You were trying to carry out your phonograph to hock it."

Sweeney dropped his head into his hands. "Lord, *did* I?"

"You didn't. I made you take it back. And I made you give me the key. Your clothes are all there, too, except your topcoat and overcoat. You must have taken them before that. And your typewriter. And your watch—unless you got it on."

Sweeney shook his head slowly. "Nope. It's gone. But thanks for saving the other stuff."

"You look like hell. Want a cup of coffee? I got some on."

"It's running out of my ears," Sweeney told her. "But—yes, I'll have another cup. Black."

He studied her as she got up and waddled over to the stove. There ought to be more landladies like Mrs. Randall, he thought. Tough as nails on the outside (they had to be to run a rooming house) and soft as butter inside. Most of them were tough all the way through.

She came back with the coffee and he drank it. He got his key and went up the stairs. He got inside and got the door closed before he started to shake, and he stood there, leaning against the inside of the door until the worst of it was over. Then he made it to the washbasin and was sick at his stomach, and that helped, although the sound of the water running made his head hurt worse.

When that was over, he wanted to lie down and sleep, but instead he stripped off his clothes, put on a bathrobe, and went down the hall to the bathroom. He drew himself a hot tub and soaked in it for a long time before he went back to his room.

Before he dressed again, he rolled up the spotted and worn suit he'd been wearing and the too-small shut and socks he'd taken from the man named Goetz and put them into the wastebasket. He put on all clean clothes, including his best summer-weight suit. He put on a silk tie that had cost him five bucks and his best pair of shoes.

He straightened up the room carefully, even meticulously. He turned on the radio side of his radio-phono combination until he got a time announcement between programs and set the clock on his dresser and wound it. It was half-past eleven. Then he got his Panama hat out of the closet and went out. Mrs. Randall's door opened as he started down the stairs. She called out, "Mr. Sweeney?" and he leaned over the railing to look toward her. "Yes?"

"Forgot to tell you there was a phone call for you this morning, early, about eight o'clock. A Walter Krieg, from the paper you work for—or used to work for. Which is it?"

"Used to work for, I guess," Sweeney said. "What'd he say? What'd you say?"

"He asked for you and I said you weren't in. He said if you came back before nine to have you call him. You didn't—not that I was expecting you to—so I kinda forgot it. That's all that was said."

Sweeney thanked her and went on out. At the corner drugstore he bought a half pint of whiskey and put it in his hip pocket. Then he went into the phone booth, dialed the *Blade,* and asked for the managing editor by name.

"Krieg?" he said. "This is Sweeney. Just got home. Got your message. Sober. What you want?"

"Nothing now. It's too late, Sweeney. Sorry."

"All right, it's too late and you're sorry. But what *did* you want?"

"Eyewitness story, if you're sober enough to remember what you saw last night. A beat copper said you were around when the lid came off that Yolanda Lang business. Remember it?"

"More than the lid came off, and I damn well remember it. Why's it too late? You got one edition on the street but the main one coming up and two others. The home edition's not in, is it?"

"Going in in fifteen minutes. Take you longer'n that to—"

"Quit wasting time," Sweeney said. "Put a rewrite man on the phone now. I can give him half a column in five minutes. Gimme Joe Carey; he can take it fast."

"Okay, Sweeney. Hang on."

Sweeney hung on, getting his thoughts organized, until he heard Joe's voice. Then he started talking, fast.

When he was through, he put the receiver back on the hook and leaned weakly against the wall of the phone booth. He hadn't asked to have Walter

Krieg put back on the line; that could wait. He'd do better going in and seeing Walter personally.

But not yet, not just yet.

He went back to his room and put the little half pint bottle of whiskey on the arm of the comfortable Morris chair and a shot glass beside it. He hung tip his suit coat and Panama, and loosened his collar and tie.

Then he went over to the phonograph and squatted down on his haunches in front of the shelf of albums. He studied the titles. Not that it-mattered; he knew which one he was going to hear: the Mozart 40.

No, you wouldn't have thought it to look at him, maybe, but that was Sweeney's favorite—the *Symphony No. 40, in G Minor, K. 550.* He stacked the three records on the phonograph, flicked the switch to start the first one, and went over to the Morris chair to sit and listen.

The first movement, allegro molto.

Why should I tell you anything about Sweeney? If you know the Mozart 40, the dark restlessness of it, the macabre drive behind its graceful counterpoint, then you know Sweeney. And if the Mozart 40 sounds to you like a gay but slightly boring minuet, background for a conversation, then to you Sweeney is just another damn reporter who happens, too, to be a periodic drunk.

But let it pass; what you think and what I think have no bearing on this; on Sweeney unscrewing the top of the half pint bottle and pouring himself a drink. Drinking it.

There are strange things and there are stranger ones. And one of the strangest? A wooden box containing oddments of copper wire and metal plates, a half-dozen spaces of the nothingness called a vacuum, and a black wire which plugs into a hole in the wall from whence cometh our help, whence flows a thing which we call electricity because we do not know what it is. But it flows and inorganic matter lives; a table is prepared before you and revolves, bearing a disk; a needle scrapes in a groove.

A needle dances in a groove and a diaphragm vibrates, and the air about you vibrates. And the thoughts of a man a century and a half dead press upon you; you sit in light and the shadow of the soul of a man long dead. You share the troubled thoughts of a dapper little court musician in a horrible financial mess, perhaps feeling the end of his life was near and working at prodigious speed, turning out in a few weeks the greatest symphony he ever wrote.

Yes, there are strange things. And there was Sweeney, pouring his second drink as the third disk dropped and the second movement started, the lighter andante.

He drank them neat, the third side of the album and the second drink. He sighed and pushed himself up out of the chair; the pain in his head was still there and the pain in his soul, but the shaking of his hands was gone.

He rinsed out the glass and put away the little half pint bottle, still more than half full. He turned over the three records on the phonograph, started it again and sat back down to listen to the rest of the 40.

He closed his eyes and just listened as the second movement ended and the dark-bright minuetto-and-trio of the third movement lived all too briefly and died and gave birth to what he had been waiting for; the bitter final movement, the allegro assai, the power and the melancholy glory.

And then Sweeney sat listening to the silence, and after a while he began to chuckle almost inaudibly to himself.

He was *out* of it now, off the binge, sober. Until the next time, which might be months, might be a couple of years. However long until enough hell accumulated inside him that he'd have to soak it out; until then he could be normal and drink normally. Yes, I know, alcoholics can't do that, but Sweeney wasn't an alcoholic; he could and did drink regularly and normally and only once in a while dive off the deep end into a protracted drunk. There's that type of drinker, too, although of late the alcoholics have been getting most of the ink.

But Sweeney was out of it now, shaken but not shaking, sober. He could even get his job back, he felt sure, if he ate a little crow. He could climb out of debt in a few weeks and be back where he was, wherever *that* was.

Or—

Yes, he *was* sober. But that utterly absurd decision or resolution or whatever it had been—

What if? Why not? *Anything you want.* Didn't God have something there: anything you want if you want it badly enough to concentrate on getting it. Any little thing like a million dollars or any big thing like spending a night with—what was her name?—Yolanda Lang.

He chuckled again, and he closed his eyes and thought back and remembered and saw again that incredible scene behind glass in the State Street hallway.

After a-few seconds he quit chuckling. He told himself: Sweeney, you're asking for trouble. You'll need money, for one thing. A dime-a-dozen reporter couldn't make the grade with that babe. And for an in, you'll have to hunt a ripper. And you might find him.

And that would be bad, Sweeney knew, because Sweeney had a horror—almost a phobia—of cold steel, cold sharp steel. Razor-edged steel in the hands of a madman, a homicidal maniac. A razor-like knife that can slash across your abdomen and spill your guts out on the sidewalk where they won't be a bit of use to you, Sweeney.

Sure, he told himself: You're a God damned fool, Sweeney.

But he'd known that for a long tune.

CHAPTER 3

SWEENEY headed for the *Blade*.

There's a nice pun in that, if you don't mind your puns obvious. *The Blade*. If you saw that pun yourself, forgive me for pointing it out. *You* got it, yes, but somebody else would have missed it. It takes all kinds of people to read a book.

Some people, for instance, see with their eyes; they want descriptions. So, if it interests you (it doesn't interest me) William Sweeney was five feet eleven inches tall and weighed a hundred and sixty-three pounds. He had sandy hair that was receding at the front and getting a little thin on top, but was mostly still there. He had a long thin face, vaguely horse-like but not, on the whole, unpleasing to the uncritical eye. He looked to be about forty-three, which is not strange because that is how old he really was. He wore glasses with light-colored shell rims for reading and working; he could see all right without them for any distance over four or five feet. For that matter, he could work without them if he had to, although he'd get headaches if he did it too long. But it was well that he *could* do without them for a while, because he was going to have to. They'd been in his pocket two weeks ago when he'd started his serious drinking and only God (I don't mean Godfrey) knew where they were now.

He threaded his way across the city room and into the office of the managing editor. He sat down on the arm of the chair across the desk from Krieg. He said, "Hi, Walter."

Krieg looked up and grunted, then finished the letter in his hand and put it down. He opened his mouth and closed it again.

Sweeney said, "I'll say it for you, Walter. First, I'm a son of a bitch to have let you down and gone on a binge without giving you notice. I'm through. You can't mess with guys like me. I'm an anachronism. The days of the drunken reporter are over and a modern newspaper is a business institution run on business lines and not a *Front Page* out of Hecht by MacArthur. You want men you can count on. Right?"

"Yes, you son of—"

"Hold it, Walter. I said it for you, all of it. And anyway, I wouldn't work on your damn pager unless you hired me to. How was the eyewitness story?"

"It was good, Sweeney, damn good. That was a break in a million, your being there."

"You say a cop mentioned I was there. I didn't see one I recognized. Who was it?"

"You'll have to ask Carey; he handled the story. Look, Sweeney, how often do you go on a bat like that? Or are you going to tell me that was the last one?"

"It probably wasn't. It'll happen again; I don't know when. Maybe not for a couple of years. Maybe in six months. So you wouldn't want me to work for you. All right. But since I'm *not* working for you, I got a little check coming for that eyewitness account. I'll let you do me one last favor, Walter. You can give me a voucher to get it now instead of putting it through the channels. That story was worth fifty bucks, if Carey wrote it like I told it to him. Will you settle for Twenty-five?"

Krieg glared at him. "Not a damn cent, Sweeney."

"No? And why the hell not? Since when have you been *that* much of a lousy—"

"Shut up!" The managing editor almost roared it. "God damn it, Sweeney, you're the toughest guy to do a favor for I ever saw. You won't even give me the satisfaction of bawling you out; you take the words out of my mouth so I can't say 'em.. Who told you you were fired? *You* did. The reason you don't get paid for that piddling little story you gave over the phone is that you're still on the payroll. You've lost two days' pay, that's all."

"I don't get it," Sweeney said. "Why two days? I been gone two weeks. What's two days got to do with it?"

"This is a Thursday, Sweeney. You started your drunk two weeks ago tonight and didn't come in Friday morning. Or Saturday. But you had two weeks' vacation coming. Maybe you forgot; you were on the list for September. I gave you a break by switching your dates so you started your vacation a week ago last Monday. You're still on your vacation right now and you're not due back for a few more days yet. Monday, to be exact. Here." Krieg yanked open a drawer of his desk and pulled out three checks. He held them across to Sweeney. "You probably don't remember but you came in to try to get your last check, only we didn't give it to you. It's there, two days short, and two full vacation week checks."

Sweeney took them wonderingly.

Krieg said, "Now get the hell out of here until Monday morning and report for work then."

"The hell," said Sweeney. "I don't believe it"

"Don't then. But—no bull, Sweeney—if it happens again before your *next* vacation, next year, you're through for good."

Sweeney nodded slowly. He stood up.

"Listen, Walter, I—"

"Shut up. Beat it."

Sweeney grinned weakly, and beat it.

He stopped at Joe Carey's desk and said "Hi," and Joe looked up and said, "Hi, yourself. What gives?"

"Want to talk to you, Joe. Had lunch yet?"

"No. Going in—" He looked at his wrist watch. "—in twenty minutes. But listen, Sweeney, if it's a bite you've got in mind, I'm broke as hell. Wife just had another kid last week and you know how that is."

"No," said Sweeney. "Thank God I don't know how that is. Congratulations, though. I presume it's a boy or a girl."

"Yeah."

"Good. Nope, it isn't a bite. Miraculously, I'm solvent There is a God. In fact, do I owe you anything?"

"Five. Two weeks ago last Wednesday. Remember?"

"Vaguely, now that you mention it. So let's eat at Kirby's; I can cash a check there and pay you. I'll wander on down and meet you there."

Sweeney cashed the smallest of the three checks at the bar in Kirby's and then went over to a table to wait for Joe Carey. The thought of food still nauseated him; eating anything at all was going to be so bad he'd rather get it over with before Joe came in. Watching Joe eat was going to be bad enough.

Sweeney ordered a bowl of soup as the least of evils. It tasted like hot dishwater to him, but he managed to get most of it down and shoved the bowl aside as Joe came in and sat down across the table.

He said, "Here's your five, Joe, arid thanks. Say, before I forget, who was it saw me over on State Street last night? I thought I didn't know either of the coppers I saw there."

"Harness bull by the name of Fleming. Pete Fleming."

"Oh," Sweeney said. "I remember now; I met him on Clark Street before that. Let's see—I was walking south on Clark so he must have been going north. I walked south a few more blocks, cut over east and walked north on State. But I didn't see him."

"Probably got there as you were leaving. The car that answered the call— the cops in it were named Kravich and Guerney—cut in their siren on the way. Wherever Fleming was on his beat, he followed the siren and got there after they did. Thanks for the fin, Sweeney."

The waiter came up and Sweeney ordered coffee along with Carey's order.

Then he leaned across the table. He said, "Joe, what gives with this Ripper business? That's what I want to pump you about. I could dig up some of the dope from the morgue files, but you'll know more than they will. First, how long has it been going on?"

"You haven't read the papers for the last ten days?" Sweeney shook his head. "Except for what was in one morning paper today, about the Yolanda Lang business last night There were references to other killings. How many?"

"Besides Yolanda Lang, two—or it could be three. I mean, there was a slashing on the south side two months ago that might or might not be the same guy. Broad by the name of Lola Brent. There were similarities between her case and the three recent ones that make the police think maybe it ties in, but they aren't sure. There are differences, too."

"She die?"

"Sure. So did the two other dames besides this Lang woman. She's the only one who didn't get killed. Pooch saved her. But you know about that."

"What's the last word on Yolanda Lang?" Sweeney asked. "She still in the hospital?"

"Supposed to be released this evening. She wasn't hurt much. Point of the shiv just barely went through the skin. She had a spot of shock; that's all."

"So did some other people," said Sweeney. "Including me."

Joe Carey licked his lips. "You didn't exaggerate that story any, Sweeney?"

Sweeney chuckled. "I underplayed it You should have been there, Joe."

"I'm a married man. Anyway, the cops are going to keep a guard on the Lang femme."

"A *guard?* Why?"

"They figure the killer might be inclined to go back after her because he might think she could put the finger on him. Matter of fact, she can't, or says she can't. A man, tallish, in dark clothes is the best she can do."

"The light was off in the hallway," Sweeney said. "The Ripper's waiting by the back door, at the foot of the stairs, probably standing outside it, holding it a little ajar. He hears her footsteps clicking along the hallway, steps inside and slashes. Only the pooch jumps past her after the guy and he jerks back through the door, almost missing the woman completely with the shiv and just barely gets away from the dog."

"It adds up," Sweeney said. "He'd be able to see her silhouetted against the light from outside through the front door, but he'd just be a shadow to

her. The point is, was he after Yolanda Lang or was he just waiting for whoever came along?"

Carey shrugged. "Could be either way. I mean, she lived there and he
could have been waiting for her because she was coming home after her
last show. On the other hand, if he knew much about her, he knew the
pooch would be along and it looks like he didn't figure on that. He *could*
have, though. Known, I mean, the dog would-walk behind her in the hallway and figure he could slash and get back out the door before the dog got
him. But, if that was it, he missed his timing."

"She got home that time every night?"

"Every week night. She's on last at one-thirty week nights. They have
shows later on Saturday and Sunday nights. She doesn't always go right
home after the last show, though, she said. Sometimes stays around El
Madhouse—that's the night club she's playing—know it?"

Sweeney nodded.

"—sometimes stays around for drinks or what not till they close at three.
Or sometimes has dates and goes out after the show. A dame like that
wouldn't be lonesome except when she wanted to be."

"Who's handling it—outside, I mean."

"Horlick, only he starts vacation Monday. I don't know who Wally will
put on after that."

Sweeney grinned. "Listen, Joe, do me a hell of a big favor, will you? I
want to work on it. *I* can't very well suggest it to Krieg, but you can, next
time you talk to him. Suggest I got an inside start with that eyewitness business and since Horlick's leaving Monday and I'm coming back then, why
not let me do the leg work. He'll fall for it if you suggest it. If *I* ask him—
well, he might not let me, just to be cussed."

"Sure, I can do that, Sweeney. But—you'll have to bone up on the details
on the other cases, and get in with the cops. They got a special Ripper
detail, by the way, working on nothing else. Cap Bline of Homicide's running it and got men under him. And the crime lab's analyzing everything
they can get their hands on, only there hasn't been much to analyze."

"I'll be up on it," Sweeney said. "Between now and Monday I'll study
those files and get in with the cops."

"Why? On your own tune, I mean. You got an angle, Sweeney?"

"Sure," Sweeney lied. "Got the assignment from a fact detective mag to
write up the case, once it's solved. They don't handle unsolved cases, but
it's promised to me once the case is cracked. Ought to get a few hundred
out of it. Joe, if you talk Krieg into giving me the case, so I'll have all the

facts ready to write once they get the guy, I'll cut you in for ten per cent. Ought to get you somewhere between twenty and fifty."

"What have I got to lose? Sure, I was going to do it for nothing."

"But now you'll be convincing," Sweeney said. "For a start, what are the names of the other dames who were slashed, the ones who died? You said the one on the south side a couple months ago was Lola Brent?"

"Check. Ten days ago, Stella Gaylord. Five days ago, Dorothy Lee."

"Any of the others strip teasers or show girls?"

"First one, this Lola Brent, was an ex-chorine. Living with a short-con man named Sammy Cole. Cops figured he killed her, but they couldn't prove it and they couldn't crack him. So they threw the book at him on some fraud charges that came out, and he's still in the clink. So if he *did* kill Lola, he didn't kill the others or make the try for Yolanda."

"What were the other two gals?"

"Stella Gaylord was a B-girl on West Madison Street. The Lee girl was a private secretary."

"How private? Kind that has to watch her periods as well as her commas?"

"I wouldn't know," Carey said. "That didn't come out. She worked for some executive with the Reiss Corporation. Don't remember his name. Anyway, he was in New York on a buying trip."

Joe Carey glanced up at the clock; he'd finished eating. He said, "Look, Sweeney, those are the main points. I haven't got time to give you any more; I got to get back."

"Okay," Sweeney said. "What hospital is the Lang dame in?"

"Michael Reese, but you can't get in to see her. They got cops six deep in that corridor. Horlick tried to get in and couldn't."

"You don't know when she'll be back at El Madhouse?"

"Nope. Her manager could tell you. Guy by the name of Doc Greene."

"What's the dope on him?"

"Listen, Sweeney, I got to get back. Ask *him* what the dope on him is."

Carey stood up. Sweeney reached for his check and got it. "I'm paying this. But tell me where I can locate this Greene character. What's his first name?"

"Dunno. Everybody calls him Doc. But wait—he's in the Goodman Block, Greene with a final *e*. You can find him from that. Or through the El Madhouse proprietor. He books all their acts, I think. So long."

Sweeney took a sip of his coffee, which he'd forgotten to drink, and it was cold. He shuddered with revulsion at the taste of it, and got out of Kirby's quick.

He stood in front a moment, hesitating which way to go, then headed back for the *Blade*. He didn't go to the editorial offices this time, though. He cashed his two other pay checks at the cashier's window and then went to the stack room. He looked through papers of about two months before until he found the one that broke the story on the murder of Lola Brent. He bought that one and all the finals for a week following, and he bought finals for each of the past ten days.

It made quite a stack of papers, even when he'd thrown the stuffing out of the Sunday ones. He caught a cab to take them home.

On the way in, he knocked on Mrs. Randall's door; he paid her the thirty-six dollars he owed her, and paid for two weeks in advance.

Upstairs in his room, he put the pile of papers on his bed, and then, outside in the hall, he looked up Greenes until he found one in the Goodman Block. J. J. Greene, thtrcl.agt. He called the number and, after brief argument with a secretary, got J. J. Greene.

"Sweeney, of the *Blade*," he said. "Could you tell me when your client is being released from Michael Reese?"

"Sorry, Mr. Sweeney, the police have asked me not to give out any information. You'll have to get it from them. Say, are you the reporter who wrote that eyewitness story in today's *Blade!*"

"Yes."

"Nice story. And swell publicity for Yolanda. Too bad she's on the dotted line for three more weeks at El Madhouse, or I could get her on for bigger dough."

"She'll be back dancing in less than three weeks, then?"

"Off the record, nearer three days. It was just a nick."

"Could I drop around and talk to you, Mr. Greene? At your office."

"What about? The police told me not to talk to reporters."

"Not even pass the time of day if you met one on the street? I never saw an agent yet that wouldn't talk to reporters. Maybe I even want to give some of your other clients publicity, and what could the cops find wrong with that? Or have they got something on you?"

Greene chuckled. "I wouldn't invite you here if the cops say not. But I'm leaving the office in about twenty minutes and I generally have a drink at one of the places I book. I have an idea that today I might stop in El Madhouse on my way north. In that case I'd be there in a little over half an hour. If you should happen to drop in—"

"I might just happen to," Sweeney said. "Thanks. Off the record, I take it Miss Lang still is at Michael Reese?"

"Yes. But you won't be able to see her there."

"Won't try it then," Sweeney said. "So long." He hung up the receiver and wiped the sweat off his fore head with a handkerchief. He went back into his room and sat very quietly for five minutes or so. When he thought he could make it, he pushed himself up out of the chair and left.

The sun was very hot and he walked slowly. On State Street, he stopped in a florist's shop and ordered two dozen American Beauties sent to Yolanda Lang at the hospital. After that, he kept plodding steadily through the bright heat until he reached El Madhouse, on Clark near Grand.

There wasn't a uniformed doorman, with a persuasive voice, in front at this hour of the late afternoon; there wouldn't be until mid-evening, when the periodic floor shows were about to start. There were the posters though:

6 Acts 6
Yolanda Lang and Devil
in
the Famous
Beauty and the Beast
Dance!

And, of course, there were photographs. Sweeney didn't stop to look at them. He walked from the blazing heat into the cool dimness of the outer bar, separated from the room with tables and the stage, where a cover charge topped higher prices.

He stopped inside, barely able at first to see, blinded by the transition from sunlight glare to neoned dimness. He blinked, and looked along the bar. Only three persons sat there. At the far end, a badly intoxicated man drooled over a too-sober blowzy blonde. Half a dozen stools away, a man sat alone, staring at his reflection in the dim blue mirror back of the bar, a bottle of beer and a glass in front of him. He sat there as though he was carved of stone. Sweeney felt pretty sure he wasn't Doc Greene.

Sweeney slid onto a stool at the end of the bar. The bartender came over.

"Greene been in?" Sweeney asked. "Doc Greene?"

"Not yet today." The bartender rubbed the clean bar with a duty towel. "Sometimes comes in around this time, but today I dunno. With Yo in the hospital—"

"Yo," said Sweeney meditatively. "I like that. Gives everybody a southern accent. People turn to her at the bar and ask 'And what's Yo having to drink,' huh?"

"A good question," said the bartender. "What *is* yo having to drink?"

"Well," said Sweeney, and thought it over. He had to get some nourishment into him somehow, a little at a time, until his appetite came back and he could look at a full meal without flinching. "Beer with an egg in it, I guess."

The bartender moved away to get it, and Sweeney heard the door behind him open. He looked around.

A moon-faced man stood just inside the doorway. A wide but meaningless smile was on his face as he looked along the bar, starting at the far end. His eyes, through round thick-lensed glasses, came to rest on Sweeney and the wide smile widened. His eyes, through the lenses, looked enormous.

Somehow, too, they managed to look both vacant and deadly. They looked like a reptile's eyes, magnified a hundredfold, and you expected a nictitating membrane to close across them.

Sweeney—the outside of Sweeney—didn't move, but something shuddered inside him. For almost the first time in his life he was hating a man at first sight. And fearing him a little, too. It was a strange combination of strange ingredients, for hatred—except in an abstract sort of way—was almost completely foreign to William Sweeney. Nor is fear a commonplace to one who seldom gives enough of a damn about anybody or anything to be afraid of him or it.

"Mr. Sweeney?" said the moon-faced man, more as a statement than a question.

Sweeney said, "Sit down, Doc."

He put his hands in his pockets, quickly, because he had a hunch the shakes were going to come back.

CHAPTER 4

THE moon-faced man slid onto the stool around the turn of the bar from Sweeney, so the two of them faced one another. He said, "That was an excellent story you wrote about—what happened last night, Mr. Sweeney."

Sweeney said, "I'm glad you liked it."

"I didn't say that I liked it," Greene said. "I said it was an excellent story. That is something else again."

"But definitely," said Sweeney. "In this particular case, wherein lies the difference?"

Doc Greene leaned his elbows on the bar and laced pudgy fingers together. He said, judiciously, "A man, Mr. Sweeney, might enjoy a bit of voluptuous description of a woman; in other cases he might not enjoy reading it. For example, if the woman was his wife."

"Is Yolanda Lang your wife?"

"No," said the moon-faced man. "I was merely, you will recall, giving that as an example. You've ordered something?"

Sweeney nodded, and Greene looked at the bartender and held up one finger. The man came with Sweeney's beer-and-egg and put a shot glass in front of Greene.

While the shot glass was being filled, Sweeney cautiously took a hand out of his pocket and rested the tips of his fingers against the front of the bar. Carefully, so the shaking wouldn't show, he began to walk his fingers up the front of the bar, over the edge, and toward the glass in front of him.

His eyes watched the ones that looked so huge through the thick spectacles.

Greene's smile had gone away; now it came back, and he lifted his shot glass. "To your bad health, Mr. Sweeney."

Sweeney's fingers had closed around his own glass. He said, "To yours, Doc," and his hand was steady as he lifted the glass and took a sip. He put it back down and took his other hand out of his pocket. The shakes were gone.

He said carefully, "Perhaps you would like to cause my health to deteriorate, Doc. If you want to try, it would be a pleasure to oblige."

The moon-faced man's smile got wider. "Of course not, Mr. Sweeney. When I became a man, I put away childish things, as the great bard says."

"The Bible," said Sweeney. "Not Shakespeare."

"Thank you, Mr. Sweeney You are, as I feared when I read that story under your by-line, an intelligent man. And, as I guessed from your name, a stubborn Irishman. If I told you to —let us descend to the vernacular—if I told you to lay off Yolanda, it would just make you that much more stubborn."

He held up a finger for a refill of the shot glass. He said, "A threat of any sort would be silly. If would be equally useless to point out to you the futility of your trying to make my —ah—client. As you may have—indeed as you *did*—notice, Yolanda is not unattractive. It has been tried by experts."

"You flatter yourself, Doc."

"Perhaps. Perhaps not. We aren't discussing my relations with Yolanda."

Sweeney took another sip of his drink. He said, "It occurs to me to wonder. Just what *are* we discussing? I take it that you didn't meet me here to discuss publicity for any of your other—ah—clients. And you say yourself that threats would be as futile as pointing out to me the futility of what you seem convinced I have in mind. So why did you come here?"

"To meet Mr. Sweeney. The moment I read that story of yours I knew—I am something of a psychiatrist—that you were going to be a thorn in my

side. There was an ineffable *something* about that story—So might Dante
have written of Beatrice, so might Abelard have written of Heloise."

"And so," said Sweeney, "might Casanova have written of Guinevere, had
they lived in the same century and had he ever seen her with her panties
off." He grinned. "You know, Doc, I hate you so damn much I'm beginning
to like you."

"Thank you," said Greene. "I feel the same about you; each of us admires
the other's capabilities, let us say. Or you will admire mine when you get
to know me better."

"Already," said Sweeney, "I admire your line of patter. Immensely. The
only thing I hate about you is your guts."

"And may the Ripper never expose them to the public gaze," Greene said.
"Not that that seems likely, for thus far he has seemed to specialize in ten-
derer morsels." He smiled broadly. "Isn't civilization a marvelous thing,
Mr. Sweeney? That two men can sit like this and insult one another, ami-
cably but sincerely, and enjoy the conversation? If we followed the cus-
toms of a century or two ago, one of us would have struck the other across
the face with the back of a hand before now, and one of us would be fated
to die before the sun rises very far above tomorrow's horizon."

"A beautiful thought, Doc," Sweeney said. "I'd love it. But the authori-
ties *are* fussy about such things. But back to Yolanda. Suppose you read
correctly between the lines of my story. What are you going to do about it?
Anything?"

"Of course. For one thing, I shall put every possible pitfall in your path.
I shall warn Yolanda against you—not obviously, of course, but subtly. I'll
make her think you're a fool. You are, you know."

"Yes," said Sweeney. "But she may discount the information, since it
comes from a bastard. You are one, you know."

"Your intuition surprises me, Mr. Sweeney. As it happens, I really am, in
the literal sense of the word. Quite possibly in the figurative sense also, but
that is irrelevant. Or perhaps I should say that there is a strong probability
that I was born of unwed parents; all I actually know is that I was brought
up in an orphan asylum. I, myself, made me what I am today."

"Only you could have done it," Sweeney said. "You gratify me. I didn't
expect a compliment. But that was a digression. In addition to putting pit-
falls in your path, I am going to help you."

Sweeney said, "Now you have me really worried."

The moon-faced man tented his fingers into a steeple. He said, "You
intend to find the Ripper. It's natural that you'll try, first because you're a
reporter, but second and more important—to you—you think it will give

you an in with Yolanda. Trying will automatically bring you in contact with her—not as close a contact as you have in mind, maybe, but it will give you an excuse to meet her and talk to her. Also you think that if you *do* find the Ripper, you'll be a conquering hero and she'll fall into your arms in gratitude. Am I correct?"

"Keep talking," Sweeney said. "As if I need to suggest it."

"So. You've got two reasons for finding him. I've got two reasons for helping you. One—" He held up a fat finger. "—If you do find him, he might stick a knife in you. I think I'd like that. I hate *your* guts, too, Mr. Sweeney."

"Thank you kindly."

'Two—" Another finger joined the first. "—the police just might have something in thinking the killer will come back to finish the job on Yolanda. Despite the fact, and the newspapers' reporting of the fact, that Yo can't recognize him on a bet, he may decide to take a chance and play safe by killing her. That I would *not* like."

"That I can understand," Sweeney said. "Also I like it better than your first reason."

"And I don't think, Mr. Sweeney, that finding him will get you to first base with Yolanda. At least, I'll take a chance on that."

"Fine, Doc. One little thing, though. The police force of Chicago outnumbers me, considerably. Just out of curiosity, what makes you think that I, with my little slingshot, might do more than the whole blue army?"

"Because you're a crazy damn Irishman. Because you're a little *fey;* I suspected that from a sentence or two in your story, and I know it now. Because God loves fools and drunkards, and you're both.

"Also because, under the sodden surface, you've got a hell of a keen brain, Mr. Sweeney; another thing I suspected before and know now. And you've got a crazy warped streak in you that might take you places where the police wouldn't think to go. Like the simpleton who found the horse by thinking he was a horse and going where he'd go if he really were a horse. Not that I would compare you to a horse, Mr. Sweeney. At least not to *all* of a horse."

"Thank you. I am a horse's ass with a hell of a keen brain. Tell me more," he said eagerly.

"I think I could. I really *am* a psychiatrist, Mr. Sweeney, although not a practicing one. An unfortunate occurrence in what would have been my last year of internship got me kicked out on my ear. It occurred to me that satyriasis might be a logical prescription for nymphomania. We had a patient who was quite an advanced satyr, Mr. Sweeney, and I took the liberty of introducing him into the room of an enthusiastic nympholept and leaving them together for an extended period. My superiors were quite stuffy about it."

"I can understand that," Sweeney said.

"Ah, had they only known some of the other experiments I tried, which were *not* found out. But we digress."

"We do indeed," said Sweeney. "So you're going to help me find the Ripper. So go ahead and help."

Greene spread his hands. "It isn't much. I didn't mean that I have the killer's name and address in my notebook, ready to turn over to you. I merely meant that I'll gladly work with you, Mr. Sweeney; I'll give you such facts and data as I have. And, since you'll want to talk to Yolanda, I'll see that you do. You might have trouble doing even that, with the police on guard around her, as they will be."

He looked at his wrist watch. "Unfortunately, I haven't more time now. A business appointment. One must eat. Could you, Mr. Sweeney, meet me here tomorrow afternoon, about this same time?"

Sweeney frowned. He said, "I don't know. Maybe you're just wasting my time. Have you really got anything?"

"I've got Yolanda," Greene said. "She'll be released from the hospital by then. I'll bring her here with me. You'll be here, of course?"

"I'll be here, of course," said Sweeney.

"Good. We may be seeing quite a bit of one another. Let us, then, dispense with the amenities. Let us not say hypocritical good-byes. My two drinks were on you. Thank you for them, and the hell with you."

He walked out.

Sweeney took a deep breath. He let it out slowly.

The bartender strolled over. He said, "That'll be a dollar and a quarter. Don't you want your beer?"

"No. Pour it down the drain. But bring me a bromo and a shot."

"Sure. Mixed?"

"Not mixed."

He put two dollar bills on the bar. When the bartender came back, Sweeney said, "Quite a character, that Doc Greene."

"Yeah. Quite a character."

"What puzzles me about him is this." Sweeney said. "Those seemed to be his own teeth he was wearing; they weren't regular enough for false ones. How the hell could a guy like that keep his own teeth that long?"

The bartender chuckled. "Maybe it's them eyes of his. Like a hypnotist. I think a guy'd have to be pretty brave to take a poke at Doc. *I'd* rather nor tangle with him. Funny, though, the way women go for him. You wouldn't think it."

"Including Yo?" Sweeney asked.

"I wouldn't know about Yo. She's a funny dame to figure out." He took Sweeney's bills and rang up a dollar eighty, putting two dimes on the bar.

Sweeney added a quarter to it and said, "Have one with me."

"Sure. Thanks."

"Skoal," said Sweeney. "Say, who's running El Madhouse now? Is it still Harry Yahn's?"

"Yahn owns it, or most of it, but he isn't running it. He's got another place over on Randolph."

"Sucker joint, like El Madhouse?"

The bartender smiled faintly. "Not this kind of sucker joint."

"Oh," said Sweeney. "It'd be a little bar with a big back room and if you know a guy named Joe at the door, you can leave your shirt in the back room."

The blowzy blonde at the far end of the bar was tapping the bottom of her glass on the wood impatiently. The bartender said, "The guy at the door is named Willie." He went down to mix a drink for the blonde.

Sweeney poured the bromo back and forth between the two glasses and drank it.

Then he got up and went into gathering dusk on Clark Street. He walked south, toward the Loop. He walked slowly, aimlessly, trying to think and not quite succeeding. This stage of recovery he knew well. His mind was fuzzy, his thoughts were ghosts that walked in thick fog. But his physical senses were almost blindingly vivid; the honk of auto horn and the clangor of trolley bells were terribly loud; everything he saw was seen vividly and in sharp focus; odors ordinarily not noticed were nauseatingly strong.

He had to eat, and soon, to get his strength back. Only solid food in him would get rid of the fog, free him of the sensation of light-headedness and dissipate the physical weariness that was beginning to penetrate, it seemed, to the very marrow of his bones.

All that, and the throbbing headache, still with him.

He thought how very nice it would be to die, quietly and painlessly, without even knowing it was going to happen; just to go to sleep and never wake up. Sleep, too, could be good, but you always woke up to confusion and complication and the thousand little unpleasantnesses that periodically mount up to one vast unpleasantness from which only immersion in alcohol could bring surcease.

Only now, today, there wasn't that. The one drink he'd taken back at El Madhouse bar hadn't brought any desire for another to keep it company. It hadn't either cleared his mind or fogged it further. It hadn't even tasted good, or bad.

The bridge, when he reached it, was better. There was a cool breeze across it; he stood looking out over the river and letting the breeze blow into his face.

When he turned back, an empty taxi was coming. Sweeney hailed it, and gave his home address.

In his room, he slid the bottom newspaper out from under the stack on the bed and sat down, in the Morris chair. He found the story of the first murder—the murder of the ex-chorine, Lola Brent. Six inches on page two, not much in the way of detail.

There hadn't been a Ripper, then. It was just a story of a woman—a not very important woman, at that—who had been found, dead, in the areaway between two buildings on Thirty-Eighth Street. A knife or a razor had been the weapon used. The crime had occurred in daylight, between four and five o'clock in the afternoon. There had been no witnesses. A child returning home from a playground had discovered the body. Police were seeking a man with whom Lola Brent was alleged to have been living.

Sweeney took up the next paper. The story had a little better play in that one, and there were two pictures. One was of Lola Brent. She was blonde, and beautiful. She didn't look the thirty-five years the story said she was; you'd have taken her for early twenties.

The other picture was that of the man the police had arrested, Sammy Cole. He had black, curly hair and a face that was handsome in the ruggedly honest way that is a con-man's stock in trade. He denied killing Lola Brent, and was being held on an open charge.

The following day's story was a brief rehash; the only new angle was that Sammy Cole had confessed to several counts of operating a confidence game. The following several papers brought out nothing additional.

The Lola Brent crime had then, it appeared, faded into limbo, unsolved. There was nothing at all concerning it in the last two papers of the week's series starting two months before. There wouldn't, Sweeney knew, have been any mention of it—of importance—in the five and a half weeks' papers that he didn't have, the gap in between his first series and the series starting ten days ago.

He picked up the paper of ten $lays before and skimmed rapidly through the story of the murder of Stella Gaylord, the B-girl from Madison Street. He didn't try to memorize details here; he was going to concentrate on one crime at a time. He was looking, now, only for further mention of the killing of Lola Brent. He found it on the second day after the Stella Gaylord murder; it was then first suggested that the crime might be a psychopathic one, perpetrated by the same killer who had slashed Lola Brent six and a half weeks before.

The next day's lead was a build-up of that idea, with a comparative description of the wounds inflicted upon the two women. Each had been killed by a horizontal slash across the abdomen, but the weapon had not been the same one. The knife that had killed Lola Brent had been no sharper than average, but the blade that had slashed Stella Gaylord had been razor keen.

Sweeney skimmed through the rest of the papers, looking, this time, only for additional details about the Lola Brent case; one at a time was all his mind would handle and absorb in its currently fuzzy condition. Apparently, no further discoveries of importance had been made on the Brent case. The police were still not too sure that the killer of Lola Brent was the same homicidal maniac who had killed Stella Gaylord and five days later, Dorothy Lee. But there wasn't any doubt about the latter two having been killed by the same hand.

Sweeney put down the last—the most recent—of the papers and tried to think. He now knew everything that had been given out to the papers on the Brent murder, but none of it seemed helpful. For that matter, what *could* be helpful—short of a lucky guess—when you were hunting a killer who killed without motive? Without motive, that is, applicable to the particular victim and not to any woman who was blonde and beautiful. Yes, there was that in common. The three who had been killed, as well as Yolanda Lang, had all been blonde and beautiful.

Sweeney went to the phone in the hall and dialed a number. When he got the man he wanted, he asked, "Sammy Cole, the guy that Lola Brent was living with, still in the jug here in Chicago?"

"Yeah," said the man to whom Sweeney was talking. I won't mention his name because he's still holding down the same job and doing right well at it, and this would get bun in trouble. Sweeney, you see, had something on him, and reporters aren't supposed to have anything on important public officials. They often do.

He said, "Yeah, we're still holding him. We could have salted him away before this, but returns are still coming in. Every once in a while we tie him *in* to a fraud charge and get it off the books."

"I'd like to talk to him," Sweeney said. "Tonight."

"Tonight? Look, Sweeney, can't you wait till regular hours tomorrow? It's after seven o'clock and—"

"You can fix it," Sweeney said. "I'll grab a taxi and be there quick."

That is how, within half an hour, Sweeney was sitting on the warden's desk and Sammy Cole sat on a straight chair a few feet away from him. They were alone in the office. Sammy Cole was recognizable from the newspaper picture of him Sweeney had seen shortly before, but barely recognizable. He still had black hair but it was cut too short to be curly. His face was ruggedly sullen instead of ruggedly honest.

"I told 'em," Sammy Cole said. "I told 'em every Goddam thing. I spilled my guts because I'd like to see whoever bumped Lola take the hot squat. There was the off chance it did tie in with something she'd been doing, see? So I spilled my guts and what does it get me? Enough raps so when I get out, if I get out, I'll be peddling pencils."

"Tough," Sweeney said. An envelope and a pencil came out of his pockets and he wrote "Want a drink?" on the back of the envelope and showed it to Sammy Cole.

"Jesus," said Sammy Cole, not at all irreverently. It would have been ambiguous to anyone listening in on a bug, but Sweeney took the half pint bottle, still two-thirds full, that he'd bought earlier at the drugstore out of his hip pocket and handed it to Sammy Cole. Sammy Cole handed it back empty and wiped his lips with the back of his hand. He said, "What you want to know?"

"I don't know," Sweeney told him. "That's the trouble; I don't know. But I got to start somewhere. When'd you see Lola last?"

"That morning—almost noon, I guess—when she went to work."

'To work? Were you that far down, Sammy?"

"Well—yeah and no. I was working on something that would have come through big. I was tired of hand-to-mouthing on the short-con stuff. What I was doing would have got us Florida for the winter, and a real stake. Laugh it off, but I was going to turn straight. For Lola. She didn't like the grifts. So she was keeping us eating while my deal came through."

"Was she tied in on the big deal?"

"No. That was strictly me. But we worked out a little racket for her that brought in peanuts. A hundred or so a week for a few days' work. That's what she was on that day."

"Where? What was it?"

Sammy Cole wiped his lips again and bent sidewise to look questioningly in the direction of Sweeney's hip pocket. Sweeney shook his head and spread his hands.

Sammy Cole sighed. He said, "A gift shop on Division Street. Raoul's Gift Shop. That was her first day there, so I dunno much about it except what she told me, from applying for the job the day before, and what little I saw when I dropped in at six. That was part of the racket. This Raoul is a faggot."

"How would that tie in with a racket for Lola, Sammy? Unless you came in later?"

"Naw, nothing like that. I just mentioned—it. All there was to the racket was Lola'd get a job selling stuff somewhere, preferably a place where she'd made a few big sales, not dime store stuff. Small store, usually, where she'd be alone when the boss went out to eat or something and left her alone a little. She'd drag down on some sales—ten bucks, fifty bucks, whatever the traffic would bear. We played extra safe because she wasn't on the blotter and I wanted to keep her off. I'd drop in later at a time we'd set and she'd slip me the moolah. She never had it on her for more'n a few minutes; she'd stash it somewhere after she dragged it down and get it just a minute before I was due to come in. It was safe as houses. Soon as she saw a mooch beginning to look suspicious at her, she'd do a fadeout; never worked anywhere longer'n a few days. Then she'd lay off a while and— well, you got the picture."

Sweeney nodded. "And she got the job at Raoul's the day before. How?"

"Newspaper ad. We had good references for her; that was my department. Job was in the morning papers. She got it in the afternoon and was to start at noon the next day. They're open till nine in the evening and she was to work noon to nine, lunch hour four to five."

"How come you didn't just arrange to meet her outside, during lunch hour?"

Sammy Cole looked at Sweeney contemptuously. "Lookit the angles," he said. "First, she'd have to walk out with the moolah *on* her, and that's taking a chance. Second, if he sends her out four to five, then the pansy's taking off at five, probably. Her best time to do a little business, on her own, would be from five to six, and I get there at six. If the pansy's still gone, good; if he's there, she can still slip it to me. I buy something for two bits and she slips the dough in the paper bag with it. It's safe as houses."

"And you got there at six?"

"Sure. She wasn't there, and I figured something was on the off beat. I phoned the flat and a cop answered so I hung up quick and stayed away. Not that I guessed what had happened—whatever the hell *did* happen. But I figured she'd got caught on a larceny rap and I'd be better off on the outside, to try to get her out of it. Hell, I was nuts about the dame. I'd have raised some moolah somehow to get her a shyster and bail her out. I'd've knocked a guy over if I had to, to get her out And they still think maybe *I* killed her. Jesus."

"When'd you find out what really happened?"

"Morning papers. I'd holed in a hotel. I near went nuts. All I could think about was getting the son of a bitch that did it and chopping him up into hamburger, slow. But I didn't know how to go looking for him without walking into cops, and I wasn't going to be able to do a Goddam thing if I did that. So all I could figure was to keep under cover till the heat was off. But I guess I was too upset to be careful enough. They got me, and by the time I get outa here, the guy'll be dead of old age.

"So, Jesus God how I hate a cop, but just the same I did all I could for 'em. I spilled my guts to 'em, just on the off chance something we'd been doing would give 'em a lead."

Sammy Cole slumped tiredly down in the chair and sighed. He looked up and asked, "Got a fag?"

Sweeney handed him a package of cigarettes and a book of matches and said, "Keep them. Look, Sammy, if you hadn't been picked up, what would you have done when the heat was off? Where'd you have started?"

"With the faggot, Raoul. Maybe he had something to do with it and maybe he didn't, but I'd have picked his petals off one at a time till I was sure."

"What happened at the gift shop? Did he catch her dragging down on a sale, or what? He must have fired her if she went home, and she was found in the areaway outside your flat."

Sammy Cole said, "That I wouldn't know. The cops ask me questions; they don't tell me. All I know is what's in the papers and they don't give me any papers. You can get papers —and stuff—in stir, if you got money. But I'm broke flat."

Sweeney nodded and took a ten-dollar bill out of his wallet and handed it across. He said, "You get no dough out of me, pal, if you were hinting. Say, would Lola maybe have put the bite on some merchandise? Rings or something? Some gift shops have lots of small stuff that's valuable."

Sammy Cole shook his head definitely. He said, "That I'll guarantee; she didn't. I drummed that into her. Too many angles, too easy to get caught, too easy to have stuff traced back to you, and too hard to get more'n a twentieth of what the stuff's worth anyway. Not even a ring or a pair of earrings for herself; I drummed that into her."

"What was the long-con you were working on? Could that have tied in?"

"Nope, it couldn't. I didn't-spill that because I was working *with* a guy, and I wouldn't rat on him. The cops couldn't rubber-hose it out of me because I'm no stoolie. And anyway, it *couldn't* have tied in with what happened to Lola because neither the guy I was working with or the guy we were working *on* knew her or knew she was alive. And she didn't know them or much about them. I mean, I'd told her what the game was, but not the details or the names. See?"

"Okay, Sammy. Thanks," Sweeney said. "I can't do you any good, I guess, but I'll keep you posted. So long."

He surprised the con-man by shaking hands with him and went out of the warden's office, nodding to the turnkey who'd been standing outside the door.

A clock in the outer corridor told him it was eight-fifteen, and he stood in front of the jail, watching both ways, until a cab came along and he hailed it.

"Division Street," he said. "Well have to look up the address on the way north; I forgot to get it. It's a gift shop named Raoul's."

The taxi driver laughed. He said, "I know the joint. The guy tried to make me once. He's a queer. Say, you ain't—" he looked at Sweeney.

He said, "No, you ain't," and turned back to the wheel.

CHAPTER 5

SWEENEY stood looking into the window of Raoul's gift shop. Presumably he was staring at the array of merchandise in the display; mostly he was watching over the low partition at the back of the window. Two customers, both women, were within. With Raoul, the proprietor, that made the feminine complement of the shop one hundred per cent. No one would ever have to wonder about Raoul.

Sweeney studied the window and saw that it was not, in the fashion of many gift shops, cluttered with junky bric-a-brac and cheap miscellany. The items displayed were few and good. There were foo dogs from China, thunderbirds from Mexico, costume jewelry that was in good taste if a bit blatant, a pair of brass candlesticks of exquisitely simple design; there wasn't a single thing in the window that Sweeney could have taken exception to—except possibly the prices, and they weren't shown. His opinion of Raoul went up several notches.

One of the women inside made a purchase and came out. The other was obviously browsing and Raoul, after apparently offering to help her, relaxed gracefully against the counter.

Sweeney went inside. The proprietor, smiling a proprietary smile, came forward to meet him. The smile turned to a slight frown when Sweeney said, "From the *Blade*. Like to talk to you about Lola Brent," but he walked with Sweeney to the back of the shop, out of earshot of the remaining customer.

Sweeney asked, "She got the job when? The day before?"

"Yes. Several came in answer to an advertisement I put in the paper. Your paper, the *Blade*. She had excellent references from a gift shop in New York; I didn't guess they were fraudulent. She was well dressed, had a pleasing personality. And she was free, ready to start work at once. I told her to come in the next day."

"And she did, at noon?"

"Yes."

"And what happened? You caught her dragging down on a sale and fired her?"

"Not exactly. I explained it all to the police."

Sweeney said, "I could get it direct from them, but I'd rather not. If you don't mind too much."

Raoul sighed. He said, "From twelve until a little after three we were both in the store. There weren't many customers and I spent most of the time acquainting her with the stock, the prices, telling her things she should know about the business. At about a quarter after three I had to leave for a short while, on a personal matter. I was gone a little over half an hour. When I returned, I asked what business she'd done while I was gone and she told me that only one customer had been in the store and that he had bought a pair of six-dollar bookends. That was the only amount that had been rung up on the register. But then I noticed that something else was missing."

"What was it?"

"A figurine, a statuette, which had been priced at twenty-four dollars. It had stood on the shelf over there." Raoul pointed. "It just happened that that particular statuette had been standing a bit askew and I had straightened it shortly before I had left on my errand. Shortly after my return, I chanced to notice that it was no longer there. There had been three figures on that shelf, and now there were only two, with the two moved closer together to avert leaving a conspicuous gap between them. So I asked Miss Brent if she had moved the statuette and she denied knowledge of it."

He sighed gently. "It was embarrassing, of course. I knew she could not be telling the truth, because—just as it happened—I was certain it had been there when I left."

"It couldn't have been shoplifted?"

"Hardly possible. The figure was ten inches high and, although slender, the arms of the figure were extended forward; it would have been a difficult object to conceal under a coat, and it would not have gone into a pocket at all. It was not the sort of object that is chosen by shoplifters, I assure you. Besides, Miss Brent had told me that only one person had been *in* the store. There was no doubt to my mind at all, Mr.—ah—"

"Sweeney. You accused her of having sold it and kept the dough."

"What else could I do? I told her that I had no desire to prosecute, and that if she would permit me to search her thoroughly back in the stock room, I would permit her to go, without calling the police."

"You found the money on her?"

"No. When she saw that I really meant to call the police unless, she confessed and really meant to let her go if she did, she admitted the theft. She had the money, a twenty-dollar bill and four ones, to the top of her stocking. A woman's repository."

"Then you didn't have to search her. Or did you?"

"Of course I did. I had missed that particular item and she had confessed selling it, but—since she was admittedly dishonest—how did I know that that was the only item she had sold beside the bookends? I couldn't inventory the stock. She might also have made, let us say, a fifty-dollar sale of costume jewelry and concealed the money to her other stocking or to her brassiere or somewhere."

"Had she?"

"No. At least I found no money except a few dollars to her purse which I was willing to believe was her own property. She was—ah—a little sullen about being searched, but she was reasonable when she saw my reason for insisting. Also she was not sufficiently naive to think that I wished to do so for any ulterior motive, if you understand what I mean."

"I understand what you mean," said Sweeney. "So it would have been about four o'clock when she left?"

"Yes. Not later than fifteen minutes after four. I did not notice the time exactly."

"She left alone?"

"Of course. And to anticipate your next question, I did not notice whether she met anyone outside. Naturally, knowing her to be dishonest, I kept my eyes on her as far as the door but not beyond. I did not notice which direction she went. But of course she must have gone directly to her home, because I understand she was found dead in the areaway there at five o'clock. She would have had to transfer to get there, and go through the Loop; it would have taken at least half an hour from here, possibly longer."

"Unless she took a cab or someone gave her a lift."

"Of course. The taxi is not too likely, judging from the small amount of money she had in her purse."

Sweeney nodded. "Being picked up isn't too likely either. Her man was to meet her here in the store at six, but he'd hardly have been around the neighborhood as early as four-fifteen."

Raoul's eyebrows rose a little. "He was to meet her here?"

"Yeah. To pick up whatever she'd dragged down by then."

"Indeed? The police didn't tell me that."

Sweeney grinned. "The police don't go out of their way to tell people things. That's why I wanted to talk to you about this instead of to them. Did Lola Brent, by the way, seem to recognize anybody who did come in that afternoon, while you were here?"

"No. I'm reasonably sure she didn't."

"What was the statuette? A woman's figure, I take it, but with or without clothes?"

"Without. Very definitely without, if you understand what I mean."

"I guess I do," Sweeney said. "Even some women, let alone statues, manage to be nakeder without clothes than others do. It's a gift."

Raoul raised his hands expressively. "I do not mean to imply, Mr. Sweeney, that the statuette was in any sense of the word pornographic or suggestive. It was, rather, quite virginal —in a very peculiar way."

"You intrigue me," said Sweeney. "How many ways of being virginal are there? I thought I knew everything, but—"

Raoul smiled. "There are many ways of expressing a single quality. Of, as it were, getting it across. Virginity, in this case, is expressed through fear, horror, loathing. Virginity—or perhaps I should say virginality—"

"What's the difference?" Sweeney asked, and then answered himself, "Wait, I think I get you. One is physical and the other is mental. Right?"

"Of course. They, may or may not coincide. Many married women are virginal, although they are not virgins. They have never really been *touched;* the physical act alone—And then again, a maiden who is *virgo intactas* may be far from virginal if her thoughts—ah—you see what I mean?"

"I do," Sweeney said. "But we wander from the statuette."

"Not far. Would you care to *see* the statuette? Not the one Miss Brent sold, of course, but a duplicate of it. I ordered two and liked them so well that I have one in my apartment in the next block. It's closing time now and—I assure you I have *no* ulterior motive, Mr. Sweeney."

"Thanks," said Sweeney. "But I don't believe it's necessary. The statuette itself could hardly have anything to do with the crime."

"Of course not. I merely thought it would interest you abstractly." He smiled. "It is, incidentally, known as a Screaming Mimi."

"A what?"

"A Screaming Mimi. Girl's name—M-i-m-i. A rather obvious pun, of course, on the screaming meamies, if you know what they are."

"Intimately," said Sweeney. "And, if I may, I'm going to change my mind; I *would* like to meet this Mimi, Mr.—Is Raoul your last name?"

"Reynarde, Mr. Sweeney, Raoul Reynarde. If you'll pardon me just a moment—"

He walked over to the remaining customer to tell her it was closing time. Sweeney followed her to the door and waited there until Reynarde had turned out the lights. They walked a block and a half east on Division Street and up two flights of stairs to the apartment.

"I can't ask you to stay long, Mr. Sweeney," Reynarde said, as he nicked on the light inside the door. "I—ah—have a guest coming. But we'll have time for a drink. May I make you a highball?"

"Sure, thanks," said Sweeney. "But where is Mimi?"

"On the mantel yonder."

Sweeney's gaze, which had been roaming about the beautifully furnished—if a bit feminine—apartment, came to rest on a ten-inch-high statuette over the fireplace. He crossed the room and stood looking at it.

He saw now what Reynarde had meant. Definitely there was a virginal quality about the slim nude figure, but that you saw afterward. "Fear, horror, loathing," Reynarde had said, and all of that was there, not only in the face but in the twisted rigidity of the body. The mouth was wide open in a soundless scream. The arms were thrust out, palms forward, to hold off some approaching horror.

"An exquisite thing," said Reynarde's voice from across the room, where he poured drinks at a little mahogany cabinet that was complete down to an ice-cube unit. "It is made of a new plastic that can't be told from ebony, unless you pick it up. The dull gloss is the same as ebony's, to the eye. If that figure were what it looks to be, hand-carved ebony, and original, it would be worth a lot of money." He waved a hand around the room. "Most things you see here *are* originals. I prefer them."

Sweeney grunted. "I don't agree with you there. I'd rather any day have a Renoir print than an art school original. But that's a matter of taste. Could you get me one of these?"

Reynarde's voice came from just behind Sweeney. "Your drink, Mr. Sweeney. Yes, I can get you a Screaming Mimi, or I think I can. The company that makes them—a small concern in Louisville, Kentucky, of all places—may possibly have some left. They generally make a few hundred of an item like that. But if you really want it, I may sell you that one. Although it has been on my mantel, it is still virginal."

He laughed. "Or I can, if you think that makes it second hand, return it to the store and sell it to you from there. One advantage of being a dealer, Mr. Sweeney; I need never grow tired of an art object or bit of bric-a-brac. Often I keep objects from the store here until I tire of them and then exchange them for others. I think that I am growing a little weary of the little lady by now. Your health, sir."

Sweeney drank absent-mindedly, without taking his eyes off the statuette, emptying the glass at a single draught. He said, "Before you change your mind, Mr. Reynarde—" He put his glass down on the mantel and counted twenty-four dollars out of his wallet.

"How," he asked, "did it get named? Is that your name for it, or the company's?"

Reynarde pursed his lips. "I don't believe I re—Oh, yes. The name came from the company that made it, but unofficially, as it were. The salesman told me that the catalogue code number for it is SM-1, and someone in their office with a sense of humor decided the SM stood for Screaming Mimi."

"Who did the statuette? The original, I mean."

"That I do not know. The company is the Ganslen Art Company. They make mostly bookends and chess sets, but they do some work in small statuary, often surprisingly good at the price. Shall I wrap the figure for you?"

Sweeney chuckled. "Put pants on Mimi? Never. I'll carry her naked through the streets."

"Another drink, Mr. Sweeney?"

"Thanks, no. I think Mimi and I must be going." He nicked up the statuette gently.

Reynarde said, "Sit down, Mr. Sweeney," and himself sank into an overstuffed chair, although Sweeney remained standing. He said, "Something interests me, Mr. Sweeney, despite the fact that it is none of my business at all. Are you a sadist?"

"Me?"

"You. I am curious because of the appeal that statuette has for you. The thing is an orgy of masochism; it would appeal, in my opinion, only to a sadist."

Sweeney looked at him thoughtfully. He said, "No, I'm not a sadist. I can see your point about the appeal of the figure; I don't know the answer. The instant I saw it, I knew I wanted to own it, but I haven't the slightest idea why."

"Its appeal as an object of art?"

"No, not that. It's well done, cleverly executed, but it isn't great art."

Reynarde pursed his lips. "Perhaps some subconscious association?"

"It could be," Sweeney said. "At any rate, thank you and I must be going."

Reynarde walked to the door with him and bowed slightly as they parted.

As the door closed behind him, Sweeney wondered why he *had* wanted the statuette. And why, in particular, he had resented Raoul Reynarde's probing into his reason for wanting it. He looked at the statuette in his hand, and shivered a little—mentally if not physically. It was neither pretty nor sensuous. Damn it, Reynarde was right; it would appeal only to a sadist, or to someone who had *some* abnormality in him. And yet he, Sweeney, had paid over twenty-four dollars of good money to take it home with him. Was he punch-drunk?

No, he wasn't. The fog inside his head was lifting, definitely. And through the fog, he almost had a glimpse of something that might have been die association Reynarde had suggested. Then the fog came down again.

Well, it would come back. Sweeney sighed and started for the stairway. Coming up the stairs was a plump, beautiful young man with blond curly hair. They passed in the hallway, and the young man looked curiously at the statuette Sweeney was carrying but made no comment. He rang the bell of Reynarde's apartment.

Sweeney went on down the stairs.

Outside, and the dark night was bright with lights, the air hot and humid. Sweeney walked west on Division Street and then south on Dearborn.

He wondered how long he could keep going like this; how long he would *have* to keep going before he could eat and then sleep. The nausea was back with him now. Food was a disgusting thought, but it was a hurdle to be taken, a hurdle that *had* to be taken.

Eventually.

At Chicago Avenue he turned half a block west and went into a small clean restaurant and sat down at the counter. A man in a white apron that made Sweeney think of a surgeon came up on the other side of the counter and stood there. He stood there scaring at the black statuette Sweeney had placed on the counter in front of him.

"Mimi," Sweeney said, "meet Joe. Joe, meet Mimi. Or is your name Joe, Joe?"

The counterman grinned uncertainly. He said, "It's close. Jack. What's wrong with the little lady?"

"She is screaming," Sweeney said. He felt as though he wanted to, himself. "Jack, could you get me a very special dinner?"

"Such as what? If we got what it takes, we can make it."

"Bread," said Sweeney. "Two slices of white bread, plain, without butter. Not too fresh, but not really stale. With the crusts left on. On a white plate. I think maybe I could eat that. The bread, I mean, not the plate. Can you do it?"

"I'll ask the cook. Coffee, too?"

"Black," said Sweeney. "In a cup."

He closed his eyes and tried to concentrate on something to keep from thinking about the smells of the restaurant, but all he succeeded in doing was concentrating on the smells. When plate and cup rattled on the counter in front of him, he opened his eyes.

He took a sip of the scalding coffee and then began to nibble on one of the slices of bread. It was all right; it would go down and stay down.

He was almost through with the second slice when the waiter came back. He stood leaning against the ledge, looking at the statuette. He said, "That thing sort of *gets* you, when you look at it. It gives you the willies. Where'd you get it?"

"From a fairy," Sweeney said. "How much do I owe you?"

"About fifteen cents. Say, know what that statue makes me think of? The Ripper."

Sweeney almost dropped his cup of coffee; he put it down carefully.

The waiter hadn't noticed. He said, "I mean, a woman being attacked by the Ripper. No dame is *that* afraid of being raped or something. But a crazy guy with a knife in his hand coming after her—and she's back in a corner maybe—"

Sweeney got up slowly. He fumbled a five-dollar bill out of his wallet and put it down on the counter. He said, "Keep the change, Jack." He grabbed Mimi firmly about the waist and went out.

Again an automobile almost ran him down as he cut diagonally across Chicago Avenue.

The fog was gone. He knew now what his hunch had been and why he'd wanted the Screaming Mimi. He should have got it when Reynarde had said the figure would appeal to a sadist; he *would* have got it then if his mind had been clear.

But it was clear as gin now. An hour or two before she'd been killed, Lola Brent had sold a Screaming Mimi. The fact that she'd dragged down on the sale had nothing to do with her death, but the fact that she'd *made* that sale had. The purchaser had been an insane sadist who had waited outside and followed her home. It had been a break for him that she'd been fired and had gone straight home, where he could close up on her in the seclusion of the areaway. Would he have tried to kill her anyway, during her lunch hour, if she'd stayed on the job?

His mind was clear now, but his body felt like hell. He walked faster. He could sleep now, and he *had* to sleep. He had to get home before he fell down.

CHAPTER 6

IN THE MORNING, it was Friday. It was almost Friday noon. Sweeney woke and lay a while in bed, and then swung his feet out onto the floor and sat there a while. His head didn't ache. Outside of that he couldn't have found much to say for himself. The room seemed to be filled with an invisible fog. But he got his eyes focused on the clock and saw that it was eleven-forty. He'd slept about twelve hours.

On top of the radio-phono, on the half that didn't lift up, stood a little ten-inch-high black statuette. It was the figure of a naked girl, her arms thrust out to ward off a ripper, her mouth open in a silent, eternal scream. Her body, which would have been beautiful relaxed, was subtly distorted, rigid with terror. Only a sadist could have liked it. Sweeney wasn't one; he shuddered a little and averted his eyes.

But it woke him up, seeing the Screaming Mimi. It woke him up to nightmare.

It made him want a drink; it made him think nostalgically of the sodden state of nonthinking in which he'd been only two days ago—a day and a half ago. It made him wish he was back there again.

And why not? He had plenty of money. Why not go out, right now, and have a drink and another?

Heat in waves came in at the open window. His body was wet with sweat. He was breathing hard.

He stood up, making an unconscious gesture of pushing back the heat and the fog, and got a bathrobe out of the closet. He went down the hall to the bathroom and sat on the edge of the tub while it filled with cool water. Almost cold water.

Getting into it woke him. He took a deep breath and sank down into it, clear to his neck, letting the coldness of it draw the heat from his body and feeling the mist clear from his mind.

Warmth, he thought, is what man wants, what he lives for, what he works for, until he gets too much of it—and then coldness is a wonderful and refreshing thing. The thought of lying in an ever-cold grave, for instance, is a horrible thing in winter; in summer—

But that was maudlin. Like thinking of Lola Brent, the ex-chorine who had loved a con-man so much she'd taken to the grift herself, to help him. And she'd sold a small black statuette to a man who'd-looked from it to her—

Sweeney swore. What did it matter to him, that a fading ex-pony was six feet under now? She'd have been there sooner or later anyway; five years from now, fifty years. Death is an incurable disease that men and women are born with; it gets them sooner or later. A murderer never really kills; he but anticipates. Always he kills one who is already dying, already doomed.

Actually, he never hurts the one he kills. The hurt is to whoever loved him or her, and has to keep on living. The man who'd killed Lola Brent had hurt Sammy Cole more than he'd hurt Lola.

If he, Sweeney, really came to hate Doc Greene and wanted to hurt him badly—

He sat up in the tub. What if—?

But no, that was silly. Sure, someone could have hated Doc Greene enough to want to get at him by killing Yolanda— but that left the other murders out of it; Lola Brent, Stella Gaylord, Dorothy Lee. A human being (a sane human being; but then, what is sanity?) couldn't conceivably hate four men enough to kill the women they loved.

And besides, it left out sadism and Mimi, and the Screaming Mimi was the key.

He didn't put his shoulders back down into the water; he got out of the tub instead and toweled himself off.

As he finished, he watched the last of the water gurgle out of the tub, and he wondered—had he just committed a murder? Isn't a tub of water, once drawn, an entity? A thing-in-itself that has existence, if not life? But then life, in a human body, may be analogous to water in a tub; through the sewerage of veins and arteries may it not flow back into some Lake Michigan, eventually into some ocean, when the plug is pulled? Yet even so, it is murder; that particular tub of water will never exist again, though the water itself will.

He removed the evidence of the crime by rinsing out the tub, and went back to his room. He put on a pair of shorts and a pair of socks. That would be enough until he was ready to go out, in that heat.

What was next? Stella Gaylord, B-girl on Madison Street. He might as well take it chronologically. The murder of Lola Brent had been two months ago; the second murder, that of Stella Gaylord, had been ten days ago.

He put the stack of old newspapers on the chair, where he could reach it from the bed, and propped the pillow up against the footboard.

Why not music? he thought. It always helped him concentrate; he could, for some strange reason, better remember what he read if he read it against a background of music. It was more vivid that way. The use of music was one thing the movie makers had discovered.

He studied the shelf of albums, wondering what would go well with the murder of a B-girl. Something vast and mysterious, perhaps. His hand hesitated at Sacre du Printemps and moved on. Strauss' Death and Transfiguration? The fath-etique? No, very beautiful but too corny. His hand went back to Death and Transfiguration. He put the records on and started the machine, then lay down on the bed and picked up the first paper, the one of ten days ago, that broke the Gaylord murder story..

It was on page one, but in the bottom right corner, six inches of type under a one-column head:

**BODY OF GIRL
SLAIN WITH KNIFE
IS FOUND IN ALLEY**

Sweeney read the six inches of type and decided that, as far as really important details were concerned, they might as well have let the headline stand alone.

Oh, there was the woman's name and address—on West Madison Street—and the place where the murder had occurred—the mouth of an alley off Huron Street between State and Dearborn. The body had been discovered at three-thirty in the morning and, according to the physician who had examined the body, the woman had been dead less than an hour.

Apparently there had been no robbery committed and—to Sweeney's amazed amusement—the story stated that the victim had not been attacked.

Police suspected that a homicidal maniac was at large, although the Lola Brent murder had apparently been forgotten; it was not mentioned.

The following day's paper had a picture of Stella Gaylord; it was a poor picture, apparently blown up from a snapshot, and you could tell that she was pretty but that was about all. There was more about Stella, too, including the address of the West Madison Street bar where she'd been working on percentage. She had been last seen alive when she'd left there, alone, at two o'clock, an hour and a half before the discovery of her body.

And, for the first time, the murder of Stella Gaylord was tied in with the murder of Lola Brent, with the suggestion that possibly the same psychopathic killer had killed both of them.

The following day's paper had a few added details, but no new developments.

Sweeney got up to shut off the phonograph. The sight of the black statuette on top of it reminded him of something he had to do. He slipped on a bathrobe and went out into the hall, to the telephone.

He got a long distance operator and-put in a call to the Ganslen Art Company at Louisville. A few minutes later he had the general manager, a Ralph Burke, on the line.

"This is the Chicago Blade," Sweeney said. "Something about one of your statuettes has come up in connection with a murder investigation. It's an SM-1. Remember it, off-hand?"

"I'm afraid I'd have to look it up."

"Maybe this will help. It's a figure of a terrified girl; somebody at your place called it a Screaming Mimi."

"Oh, yes, certainly. I remember it now. What do you want to know about it?"

"Could you tell me how many of them you sold—and particularly how many of them you sold in Chicago?"

"We didn't sell many, I know. It didn't turn out to be a popular number at all. In fact, we never got around to listing it in our catalogue. We made a trial lot of one gross and we've got most of them left. We gave each salesman a sample six months ago and some of them sold a few. If you want to hold the line a minute I can look up how many were sold in Chicago. Or shall I call you back?"

"I'll hold the line," Sweeney said.

It was scarcely a minute before the manager's voice was back. He said, "I've got it all here—luckily we keep a separate record on each number. There were—uh—two sold in Chicago. Only two, and both to a place called Raoul's Gift Shop. Altogether we sold about forty of them—mostly on the East and West Coasts. Want the exact figures?"

"Thanks, no," Sweeney said. "What does the SM-1 designation mean, if anything?"

"The SM part doesn't; it's just our serial number, picked in rotation. Our number before that was SL and the one after it was SN. The figure one is the size and finish. If we'd put it out in other sizes and materials, they'd have been SM-2, SM-3, and so on. But we won't, in this case. Unless, the first time our salesmen carry it, they take orders for several gross, we drop the number from our line and don't even catalogue it. It wouldn't pay. And we make only the very popular things in various sizes and styles."

"What will you do with the hundred-odd Mimis you have left?"

"We'll get rid of them next year, in with mixed lots. If a customer orders, say, a dozen mixed figures, our choice, he gets them about half the usual list price; we get rid of our odd lot and remainders that way. At a loss, of course, to us—but it's better than throwing them away."

"Of course," Sweeney said. "Do you recall who nicknamed SM-1 the Screaming Mimi?"

"Our bookkeeper; it's a hobby of his to try to think up names that match the figures and the letter designations—says it helps him remember which is which." The manager chuckled. "He hits well once in a while. I remember our number SF. He called it Some Fanny, and it was."

"I'm tempted to order one," said Sweeney. "But back to Mimi. Who designed her, or sculptured her, or molded her?"

"Fellow by the name of Chapman Wilson. Artist and sculptor, lives in Brampton, Wisconsin. He modeled it in clay."

"And sent it to you?"

"No, I bought it from him there, in Brampton. I do the buying myself, make trips several times a year. We've got quite a few artists we buy from and it's much more practical to go to their studios to look over what they have than to have-a lot of stuff shipped here and have to ship most of it back. I bought SM-1 from him about a year ago, and two other numbers. I guessed right on the others; they're selling okay."

"This Chapman Wilson—did he model Mimi from life, or what?"

"Don't know; didn't ask him. The original was in clay, same size as our copies, about ten inches. I took a chance on it because it was unusual. Something unusual may go over really big, or it may not sell at all. That's a chance we take."

"Know anything about Chapman Wilson personally?"

"Not much. He's rather an eccentric, but then a lot of artists are."

"Married?"

"No. At least, I don't think so. Didn't ask him, but I didn't see a woman around, or any sign of one."

"You say he's eccentric. Could you go as far as psychopathic, maybe?"

"I don't think so. He's a little screwy, but that's all. Most of his stuff is pretty routine—and sells fairly well."

"Thanks a lot," Sweeney said. "Guess that's all I need to know. Goodbye."

He checked the charges on the call so he could settle with Mrs. Randall and went back to his room.

He sat down on the edge of the bed and stared at the black statuette. His luck had been better than he had hoped—only two Mimis had come to

Chicago. He was looking at one of them. And the other— Maybe the Ripper was looking at it now.

The luck of the Irish, Sweeney thought. He'd been working on the case a day and had a lead the cops would give their eye teeth for.

And besides that, he felt pretty good for the shape he was in. He was even getting mildly hungry; he'd be able to put away a meal today.

He got up and hung his bathrobe on the hook, stretched luxuriously.

He felt swell. He grinned at Mimi. He thought, we're a jump ahead of the cops, Baby, you and I; all we got to do is find your sister.

The little black statuette screamed soundlessly, and Sweeney's grin faded. Somewhere in Chicago another Mimi was screaming like that—and with better cause. A madman with a knife owned her. Someone with a twisted mind and a straight razor.

Someone who wouldn't want to be found by Sweeney.

He shook himself a little, mentally, to get rid of that thought, and turned to the mirror over the washbowl. He rubbed a hand over his face. Yes, he'd better shave; he'd be meeting Yolanda late in the afternoon, if Doc Greene was as good as his word. And he had a hunch the agent would be.

He held out his hand and looked at it; yes, it was steady enough that he could use his straight razor without cutting himself. He picked up the shaving mug from the shelf above the washbowl and ran hot water into it, working up a lather with the brush. He lathered his face carefully and then looked, and reached, for the razor. It wasn't there, where it should have been lying.

His band stayed that way, a few inches above the shelf, frozen like Mimi's scream, until he made a conscious effort to pull it back.

He bent forward and looked, very carefully and disbelieving, at the mark in the thin layer of dust, the mark that was just the shape of the razor.

Carefully he wiped the lather off his face with a wetted towel* and dressed.

He went downstairs. Mrs. Randall's door was ajar and she said, "Come on in, Mr. Sweeney."

He stood in the doorway. "When did you dust in my room last, Mrs. Randall?"

"Why—yesterday morning."

"Do you remember if—" He was going to ask if she remembered seeing the razor and then realized he didn't have to ask that. Whether she remembered or not, that fresh spot in the dust was proof that the razor had been there after the dusting. He changed his question. "Was anybody in my room yesterday evening, or yesterday after I left?"

"Why, no. Not that I know of, anyway. I wasn't here yesterday evening; I went to a movie. Is something missing?"

"Not anything valuable," Sweeney said. "I guess I must have taken it while I was drunk, the last time I was here. Uh —you haven't been in my room at all since yesterday morning?"

"No, I haven't. Are you going out this afternoon? Ill want to make your bed, and if you're going to be around anyway, I might as well do it now."

"Ill be leaving in a few minutes. Thanks."

He went back up to his room and closed the door. He struck a match and examined the mark in the dust minutely. Yes, there was some dust in the bare patch that was the shape of the closed razor, about half as much as in the surrounding area. Then the razor had been there for a while after the dusting. It must have been taken late yesterday afternoon or yesterday evening.

He sat down in the Morris chair and tried to remember whether he'd seen the razor at all, either last night when he'd come home with Mimi or earlier in the day when he'd been in his room to change clothes. He couldn't remember seeing it. He hadn't looked for it, of course; he'd shaved at Goetz's room, with Goetz's electric razor.

Was anything else missing? He went over to the dresser and opened the top drawer in which he kept small miscellaneous items.

The contents looked intact until he remembered that there'd been a two-bladed penknife in the drawer.

It wasn't there now.

Nothing else was missing. There was a pair of gold cufflinks in the drawer, in plain sight, that was worth three or four times what the penknife was worth. And a stickpin with a zircon in it that a thief or burglar could not have been sure wasn't a diamond. But only a knife had been taken from the drawer. And only a razor from elsewhere in the room.

He looked at Mimi, and he knew how she felt.

CHAPTER 7

THE SHINING RAZOR hovered above Sweeney's throat. It descended under his chin and scraped gently upward, taking away lather and stubble, leaving a clean, smooth swath. It rose again.

"Take this Ripper business," said the barber. He wiped the razor on a piece of tissue and poised it again. "It's got the whole damn town jittery. It got me pinched last night."

Sweeney grunted interrogatively.

"Carrying a razor. I keep my good hone—I got a Swatty— at home because somebody'd walk off with it around this joint. So every once in a while I take a razor home, never thought anything of it. Put it in the breast pocket of my suit coat and the top of it shows and damn if a harness bull didn't stop me right on the street and get tough. I was lucky to be able to show identification I was a barber or he'd have run me in. Pretty near did anyway. Said for all anybody knew, the Ripper's a barber, too. But be ain't."

The razor scraped. "How do you know?" Sweeney asked.

"Throats. A barber that went nuts would cut throats with it. All day long people lay stretched out in front of him with their throats bare and their chins thrown back and he just can't help thinking how easy it'd be and how—uh—you know what I mean."

Sweeney said, "You got something there. You don't feel like cutting one today, I hope."

"Nope, not today." The barber grinned. "But once in a while—well, your mind does screwy things."

"So does yours," Sweeney said.

The razor scraped.

"One of the three dames he killed," said the barber, "used to work a block from here. Tavern down on the next corner."

"I know," Sweeney said. "I'm on my way there. Did you know the girl?"

"I seen her in there, enough to place her when I saw her picture in the paper. But I don't go in B-joints very often, not with the money I make. You get taken before you know it for five or ten bucks in percentage drinks, and what have you got. Not that I won't put out five or ten bucks if I get something for my money besides a little conversation. Me, I get enough conversation all day long. The whacks that sit in that chair!"

He put a steaming towel over Sweeney's face and patted it down. He said, "Anyway, I figure the Ripper uses a knife instead of a razor. You could use a razor like that, sure, but I figure it'd be too awkward to hold for a long hard slash across the guts like he uses. You'd have to tape the handle to get a good grip on it, and then it'd o be awkward to carry, taped open. And it'd be a dead giveaway if anybody saw it. I figure he'd use a pocketknife, one small enough he could carry it legally. A pre-war imported one with real steel in it, so he could have one of the blades honed down to a razor edge. Haircut?"

"No," said Sweeney.

"What do you figure he uses? A knife or a razor?"

"Yes," said Sweeney, getting up out of the chair. "What do I owe you?"

He paid, and went out into the hot August sunlight. He walked a block west to the address that had been given in the newspaper.

The place had a flashy front. Neon tubes, writhing red in the sun's glare, proclaimed that this was Susie's Cue. Hexagonal windows were curtained off to block the view within, but held chaste photographs of unchaste morsels of femininity. You could see in, if you tried, through a diamond-shaped glass in the door.

But Sweeney didn't try; he pushed the door open and went in.

It was cool and dim inside. It was empty of customers. A bartender lounged behind the bar and two girls, one in a bright red dress and the other in white with gold sequins, sat on stools together at the far end of the bar. There were no drinks in front of them. All three looked toward Sweeney as he entered.

He picked a stool in about the middle of the tow and put a five-dollar bill on the mahogany. The bartender came over and one of the girls—the one in red—was getting off her stool. The bartender beat her there and Sweeney had time to ask for a rye and seltzer before the girl, now on the stool beside him, said "Hello."

"Hello," Sweeney said. "Lonesome?"

"That's my line; I'm supposed to ask that. You'll buy me a drink, won't you?"

Sweeney nodded. The bartender was already pouring it. He moved away to give them privacy. The girl in the red dress smiled brightly at Sweeney. She said, "I'm awfully glad you came in. It's been dead as a doornail in this joint ever since I got here an hour ago. Anyway you don't look like a jerk like most of the guys come in here. How'd you like to sit over in one of the booths? My name's Tess, so now we're introduced. Let's move over to one of the booths, huh, and Joe'll bring us—"

"Did you know Stella Gaylord?"

Stopped in mid-sentence, she stared at him. She asked, "You aren't another shamus, are you? This place was lousy with 'em, right after what happened to Stella."

"You did know her, then," said Sweeney. "Good. No, I'm not a shamus. I'm a newspaperman."

"Oh. One of those. May I have another drink, please?"

Sweeney nodded, and the bartender, who hadn't gone far, came up to pour it.

"Tell me about Stella."

'Tell you what?"

"Everything you know. Pretend I never heard of her. For all practical purposes, I haven't. I didn't work on the case. I was on vacation when it happened."

"Oh. But you're working on it now?"

Sweeney sighed. He'd have to satisfy her curiosity before he could satisfy his own. He said, "Not for the paper. I'm going to write it up for a fact detective magazine. Not just Stella Gaylord, but the whole Ripper business. As soon as the case is cracked, that is. The true detective mags don't buy unsolved cases. But I'll have to be ready to write it up quick, once the thing breaks."

"Oh. They pay pretty well for something like that, don't they? What's in it for me?"

"A drink,". said Sweeney, motioning to the bartender. "Listen, sister, I'll be talking to about fifty people who knew Stella Gaylord and Dorothy Lee and Lola Brent, and to coppers who worked on it, and to other reporters. Wouldn't I be in a beautiful spot if I gave everybody a slice of it? Even if the case does break and I do sell the story, I'd come out behind, see?"

She grinned. "It never hurts to try."

"That it doesn't. And, incidentally, I will split with you if you can crack the case so I can sell it. You don't happen to know who killed her, do you?"

Her face hardened. "Mister, if .1 knew that, the cops would know it. Stella was a good kid."

"Tell me about her. Anything. How old she was, where she came from, what she wanted, what she looked like—anything."

"I don't know how old she was. Somewhere around thirty, I guess. She came from Des Moines, about five years ago, I think she told me once. I knew her only about a month."

"Was that when you started here, or when she did?"

"When I did. She'd been here a couple of months already. I was over on Halsted before that. It was a worse joint than this, for looks, but I made better dough. There was always trouble there, though, and God, how I hate trouble. I get along with people, if they get along with me. I never start—"

"About Stella," said Sweeney. "What did she look like? I saw the newspaper picture, but it wasn't very good."

"I know. I saw it. Stella was kind of pretty. She had a beautiful figure, anyway; she tried to get into modeling once, but you got to have contacts. She was about thirty; her hair was kind of a darkish blonde. She ought to've hennaed it, but she wouldn't. Blue eyes. About five-five or so."

"What was she, inside?" Sweeney asked. "What was she trying to do?"

The red dress shrugged. "What are any of us trying to do? Get along, I guess. How'd I know what she was like inside? How'd anybody know? That's a funny question for you to ask. How's about another drink?"

"Okay," said Sweeney. "Were you working here with her the night she was killed?"

"Yeah. I told the cops what I knew about that."

"Tell me, too."

"She made an after-date. After two, that is; we closed at two. It was with a guy that was in around ten or eleven o'clock and talked to her for half an hour or so. I never saw him before, and he hasn't been in since."

"Did he pick her up at two?"

"She was going to meet him somewhere. His hotel, I guess." She turned and looked at Sweeney. "We don't do that with anybody. But sometimes, if we like a guy—well, why not?"

"Why not?" Sweeney said. "And you girls don't make much at this percentage racket, do you?"

"Not enough to dress the way we got to dress. And everything. This ain't a nice racket, but there are worse ones. At least we can pick which men we want to go out with, and we get ten or twenty propositions a day." She grinned at him impudently. "Not often this early, though. Yours will be the first today, when you get around to it."

"If I get around to it," Sweeney said. "What do you remember about the guy she was going to meet?"

"Practically nothing because I didn't notice him. After he went out, Stella came back to me—I was sitting alone just then for a few minutes—and mentioned she was meeting him after two and—what did I think of the guy. Well, I'd just glanced at him sitting there with her before and all I remembered was that he was pretty ordinary looking. I think he had on a gray suit. He wasn't specially old or young, or tall or short or fat or anything or I'd probably have remembered. I don't think I'd know him again if I saw him."

"He didn't have a round face and wear thick glasses, did he?"

"Not that I remember. I wouldn't swear he didn't. And I'll save you one thing; nobody else around here noticed him or has any better idea. That's one thing the coppers dogged everybody about. No use asking George, behind the bar, or Emmy—that's the girl in the white dress. They were both here that night, but they didn't remember as much about it as I did."

"Did Stella have any enemies?"

"No. She was a nice kid. Even us girls who worked with her liked her, and mister, that's something. And to beat your next question, no, she didn't have any serious men friends and she didn't live with anybody. I don't mean she never packed an overnight bag, but I mean living with anybody, serious."

"She have a family, back in Des Moines?"

"Her parents were dead, she said once. If she had any other relatives anywhere she never talked about them. I don't guess she had any she was close to."

"The address on West Madison where she lived. That would be about three blocks from here, wouldn't it? What is it, a hotel or rooming house?"

"A hotel, the Claremore. It's a dive. Can I have another drink?"

Sweeney crooked a finger at the bartender. He said, "Mine, too, this time."

He shoved his Panama back on his head. "Look, Tess, you've told me what she looked like, what she did. But what was she? What made her tick? What did she want?"

The girl in the red dress picked up her glass and stared into it She looked at Sweeney, then, squarely for the first time. She said, "You're a funny kind of guy. I think I could like you."

"That's swell," said Sweeney.

"I even like the way you said that. Sarcastic as hell, but—I don't know what I mean. You meet all kinds of guys in a business like this, and—" She laughed a little and emptied her glass. She said, "I suppose if *I* got myself killed by a ripper, you'd be interested in finding out what made *me* tick, what *I* really wanted. You'd—Oh, hell."

"You're a big girl now," Sweeney said. "Don't let it get you down. I *do* like you."

"Sure. Sure. *I* know what I am. So let's skip it. I'll tell you what Stella wanted. A beauty shop. In a little town somewhere, a long way from Chicago. Go ahead and laugh. But that's what she was saving up her money for. That's what she wanted. She saved her money, working as a waitress, and then got sick and it went. She didn't like this racket any more than the rest of us, but she'd been at it a year and in another year she'd've had enough saved up to make a break for herself."

"She had money saved up then. Who gets it?"

The girl shrugged. "Nobody, I guess, unless some relative shows up. Say, I just remembered something. Stella had a girl friend who's a-waitress near where she was killed. An all-night restaurant on State just north of Chicago Avenue. And she nearly always, had something to eat after she got off at two. I told the cops maybe she went from here to that restaurant for a sandwich before she kept her date with the mooch. Or maybe she met him at the restaurant instead of at his hotel room or whatever."

"You don't know the waitress* name, do you?"

Tess shook her head. "But I know the restaurant. It's the third or fourth door north of Chicago Avenue, on the west side of State."

Sweeney said, "Thanks, Tess. I'd better push along." He glanced at the money on the bar, three singles and some change left out of the ten he'd put there. "Put it under the mattress. Be seeing you."

She put a hand on his arm. "Wait. Do you mean it? Will you come back?"

"Maybe."

Tess sighed, and dropped her hand. "All right, then, you won't. I know. The nice guys never do."

When Sweeney stepped out to the sidewalk, fee impact of the heat was almost like a blow. He hesitated a moment and then walked west.

The Claremore Hotel, from the street, was just a sign and an uninviting stairway. Sweeney trudged up the steps to a tiny lobby on the second floor.

A swarthy, stocky man who hadn't shaved for at least two days was sorting mail behind a short counter. He glanced at Sweeney and said, "Filled up." He looked down at the mail again.

Sweeney leaned against the counter and waited.

Finally the stocky man looked up again.'

"Stella Gaylord lived here," Sweeney said.

"Jesus God, another cop or a reporter. Yeah, she lived here. So what?"

"So nothing," said Sweeney.

He turned and looked down the dim corridor of doors with peeling paint, at the uncarpeted stairs leading to the floor above. He sniffed the musty air. Stella Gaylord, he thought, must have wanted that beauty shop pretty bad to have lived in a hole like this.

He looked back at the stocky man to ask a question and then decided, to hell with it.

He turned and walked down the stairs to the street.

The clock in the window of a cheap jewelry store next door told him he still had over an hour before his appointment with Greene and Yolanda Lang at El Madhouse.

It also reminded him that he still didn't have a watch, and he went in and bought one.

Putting change back in his wallet, he asked the jeweler, "Did you know Stella Gaylord?"

"Who?"

"Such is fame," Sweeney said. "Skip it."

Outside, he flagged a cab and rode to State and Chicago. The waitress who had been Stella's friend wouldn't be on duty now, but maybe he could get her address, and maybe he could learn something anyway.

The restaurant was called the Dinner Gong. Two waitresses were working behind the counter and a man in shut sleeves, who looked as though he might be the proprietor, was behind the cash register on the cigar counter.

Sweeney bought cigarettes. He said, "I'm from the *Blade*. You have a waitress here who was a friend of Stella Gaylord. Is she still on the night shift?"

"You mean Thelma Smith. She quit over a week ago. Scared stiff to work in this neighborhood, after what happened to the Gaylord girl."

"You have her address? Thelma's, I mean?"

"No. She was going out of town; that's all I know. She'd been talking about going to New York, so maybe that's where."

Sweeney said, "Stella was in here that night, wasn't she?"

"Sure. I wasn't on then, but I was here while the police were talking to Thelma. She said Stella came here a little after two o'clock and had a sandwich and coffee and then left."

"She didn't say anything to Thelma about where she was going?"

The proprietor shook his head. "But it was probably somewhere near here, or she wouldn't have come way up here from Madison for a sandwich. She was a chippie; the cops figure it she had a hotel-room date somewhere around here after she got through at the bar she worked at."

Sweeney thanked him and went out He was pretty sure it wouldn't pay to try to trace Thelma Smith; the police had already talked to her. And if there'd been anything suspicious about her leaving town, they'd be doing the tracing.

While he was waiting for a chance to get across the traffic on Chicago Avenue, he remembered something he'd forgotten to ask Tess. When he got across the street he phoned Susie's Cue from the corner drugstore and asked for her.

"This is the guy you were talking to half an hour ago, Tess," he told her. "Just remembered something. Did Stella ever say anything about a statuette—a little black statuette of a woman, about ten inches high?"

"No. Where are you?"

"I'm lost in a fog," Sweeney said. "Were you ever up to Stella's room?"

"Yes, once just a few days before she—before she died."

"She didn't have a statuette like that?"

"No. She had a little white statuette on her dresser, though. A Madonna. She'd had it a long time, I remember her saying. Why? What gives about a statuette?"

"Probably nothing. Tess, does 'Screaming Mimi' mean anything to you?"

"I've had 'em. What is this, a gag?"

"No, but I can't tell you about it. Thanks, anyway. I'll be seeing you sometime."

"I'll bet."

When he left the drugstore he walked west to Clark Street and south to El Madhouse.

CHAPTER 8

SHE LOOKED just like the picture of her that had been in Sweeney's mind, except, of course, that she wore clothes. Sweeney smiled at her and she smiled back and Doc Greene said, "You'll remember her, Sweeney. You've been staring ever since you sat down."

Yolanda said, "Pay no attention to him, Mr. Sweeney. His bark is worse than his bite."

Greene chuckled. "Don't give Sweeney an opening like that, my sweet. He already suspects that I have canine ancestry." He stared at Sweeney through the thick glasses. He spoke softly: "I *do* bite."

"At least," said Sweeney to Yolanda, "he nips at my heels. I don't like him."

"Doc's all right, Mr. Sweeney. He grows on you."

"He'd better not try to grow on *me.* Doc, do you shave with a straight-edge razor?"

"As it happens, yes."

"Your own, or do you borrow other people's?"

Behind the heavy lenses, Doc Greene's eyes narrowed slightly. "Someone has borrowed yours?"

Sweeney nodded. "Again your perspicacity mystifies me. Yes, someone has borrowed mine. And a small knife as well. The only two keen-edged tools in the place."

"Not counting your brain, Sweeney. He left you that. Or was it there at the time of the theft?"

"I doubt it seriously. It must have been in the evening while I was out rather than while I was sleeping. I deduce that from the fact that, when I looked in the mirror this morning, there was no fine red line across my throat."

Greene shook his head slowly. "You looked in the wrong place, Sweeney. Our friend the Ripper has a strong predilection for abdomens. Did you look there?"

"Not specifically, Doc. But I think I would have noticed when I took a shower."

Yolanda Lang shuddered a little and pushed her chair back. "I'm afraid I must run along, Mr. Sweeney. I've got to talk to the maestro about a new number. You'll come to see me dance tonight? The first number is at ten."

She held out her hand and smiled at him. Sweeney took the hand and returned the smile. He said, "Wild horses and so forth, Yo. Or may I call you Yolanda?"

She laughed. "I think I prefer it. You say it as though you meant it."

She walked toward the archway leading from the tavern to the night club at the rear. The dog, which had been lying beside her chair, followed her. So did the two detectives who had been sitting at the next table.

"Makes quite a parade," Doc Greene said.

Sweeney sat down again and made circles on the table with the bottom of his glass. After a minute he looked up. He said, "Hello, Doc. I didn't know you were here."

"Getting anywhere, Sweeney? Got a lead?"

"No."

Greene sighed deeply. "My bosom enemy, I'm afraid you don't trust me."

"Should I?"

"To an extent. And to what extent? To the extent that I tell you you can. That means as far as finding the Ripper is concerned." He leaned forward, elbows on the table. "As concerns Yolanda, no. As concerns yourself, no. As concerns money, no—although that shall have no reason to arise between us. But as concerns the Ripper, yes. I shall worry about Yolanda until he is caught. I would even prefer that he is killed rather than caught, because he presumed to touch her."

"With a cold blade," said Sweeney. "Not with a hot hand."

"With anything. But that is past. It's the future that worries me. Right now there are two detectives guarding Yo all the time; three eight-hour shifts of them. But the police won't do that forever. Find me the Ripper, Sweeney."

"And after that?"

"After that, the hell with you."

"Thank you, Doc. The only trouble is that you're so completely honest that I distrust you."

Greene sighed again. "Sweeney," he said. "I don't want you to waste time suspecting me. The police got that little idea yesterday because I couldn't account for where I was when the Ripper attacked Yolanda. I don't know where I was either, except that it was on the South Side. I was with a client—a singer at the Club Cairo—until midnight and I got pretty stinking. I got home, but I can't prove when, and I don't even know when."

"That happens," Sweeney said. "But why should I believe it?"

"For the same reason the police did, you should. Because it happens I have solid alibis on two of the other three attacks. I checked back, and the police checked back on what I told them.

"Not on the Lola Brent one, two months ago; that's too far back and I couldn't figure out where I was. But they told me the second one—What was her name?"

"Stella Gaylord."

"—was the night of July 27th, and I was in New York on business. I was there from the 25th through the 30th, and on the night of the 27th I was— luckily—with some damned respectable people from dinner time until three in the morning. Don't waste time or distract me by asking what I was doing with respectable people. That's irrelevant. The police have checked it. Ask Captain Bline.

"And on the first of August, last week, at the moment this secretary, Dorothy Lee, was killed, I was here in Chicago, but it just happens I was in court testifying on a breach of contract suit against a theater manager. Judge Goerring and the bailiff and the court clerk and three lawyers—one of them mine and two of them the theater's—are all the alibi I've got on that one. "Now if you want to believe I'm half a ripper, working the first and fourth cases with a stand-in filling in for the second and third, you're welcome. But you aren't that much of a damn fool."

"You've got something there," Sweeney admitted. He took a folded piece of blank copy paper and a pencil from his pockets. "I'll even settle for *one* alibi, if it's the real McCoy. Judge Goerring's court, you say? When to when?"

"Case was called at three o'clock and ran till a little after four. Before it was called, I was in conference with all three lawyers for a good half-hour in an anteroom of the court According to the newspapers, the Lee girl left her office alive at a quarter of three to go home. She was found dead in her apartment at five and they thought she'd been dead an hour. Hell, Sweeney, I couldn't have *planned* a better alibi. She was killed right while I was on the witness stand, two miles away. Will you buy it?"

"I'll buy it," Sweeney said. "What were the lawyers' names?"

"You're a hard man, Sweeney. Why suspect me, anyway, any more than Joe Blow up there at the bar, or the guy next to him?"

"Because my room was entered last night. Only a razor and a knife were taken, and razors and knives tie up with the Ripper. Up to last night damn few people knew I had any interest in the Ripper. You're one of them."

Greene laughed. "And how did I find out? By reading that eyewitness story you wrote for the *Blade*. What's the circulation of the *Blade!* Half a million?"

Sweeney said, "Excuse me for living. I'll buy you a drink on that, Doc."

"Bourbon straight. Now, have you got a lead to the Ripper yet?"

Sweeney signaled the waiter and ordered, then answered. "Not a lead," he said. "What were the names of the lawyers, Doc?" He poised the pencil over the copy paper.

"I thought you were mostly Airedale, Sweeney, but you're half bulldog. My lawyer's Hymie Pieman, in the Central Building. The opposition was Raenough, Dane & Howell. Dane—Carl Dane, I think it is—and a young neophyte named Brady, who works for them but isn't a member of the firm yet, were the two who were in conference and present at the hearing. And the judge was Goerring. G-o-e-r-r-i-n-g. He's a Republican, so he wouldn't alibi a Ripper."

Sweeney nodded moodily. He said, "Wish I could snap out of this hangover and think straight. I'm as nervous as a cat." He unfolded the sheet of copy paper and smoothed it flat. Then he held out his right hand, back up and fingers spread wide, and put the piece of paper on it. The slight trembling, magnified, vibrated the edges of the paper.

"Not as bad as I thought," he said. "Bet you can't do any better." He looked at Greene. "In fact, five bucks you can't."

Greene said, "I should never bet a man at his own game, and I've never tried that, but you're on. You're a wreck, and I've got nerves like a rock."

Greene picked up the paper and balanced it flat on the back of his hand. The edges vibrated slightly, but noticeably less than they had on Sweeney's hand.

Sweeney watched the paper very closely. He asked, "Doc, did you ever hear of the Screaming Mimi?"

The rate of vibration of the edges of the paper didn't change at all. Watching them, Greene said, "Guess I win, Sweeney. Concede the bet?"

There'd been no reaction, but Sweeney cussed himself silently. The man who'd bought that statuette wouldn't have known the company's nickname for it; Lola Brent, as a new employee, wouldn't have known it to tell him.

Sweeney said, "A small black statuette of a woman screaming."

Doc Greene looked up from the paper, but the vibration of the edges— Sweeney's eyes stayed on the paper—didn't change.

Greene lowered his hand to the table. He said, "What is this? A gag?"

"It was, Doc. But you win the bet." Sweeney handed over the fin. "It's worth it. You answered my questions so I can believe you—for sure."

"You mean the Screaming Mimi and the black statuette? No, I never heard of either, Sweeney. A statuette of a woman screaming? One and the same thing? The statuette is called Screaming Mimi? M-i-m-i?"

"Right. And you never heard of either. I don't necessarily believe your saying so, Doc, but I do believe the edges of that piece of paper."

"Clever, Sweeney. A homemade lie detec—No, not that; a reaction indicator. I'll keep your five, but I'll buy you a drink out of it. Same?"

Sweeney nodded. Doc signaled.

Doc put his elbows on the table. He said, "Then you were lying. You have got a lead. Tell Papa. Papa might help."

"Baby doesn't want help, from Papa. Papa is too anxious to get Baby cut up with a sharp shiv."

"You underrate me, Sweeney. I think I can get it without your help. And I'm curious, now. I will if I have to."

"Prove it."

"All right." Doc Greene's eyes looked enormous, hypnotic, through the lenses of his glasses. "A small black statuette called the Screaming Mimi. Most statuettes are sold in art and gift shops. One of the girls attacked worked, for one day—the day of her murder—in an art and gift shop. I—forgot where, but the newspapers would tell me. If I look up the proprietor and ask him if he ever heard of Screaming Mimi, would it get me any-where?"

Sweeney lifted his glass. "I did underrate you, Doc."

"And I you, Sweeney, when I almost believed you that you didn't have a lead. To your bad health."

"And yours."

They drank and then Greene asked, "So do I go to the proprietor of the art store and start from there, or do you break down and tell me?"

"I might as well. Lola Brent sold a small black statuette of a screaming, terrified nude just before she was killed. There's pretty good reason to believe the Ripper was her customer, followed her home and killed her. Likely the figure set him off; it's something that would appeal only to a psycho."

"Do you like it?"

"I dislike it, but I find it fascinating. It's rather well done, incidentally. And I followed up on it. Only two were sent to Chicago. I've got one. The Ripper's got the other."

"Do the police know that?"

"No. I'm pretty sure they don't."

"I told you, Sweeney. The luck of the Irish. By the way, are you crowding your luck too far, or are you going heeled?"

"Heeled?"

"Packing a rod, toting a gun. In a word, armed. If the Ripper —anyone else—had called on me and removed my small armament of knife and razor, I'd bring up the artillery. If the Ripper knew where *my* room was, I'd sleep with a sawed-off shotgun across my chest. Or *does he know, Sweeney?*"

"You mean?"

"Yes."

Sweeney grinned. "You want my alibis? Well, I don't know anything about two months-ago. I doubt if I could check back. As for the next two murders, well, I was on a two-week drunk. Only God knows where I was and what I was doing, and I wasn't with God all the time. As for night before last, when Yolanda was attacked, I was at the scene of the crime at approximately the time of the crime. How's that for a set of alibis?"

Doc Greene grunted. He said, "I've heard better. I can't remember when I've heard worse. Sweeney, as a practical psychiatrist, I don't think you're the Ripper type, but I've been wrong. *Are* you?"

Sweeney stood up. He said, "I'm damned if I'll tell you, Doc. In the little duel of pleasantries between us, it's the one big edge I've got on you. I'm going to let you wonder. And if I am, thanks for warning me about the sawed-off shotgun."

He went outside and it was dusk. His headache was gone and he felt almost human again.

He walked south on Clark Street without thinking about where he was going, without, in fact, thinking at all. He let his mind alone and his mind let him alone, and they got along fine together. He heard himself humming and listened to himself long enough to find out what it was; it turned out to be the melody of a Brahms Hungarian dance, so he quit listening.

He watched, instead, the movies that were going on inside his head, and very nice movies they were. Yolanda sitting across the table from him, even as she had sat only minutes before; Devil, the dog, as well trained as any Seeing-Eye dog, curled up at her feet with a small but incongruous bandage on top of his head, result of a very skillful job of creasing by the detective who'd shot through the glass at him. Sweeney admired the marksmanship of that cop almost as much—but not in the same way—as he admired the next sequence in his mental movie: the beautiful body of Yolanda, seen In the spot of the other detective's flashlight.

He sighed, and then grinned. It had never occurred to him that a woman could be that beautiful. He still didn't quite believe it. He'd half expected disillusionment when he'd gone to El Madhouse to meet Doc Greene and Yolanda. He *had,* after all, been pretty drunk when he'd seen—what he'd seen some (How long was it?) forty hours ago. It would have disappointed him, but not surprised him too much, had she turned out not to look like that at all. Or if she had been beautiful but had talked with a Brooklyn accent.

But, instead, she had been *more* beautiful than he had remembered. Her face had, anyway. And, even more, there had been that intriguing air of mystery about her which, forty hours ago, he had thought was entirely subjective, due to the strange circumstances of the affair in the hallway. It hadn't been; it was really there. Yolanda Lang *had* something besides the most beautiful body he had ever seen.

He thought: Godfrey, you'd better be right. And then he grinned, because he knew damned well that Godfrey *was* right. If you wanted something badly enough you could get it.

And he was going to get it.

If he'd wondered that before he'd met and tangled with Doc Greene, he'd quit wondering after. If Yolanda were fat and forty—and she wasn't either—he'd have to carry through out of cussedness just because he and Greene hated one another so completely. Almost literally, the man made his flesh crawl.

If only he could prove that Greene was the Ripper—

But there were two alibis. The police had accepted them. Anyway, Greene had *said* the police had-become interested in him and then had accepted the alibis. But that was something he could check. That was something he *would* check.

Furthermore, he could at least start to check on it right now.

He was crossing Lake Street into the Loop and he kept on going to Randolph and turned west to the tavern, between Clark and LaSalle, where a lot of the boys from the *Blade* hung out.

None of them seemed to be hanging out there at the moment, so he ordered a shot and mixed it with soda so he could work on it a while to see if any of them were coming in.

He asked Burt Meaghan, who ran the place and who was alone behind the bar at the moment, "Think any of the boys will come around for pinochle after work this evening?"

"Be an unusual evening if they don't. Where you been keeping yourself, Sweeney?"

"Around and about. I've been on a bender, if you don't know. Doesn't anybody tell you these things, Burt?"

"Yeah, I'd heard. In fact, you were in here a few times the first week of it. Haven't seen you for over a week, though."

"You didn't miss much. Burt, do you know Harry Yahn."

"Know of him. Not personally I don't know him. I don't move in such high circles. He's got a place a couple blocks west of here that he runs himself. And an interest in a few others."

"I've been out of touch," Sweeney said. "What's the name of the place he runs himself?"

"Name on front of the tavern is the Tit-Tat-Toe; that's just the front, of course. Want an in?"

"Wouldn't need it. I know Harry from way back when. I just lost track of where he was operating."

"He ain't been there long. Month or so. 'Scuse me, Sweeney."

He went down to the other end of the bar to wait on another customer. Sweeney drew wet rings on the bar with the bottom of his glass and wondered if he'd have to see Harry Yahn. He hoped not, because monkeying with Harry Yahn was as healthy as trimming your fingernails on a buzzsaw. But he was going to need money from somewhere before this thing was over. He still had about a hundred and fifty dollars left out of the three checks Wally had given him, but that wasn't going to go very far on all he had in mind.

There was a hand on his shoulder and he turned. It was Wayne Horlick. Sweeney said, "The very guy I wanted to see most. Talk about the luck of the Irish."

Horlick grinned at him. "Costs you ten bucks to be that lucky, Sweeney. I'm glad to see you too. Ten bucks' worth."

Sweeney sighed. "From when?"

"Ten days ago. In here. Don't you remember?"

"Sure," Sweeney lied. He paid up. "And a drink for interest?"

"Why not? Rye."

Sweeney downed the last sip of the drink he'd been working on and ordered two. He said, "Why I wanted to see you, if you're curious, is that you've been working on the Ripper case."

"Yeah. The recent parts of it, anyway. I don't know who did the Lola Brent part, couple of months ago. But I got put on the second one, the Stella Gaylord murder, and been at it ever since."

"Any leads?"

"Nary a lead, Sweeney. And if I did get one I'd turn it over to the cops quick-like and cheerful-like. The Ripper's one boy I wouldn't care to meet. Except through bars after Bline gets him. Did you know they've got a special Ripper detail working on nothing else, with Cap Bline in charge?"

(

"Carey told me. Think they'll get him?"

"Sure they'll get him—if he keeps on slicing dames. But not on any clues he's left with the ones he's already cut. Say, have you talked to this Yolanda Lang dame?"

"Yes, just an hour or so ago. Why?"

Horlick laughed. "Figured you'd try—after I read that eyewitness account of yours. Nice writing there, pal. Made everybody's mouth water. Mine included. Been trying for an interview with the dame ever since, but can't get it. I figured you would."

"Why?" Sweeney asked curiously. "I don't mean why would I try, but why did you figure I'd get one if you couldn't?"

"That *story* you wrote. Far be it from me to praise anybody else's writing, Sweeney, but that was a minor classic of journalism. And what's more to the point, it's ten thousand dollars' worth of free publicity for the dame— above and beyond the publicity from getting picked on by the Ripper, and being the first one to survive a Ripper attack. Doc Greene must love you like a brother."

Sweeney laughed. "Sure. Like Cain loved Abel. Say, Horlick, anything come out about any of the cases that didn't get in the papers? I've read up on—uh—Lola Brent and Stella Gaylord; haven't got around to the third dame yet, Dorothy Lee."

Horlick thought and then shook his head. "Nothing I can think of, nothing worth mentioning. Why? You really interested? Beyond getting that interview with the strip-teaser? You don't need to explain that."

Sweeney decided to stick to the lie he'd told Joe Carey. "Had in mind to write it up for a fact detective mag. Way to do that is have all the dope ready so the minute the case is cracked, I can beat the others to the punch."

"Good idea, *if* they ever crack the case. And they will, of course, if the guy keeps on ripping. He can't be lucky forever. I hope Wally puts you on it instead of me; I don't like the job. Want me to put in a word for you?"

"Carey's going to, so you'd better not. Wally might get suspicious if we laid it on too thick. What do you know about Doc Greene?"

"Why? Going to try to pin it on him?"

"I'd love to. I love him like a brother, too. He tells me the cops got the same idea and that he was alibied on two of the jobs and they took his alibis. Know anything about it?"

Horlick shook his head. "That would have been since the Ripper tried for Yolanda, of course; in the last couple of days. No, Bline didn't tell me about investigating Greene. But then I guess they have investigated just about everyone who's ever been closely connected with any of the four dames."

"What's your impression of Greene, Horlick?"

"He gives me the creeps. Is that what you mean?"

"That," said Sweeney, "is *exactly* what I mean. For that, I'll buy you another drink. Rye?"

"Rye."

"Hey Burt, a rye for Horlick. I'll pass this one."

And he really did pass it, and wouldn't let Horlick buy back Half an hour later, he left and went home.

Mrs. Randall heard him come in and opened her door.

"Mr. Sweeney, there's a man to see you. He wanted to wait so I let him wait in my sitting room. Shall I tell him—"

A big man stepped around from behind her. He said, "William Sweeney? My name is Bline, Captain Bline."

CHAPTER 9

SWEENEY STUCK out a paw and the detective took it, but not enthusiastically. But Sweeney pretended not to notice. He said, "I've been wanting to meet you, Cap, since I heard you were on the case. Some things I want to ask you. Come on up to my room."

Bline followed him up the stairs and into the room. He sat down in the chair Sweeney pointed out to him, the overstuffed one with the creaky springs; it groaned under his weight.

Sweeney sat on the edge of the bed. He glanced at the phonograph and said, "Want some music while we talk, Cap?"

"Hell, no. We're gonna talk, not sing duets. And it's me that's going to ask the questions, Sweeney."

"What about?"

"You're asking 'em already. Look, I don't suppose you remember where you were on the afternoon of June 8th, do you?"

"No, I don't. Unless I was working that afternoon. Even then, I wouldn't know offhand if I was in the office doing rewrite, or if I was out on a job.

Unless—maybe if I checked the late editions for that day and the early ones for the next, I could spot and remember which stories I worked on."

"You didn't work on any. You didn't work, that day; you were off. I checked at the *Blade.*"

"Then all I can tell you is what I probably did, which wouldn't mean much. I probably slept till about noon, spent most of the afternoon here reading or listening to music, probably went out in the evening to play some cards and have a few drinks. Or maybe a show or a concert. That part I might possibly be able to check on, but not the afternoon, and I judge that's what you're interested in."

"Right. And how about July 27th?"

"As hopeless as the next one you're going to ask about, Cap. August 1st, I mean. God knows where I was either time, except that I'm pretty sure it was in Chicago. Haven't been out of town in the last two weeks that I know of." Bline grunted.

Sweeney grinned. He said, "Only I'm not the Ripper. Granted that I don't even know where I was or what I was doing when Stella Gaylord and Dorothy Lee were killed, I know I didn't kill Lola Brent—because I wasn't that drunk, I mean drunk enough not to remember something I did, any time in June. And I know I didn't make the pass at Yolanda Lang because I do remember Wednesday night; I was beginning to come out of it then, and feeling like hell. Ask God."

"Huh?"

Sweeney opened his mouth and then closed it again. No use getting poor old Godfrey grilled at headquarters, and Godfrey couldn't alibi him anyway, not for the exact time the attack had been made on Yolanda. He said, "A manner of speaking, Cap. Only God could prove what I was doing Wednesday night. But cheer up, if the Ripper keeps on ripping, maybe I'll have an alibi for the next one."

"That will be a big help."

"Meanwhile, Cap, and seriously, what made you come here to ask me about alibis? Did a little bird tell you? A Greene one?"

"Sweeney, you know damn well why I'm here. Because you were there in front of that door on State Street Wednesday night. The Ripper was probably in front of that door. Way we figure it, he was standing at the back door of that hallway and reached in and slashed as the dame came toward him. Only he was a couple of inches short and just nicked her, and the dog ran around her and jumped and he had to duck back and slam the door without having a chance for a second try. And then what would he do?"

"You asked it," Sweeney said. "You answer it."

"He might have got the hell out of there, of course. But if he followed the pattern of most psycho killers, he came out of the alley and walked around to the front and was in that knot of people looking through the door when the squad car came."

"Also maybe," Sweeney said, "having put in the call for the police from the tavern on the corner."

Bline shook his head. He said, "No, we found out who put in that call. Guy that had been standing at the bar there with two other guys, talking, for hours. He left there a little before . two-thirty and he was back in a few minutes. Told the guys he'd been talking to and the bartender that there was something going on in a hallway down the street. That a dame was on the floor and a big dog wouldn't let anybody open the door and go in to see what was wrong with the dame, so maybe he better phone the cops. So he did, and then he and the other two guys—all three of them this time— went-together to the place and were there when the squad car came. I've talked to all three of them—the bartender knew one and I found the others through him. They say there were about a dozen people in front of the doorway. That what you'd say?"

"Pretty close. Not over fifteen at the most."

"And the squad car coppers—even after they saw it was a Ripper job— didn't have sense enough to hold every one of them. We've located five out of the twelve or fifteen. If only we had *all* of 'em—"

"Who is the fifth?" Sweeney asked. "The three who were together and I made four; who else?"

"Guy who lived in the building. Guess he was the first one to see the woman and the dog. Came home and couldn't get in because the dog started to jump him every time he started to open the door. Other passers-by saw something was happening and stopped to look in too. When the guy from the tavern—the one who made the phone call—got there, there were six or eight people. When he got back with his two friends, there were nine or ten besides them."

"I was probably the next arrival," Sweeney said. "I got there just a minute before the squad car came. And to answer your next question, no, I didn't notice anybody else in the crowd. Couldn't identify a one of them. All I noticed was what was going on inside and what the squad car coppers did. Probably couldn't identify even them."

Bline said dryly, "We don't need them identified. I'd give a lot, though, to have every one of that crowd in front. Instead of five—and four of those five cleared."

"Not counting me?"

"Not counting you."

"What clears the man who lived in the building? The one who, according to his own story, was the first one there?"

"He's reasonably clear. Works a night shift on the *Journal of Commerce* on Grand Avenue; he's a printer. Didn't punch out on the time clock till one forty-five and it'd have taken him that long to get there; he wouldn't have had time to go in the alleyway, wait a while, and then go around to the front. Besides, he has solid alibis for all three other rippings; we checked them."

He frowned at Sweeney. "So of the five men we have located who were in that crowd in front of the door, you're the only one without an alibi for anything at all. By the way, here's your cutlery; the lab couldn't get anything on it."

He took an envelope from his pocket and handed it to Sweeney. Without opening it, Sweeney could feel that it contained his penknife and straight razor.

He said, "You might have asked me for them. Did you have a search warrant?"

Bline chuckled. "We didn't want you in our hair while we were casing the joint. As for a warrant, does it matter now?" Sweeney opened his mouth and then closed it again. He was mad enough to start something; those things being gone had given him some bad moments. On the other hand, it was going to be helpful if not necessary to have Bline friendly to him; there were things the police could do that he couldn't.

So he said, mildly, "You might have left a note. When I missed those, I thought maybe the Ripper thought I was the Ripper. Say, Cap, what do you know about this guy Greene, Doc Greene?"

"Why?"

"I kind of like to think of him as the Ripper, that's all. He tells me he's got alibis and that you've checked them. That right?"

"More or less. No alibi for Lola Brent, and the one for Dorothy Lee isn't perfect."

"Not perfect? I thought that was the one where he was testifying in court under Judge Goerring."

"The tunes don't fit perfectly. His alibi takes him up to about ten minutes after four. Dorothy Lee wasn't found dead until about five o'clock—maybe a few minutes after. The coroner said she'd been dead at least an hour when he saw her at five-thirty, but that means she could have been killed at four-thirty, twenty minutes after Greene's alibi ends. He could have made it, in a taxi, from the court to her place in that time."

"Then it's no alibi at all."

Bline said, "Not an iron-clad one, no. But there are angles. She left work at two forty-five to go home because she was sick; ordinarily she worked till five. Even if Greene knew her—and there's no proof he did—he wouldn't have known he'd find her home if he rushed there right from court. Only someone who worked with her would have known that."

"Or anyone who dropped in her office or phoned for her."

"True, but Greene didn't drop in. He would barely have had time to phone, and still get to her place by four-thirty."

Bline frowned. "You're stretching probabilities."

"Am I? Suppose Greene knew her—well. He could have had a date to pick her up at her apartment after five. But he gets through in court a little after four and goes there to wait for her. Maybe he even has a key, and lets himself in to wait, not knowing she came home sick and is already there."

"Oh, it's *possible,* Sweeney. I told you it wasn't a perfect alibi. But you've got to admit it isn't likely. The Ripper probably followed her home, seeing her on the street for the first time after she left work. Like he probably followed Lola Brent home from the gift shop. He couldn't have been waiting for Lola Brent at her place for two reasons—first, he couldn't have known she was going to be fired and come home early; second, she was living with a man, Sammy Cole; he couldn't have known Sammy wouldn't walk in on him."

"And anyway," Sweeney said, "Lola wasn't killed in her apartment but in the areaway outside the buildings. Sure, she was probably followed. And so was Stella Gaylord—followed as far as the mouth of the alley. But the Ripper doesn't always use the following technique. He didn't follow Yolanda Lang home; he was waiting for her outside that door at the back of the hallway in her building."

"You've really studied this case, haven't you, Sweeney?"

"Why not?" Sweeney asked. "It's my job."

"As I get it, you haven't been assigned to it yet. Or am I wrong?"

Sweeney considered whether to give Bline the song-and-dance about the fact detective magazine and decided not to; Bline might ask which magazine, and then check up on him.

He said, "Not exactly, Cap. But I was assigned on at least one angle of it when Wally Krieg told me to write that eyewitness account. And I figured because of that *in* I had on the case, he'd probably ask me to do more when I go back to work Monday, so I read up on the case, what's already been in the papers, and asked a few questions."

"On your own time?"

"Why not? I got interested in it. You'd still follow the case if you got taken off it, wouldn't you?"

"Guess I would," Bline admitted.

"How about Greene's other alibi, the New York one? How well did you check on that one?"

Bline grinned. "You're hell-bent to fit Greene into this, huh, Sweeney?"

"Have you met him, Cap?"

"Sure."

"That's why. I've known him a day and a half now, and I think the fact that he's still alive is pretty good proof I'm not the Ripper. If I was, he wouldn't be."

Bline laughed. "That ought to work both ways, Sweeney.: He seems to like you almost as much as you like him. And you're still alive. But about the New York alibi; we gave it to the New York police and they checked the hotel he was staying at, the Algonquin, He was registered there from the 25th through the 30th."

Sweeney leaned forward. "That's as far as you checked? The Gaylord murder was on the 27th, and it's only four hours by plane from New York to Chicago. He could have left there in the evening and been back the next morning."

Bline shrugged. "We'd have checked further if there'd been any reason for it. Be honest, Sweeney; what have you got against him except that he rubs you the wrong way? And me too, I admit it. But aside from that, he knows *one* of the four dames who were attacked. To my mind, that's damn near an alibi in itself."

"How the hell do you figure that?"

Bline said, "When we get the Ripper, I'll bet you we find he knew *all* of the four women or none of them. Murderers —even psychopathic ones— follow that pattern, Sweeney. He wouldn't have picked three strangers and one friend; take my word for it."

"And you've checked—?"

"Hell yes, we've checked. We've made up lists as complete as we could of everybody who knew each of the four women, and then we've compared the lists. There's been only one name that appeared on even two of the four lists, and that much is allowable to coincidence."

"Who is it?"

"Raoul Reynarde, the guy who runs the gift shop that Lola Brent got fired from the day she was killed. Turns out he also had a slight acquaintance with Stella Gaylord, the B-girl."

"Good God, what for?"

Bline grinned. "I see you've met him. But why not? Lots of faggots have friends who are women. You have male friends, don't you? Anyway, it was just a slight acquaintance, both according to Reynarde and to the other friends of Stella Gaylord that we checked with."

"But he could have known the other two then. It's hard to prove that he hadn't met—"

"In one case, no; we can't ask Dorothy Lee. We could only ask her other friends and none of them knew Reynarde. But we could and did ask the strip-tease dame. And Yolanda Lang doesn't know him from either name or photograph."

"You checked him for alibis?"

"Fairly good ones on two of the cases. Especially on the Lola Brent one. He couldn't have followed her home after he fired her without closing the store and there's fairly good evidence—negative evidence, anyway—that he didn't close it."

Sweeney sighed. "Wash him out, then. I still like Doc Greene."

"Sweeney, you're nuts. All you mean is that you *don't* like him. Not a thing to point to him otherwise. We've got a hell of a lot better suspect than Greene."

"You mean me?"

"You're damn right I mean you. Look, not even a shadow of an alibi for *any* murder. Your extreme interest in the case. The fact that you are psychically unbalanced—or you wouldn't be an alcoholic. And that, in one case out of the four, we can put you right at the scene of the crime at the tune of the crime. I'm not saying that's enough evidence to hang a dog on, but it is more than we've got on anybody else. If you weren't—"

"If I weren't what?"

"Skip it."

Sweeney said, "Wait, I get it. You mean if I wasn't a reporter, you'd probably drag me in and sweat me down a bit on the off chance. But you figure I'll be writing on the case and that you couldn't hold me long and once I got out the *Blades* stories would play merry hell with the captain in charge of the Ripper detail."

Bline's laugh was a little embarrassed. He said, "I guess that isn't too far off, Sweeney. But damn it, man, can't you give me something that'll let me write you off, so I won't have to waste so much tune on you? There ought to be some way you could check where you were at the time of at least one of the murders."

Sweeney shook his head. "I wish there was, Cap." He glanced at his wrist watch. "Tell you what, though. I'll do the next best thing; I'll buy you a drink. At El Madhouse. First show goes, on at ten; that's in a few minutes now. You know she's dancing again tonight already."

"I know everything. Except who the Ripper is. Sure, Sweeney, I was thinking of dropping in there tonight anyway. Let's go."

At the door, before he reached back to turn out the light, Sweeney looked at the black statuette on the radio, the slim, naked girl, arms outraised to ward off ineffable evil, a silent scream eternally frozen on her lips. He grinned at her and tossed her a kiss before he flicked off the light and followed Bline down the stairs.

They hailed a cab at Rush Street. Sweeney said "El Madhouse" to the driver and then leaned back and lighted a cigarette. He looked at Bline, sitting back, relaxed, his eyes closed. He said, "You don't really think I might be the Ripper, Cap. Or you wouldn't relax like that."

"Like what?" Bline's voice was soft. "I was watching your hands and letting you think my eyes were all the way closed. And there's a gun in my right coat pocket, the side away from you, with my hand on it. I could use it quicker than you could pull a knife, if you started to."

Sweeney laughed.

And then he wondered what was funny about it.

CHAPTER 10

EL MADHOUSE was crowded. It seemed strange to Sweeney that he hadn't thought of that. With all the publicity Yolanda Lang had received— the best of it at Sweeney's own hands —he realized that he should have realized that the joint would be jammed. As they went in the door, he could see the husky waiter stationed at the inner doorway turning people away. Over the waiter's shoulder he could see that more tables than usual had been crowded into the big back room, and that every table was crowded.

A three-piece orchestra—not good but not bad—was playing back there now, and a woman with gravel in her throat was singing a torch song, probably the first number of the floor show. But from the outer room, the barroom, you couldn't see the stage—or floor or platform, whichever it would be.

He grunted disgustedly, but Bline took him by the arm and started with him toward a table from which a couple was just rising. They got the seats and Bline said, "We don't want to go back there yet. Show's just starting, and Yolanda won't come on for forty minutes or so."

"We'll play hell getting back there at all. Unless—Yolanda told me to come around and catch the show; maybe she had more sense than I did and made a reservation for me. I'll check; you hold this seat for—" He started to get up again.

"Sit down and relax," Bline told him. "You got a police escort. Any time we want, we'll go back there, if they have to put chairs on top of tables for us. Don't think they'll have to, though; I told one of the boys to save me a place at his table, and we can crowd an extra chair in if there's room for one."

He caught a rushing waiter by the arm and said, "Send Nick over right away, will you?"

The waiter tried to pull loose. "Nick's busy. We're all going nuts tonight. You'll have to wait your—"

Bline's free hand pulled back his lapel for a brief flash of silver plate. He said, "Send Nick over."

"Who's Nick?" Sweeney asked, when the waiter had vanished into the crowd.

"Nick runs the place, nights, for Harry Yahn." He grinned. "I don't really want to see him, but it's the only way we'll get drinks right away. What you having?"

"Whiskey highball. Maybe I'll have to buy one of those badges. It's a system, if it works."

"It works," Bline said. He looked up as a dapper, stocky man came up to the table. "Hi, Nick. Everything under control?"

The stocky man grunted. "If there weren't so many deadheads in the house, we'd be doing better. Four coppers back there already taking up room, and now you come."

"And Sweeney, Nick. This is Sweeney, of the *Blade*. He comes, too. You can crowd in an extra chair for him, can't you?"

"Cash customer?"

"Cash customer," Sweeney said.

Nick smiled, and from the smile Sweeney expected him to rub his hands together, too. But instead he stuck one out to Sweeney. "I was kidding, Mr. Sweeney. It's on the house for you. I read that story you wrote. But it cost us money, too."

"The hell," said Sweeney. "How?"

"Greene. He's holding us up, and we got to pay it to cash in." He turned around and grabbed a flying waiter, the same one Bline had grabbed. "What you gentlemen having?"

"Whiskey and soda for both of us," Bline told him.

"Make it three, Charlie, and make it next," Nick told the waiter. Then he said, "Just a minute; I get a chair." He brought one from somewhere and sat down at the table with them just as the drinks came.

"Bumps," Sweeney said. "And how come Greene could hold you up; isn't Yolanda under contract?"

"Sure she is. For four more weeks. But—"

Sweeney cut in; "Doc Greene told me for three."

"Greene wouldn't tell the truth on a bet, even where it don't matter, Mr. Sweeney. If it'd been three weeks, he'd've told you four. Sure, she's under contract through September 5th, but the contract's got a clause."

"Most contracts have," Sweeney said.

"Yeah. Well, this clause says she don't have to work if she's sick or hurt. And Greene got one of the docs at the hospital to write a paper that says that because of shock she shouldn't ought to work for a week or even two weeks."

"But would she get paid for that time if she didn't?"

"Sure she wouldn't. But look what we can cash in on her if she does. Lookit the crowd tonight, and they're spending money, too. But because Doc had us by the nuts we had to offer a one-grand bonus if she'd forget she was shocked. A bonus—that's what Doc calls a bribe."

"But *is* she okay to dance this soon?" Sweeney asked. "She really was suffering from shock. I saw her face when she stood up in that hallway."

"You didn't mention her face."

"Sure, I did. Before the dog pulled the zipper. Say, Nick, how come she wasn't wearing a net bra and a G-string under that dress? I never thought to ask, but unless the police rules here have changed, she'd have been wearing them for the show."

"Wasn't she? They don't show much. I thought you was just exaggerating to make it a better story."

"So help me God," said Sweeney.

"Well, it could be. We got a pretty good dressing room with a shower here, and Wednesday was a hot night. Probably she took a shower after the last show and didn't bother to put on anything under a dress to run home in if she expected to go right to sleep. Or something."

"If it had been something, she wouldn't have been alone," Sweeney pointed out. "But we got off the track. Isn't it a bit soon for her to start dancing again?"

"Naw. If she got shocked, she was over it by the time she had a night's sleep. And the scratch was just a scratch. She'll be wearing a strip of adhesive tape six inches long, but that's what the customers are paying to see.

Well, not all they're paying to see." He pushed back his chair and stood up. "Well, I got to do things. Want to go back now? Yo won't be on for half an hour yet, but the rest of the show don't stink too much."

The voice of an emcee telling jokes came from the back room and both Sweeney and Bline shook their heads. Bline said, "We'll look you up when we want to move back."

"Sure. I'll send you two more drinks here, then."

He went away, taking his chair back to wherever it had come from.

Sweeney asked Bline, "Yolanda just do one number?"

"Right now, yes. Before the excitement, she was on twice. A straight strip tease for the third number on the show, and then the specialty with the dog for the last number. But Nick told me this afternoon that to get her to go back on right away, they agreed to let her do just the one number, the specialty, on each show. Not that that matters; they'll get as big crowds here to see her do one number a show as two."

Their drinks came. Bline looked down into his for a moment and then squarely at Sweeney. He said, "Maybe I was a little rough on you tonight, Sweeney. In the cab, I mean."

Sweeney said, "I'm glad you were."

"Why? So you can pan me in the *Blade* with a clear conscience?"

"Not that. As far as I know to date, you don't deserve any panning. Not for the way you've handled the case. But now I can hold out on you with a clear conscience."

Bline frowned. "You can't hold back any evidence, Sweeney. Not and get away with it. What is it you're holding back?" He leaned forward, suddenly intent. "Did you notice anything there on State Street Wednesday night that you didn't tell about in the write-up? Recognize anybody, maybe or notice anybody acting suspiciously? If you did—"

"I didn't. You've got the whole truth and nothing but the truth on that. I mean, if in playing around with the case and doing my own investigating and question-asking, I come on anything that you missed, it's my own business. I mean, until I get enough of it to beat you out on cracking the case."

Bline said, "Let's take it as of now. Right here and now. Will you give me your word of honor on the answer to one question?"

"If I answer it at all, I'll answer it straight. It isn't, by any chance, whether I'm the Ripper, is it?"

"No; if you *are,* I wouldn't expect a straight answer. So I'm asking this on the assumption that you're not. But by God, Sweeney, if you won't answer this, *Blade* or no *Blade,* I'm going to take you in and work on you. And the same goes if you do answer it and I ever find out it wasn't straight.

"Do you know or even think you might know, who the Ripper is? Either by sight or by name, do you even suspect anybody?"

"No, definitely not. Unless it's Doc Greene, and I haven't a damn bit of reason for that except that I'd *like* him to be."

Bline sat back. He said, "Okay, then. I've got a lot of men under me on this, and besides that we've got the whole police force keeping an eye out. If you, all by yourself, get anything we miss, it's your baby. It'd probably get you a knife in the belly, but that's your business."

Sweeney said, "Fair enough, Cap. And for those kind words —especially about the knife, I'll even forgive you for taking my razor and penknife without telling me, and scaring the pants off me when I found them gone. Why didn't you leave a note?"

"Wanted to see how you'd react. If you'd been the Ripper, and found them gone, you'd have probably been even worse scared; you'd like as not have taken it on the lam and we'd have picked you up. You know, Sweeney, I've just about decided you're not the Ripper."

"Awfully sweet of you, Cap. But I'll bet you tell that to all the boys. By the way, have I been tailed while you thought I was it?"

"Today, yes. Hadn't got around to you yet yesterday. But I'll pull *the* guy off of you now, I guess. Especially now that you know about it."

"I might suggest you put him on Doc Greene. Say, was it Doc's salesmanship that made you suspect me to begin with?"

Bline grinned. "You two really do love one another. Is that enough of an answer to your question? Well, what do you say we go in out of the rain? She'll be on in ten minutes."

They found Nick and he took them past the big waiter who guarded the portal. The gravel-voiced torch singer was at it again as they threaded their way through barely navigable aisles among the close-packed, crowded tables. No tete-a-tete tables tonight, Sweeney noticed; at least four people were at every table and five or even six were at some of them. Two hundred people, more or less, were jammed in a room whose normal complement wasn't much over half that number.

They had barely started across the room when Sweeney felt his arm gripped from behind and turned. Bline was leaning his head close. He had to yell to make himself heard above the music and the noise, but pitched his voice so it wouldn't carry past Sweeney. "Forgot to tell you, Sweeney. Keep your eyes open in here. Watch the faces and see if you see anybody you remember being by that door on State Street. Get me?"

Sweeney nodded. He turned and started following Nick again, but this time kept watching as many faces along the route as he could. He didn't think he'd remember anybody who'd shared Wednesday night's spectacle with him; all he'd really seen outside the door had been the backs of heads. But it didn't hurt to try, and Bline's idea that the Ripper might have come around to the front and joined the crowd seemed quite reasonable. Also, he agreed with the thought that the Ripper might have come here tonight.

Nick led them to a table where three men sat; one chair was empty, tilted against the table's edge. He said, "I'll send over a waiter with another chair; they can crowd you *in* here. Same to drink, both of you?"

Bline nodded, then said, "Sit down, Sweeney. Want to talk to an outpost or two before I squat."

Sweeney took the chair and glanced at his three companions, all of whom were watching the singer and paying no attention to him. One of them looked familiar; the others were strangers to him. He watched the singer. She wasn't bad to watch, but he wished he didn't have to listen to her, too.

The chair arrived, as did the drinks, before Bline came back. Sweeney moved over to make more room, and Bline said, "Sweeney—Ross, Guerney, Swann. Anything doing, boys?"

The one called Swann said, "Guy over at the corner table acts a little screwy; I been keeping an eye on him. The one with the carnation in his buttonhole. Maybe he's just a little drunk."

Bline watched that way a while. He said, "Don't think so. The Ripper wouldn't call attention to himself dressing up like that and wearing a flower, would he? And I don't think the Ripper'd get drunk."

"Thanks for that last thought," Sweeney said.

Bline turned to him. "See anybody might have been there that night?"

"Only the guy across from me there, the one you introduced as Guerney. Isn't he one of the boys from the squad car?"

Guerney had turned back at the sound of his name. He said, "Yeah. It was me that creased the dog."

"Nice shooting."

Bline said, "Guerney's one of the best shots in the department. His partner's here, too. Kravich. He's at the bar out there, watching 'em as they come and go."

"Didn't notice him."

"He noticed you. I saw him start toward you when you came in the door; then he saw I was with you and turned back. Sure you haven't seen anybody else that—"

"No," said Sweeney. "Shhhh."

The emcee was on stage—it had turned out to be actually a stage, although a small one, about eight feet deep and twelve feet wide—and was building up an introduction to Yolanda Lang and her world-famous Beauty and the Beast dance. Sweeney wanted to hear.

Not that it was worth hearing. The emcee had dropped his corny humor and was being cornier by far. It was pathetically bathetic, Sweeney thought. He tried now *not* to listen about the brave courage of the courageous little woman who had risen from a bed of pain to answer the call of her art and the demand of her public, to do for them the most wonderful, the most sensational dance in the world, with the aid of the most wonderful trained dog in the world and the most courageous, who had courageously saved his mistress's life at the risk of his own and who had also been injured but courageously had—

Sweeney couldn't take any more of it. He said to Bline, "Who does the bastard think he's introducing—Joan of Arc?"

Bline said, "Shhhh." Sweeney listened to forty-five seconds more of it and then, mercifully, it ended; nothing can last forever, not even an emcee with an unprecedented opportunity to go dramatic.

The lights dimmed, and the room was quiet. As miraculously quiet as though two hundred people were holding their breath. You could hear the click of the switch as a spotlight went on, from somewhere in the back of the room, throwing a bright circle of yellow light on the left side of the stage. Everyone watched the yellow circle of light. A drum began to throb and the tone and pitch of it pulled Sweeney's eyes away from the stage and toward the three-piece orchestra; the three-piece orchestra wasn't there. Rather, two-thirds of it wasn't there; the pianist and the sax-player had left the platform. The trap-drummer had left his traps and sat before a single kettledrum, a big one, turned low. His only weapons were two drumsticks with big well-padded heads.

Smart, thought Sweeney, and he wondered if Yolanda or her manager deserved the credit for that idea. Resonant rhythm without music. And not even the lousiest drummer can corn up a kettledrum with padded sticks, set out of reach of his cymbals, blocks and bells.

The drum throbbed a slow crescendo and the spotlight dimmed; you caught a flash of movement in the dimness, then as the yellow circle blazed bright again, she stood there full in its center, stood poised, unmoving.

And she *was* beautiful; there was no doubt of that. The picture Sweeney had been carrying in his mind had not been exaggeration, not in the slightest. He thought, now, that she was the most beautiful woman he had ever seen. And by the collective catch of breath of the audience, he knew that he was not alone in thinking so. What, he wondered, was she doing in a dive like this, on Clark Street in Chicago? Even if she couldn't dance—

She wore a gown exactly like the one she had worn for the scene in the hallway, except this one was black and that had been white. This one was better, Sweeney thought. Contrast of black and white. It was strapless, molded to every curve of her body.

She was barefoot; the black gown her only visible garment. No ribbon, no gloves, no bolero; this wasn't to be a gradual strip tease like other strip teases; it would be one blinding flash from black to white, from cloth to flesh. The drum throbbed.

You thought she was a statue there, and then—so gradually that you weren't sure at first—she moved. Merely to turn her head.

And when it was turned your eyes followed hers. You saw, as she saw, what crouched in semi-darkness on the other side of the stage. It was Devil, the dog; only he wasn't a dog at all now. He was all devil. He crouched there, his jaws slightly parted in a silent snarl of bared white teeth, his yellow eyes luminous in the dimness.

The drumbeat died down to almost-inaudibility. And in the almost-silence, the dog snarled loudly. It was the same sound, exactly the same sound, that Sweeney had heard before, two nights ago. It had put a cold chill down his spine then, and it put a cold chill down his spine now.

Still half-crouched, the dog took a stiff-legged step toward the woman. He snarled again and crouched to spring.

There was a sudden quick movement across the table from him that pulled Sweeney's eyes from the tense drama on the stage. And at the same instant that Sweeney saw the movement, Bline's big hand reached across the table and grabbed Guerney's arm.

There was a gun in Guerney's hand.

Bline whispered hoarsely, "You Goddam fool, it's part of the act. He's trained to do that; he's not going to hurt her."

Guerney whispered back, "Just in case. In case he *does* jump her. I could get him before he got her throat."

"Put back that gun, you Goddam sap, or I'll break you."

The gun went slowly back into the shoulder holster, but Sweeney saw, out of the corner of his eye, that Guerney's hand stayed on the butt of the gun.

Bline said, "Don't get trigger-happy. The dog jumps her; it's part of the act, Goddam it."

Guerney's hand came out from under his coat, but stayed near his lapel. Sweeney's eyes jerked back to the stage as a sudden intake of breath from the audience backgrounded a yip from a woman at a table near the stage, a yip like a suddenly stopped scream.

The dog was leaping.

But the woman moved, too, one step aside and the dog flew past her and down, alighted and turned in a flash of brown-ness, crouched again, and now she was in the middle of the stage as he leaped. Again she was not there when he landed.

And Sweeney wondered if that was going to go on indefinitely, but it didn't. That was the last time. The dog—as though convinced that leaping was futile—crouched now in the center of the stage, turning as she danced around him.

And she *could* dance; well, if not superlatively; gracefully, if not significantly. The dog, now no longer snarling, pivoted, his yellow eyes following every move she made.

Then, alongside the now-tamed dog, the Beast, Beauty sank to her knees and put her hand upon the dog's head, and he snarled, but tolerated the caress.

The drum throbbed, the beat accelerated. And then, as Yolanda gracefully rose to her feet, facing the audience from the center of the yellow circle of light that already, but very gradually, was starting to fade, the dog padded behind her. It reared up, as tall as she, and then as it started downward its teeth caught the tab sewed to the tag of the zipper and pulled.

And the black dress, as had the white one, fell suddenly into a circle about her feet.

She was incredibly beautiful despite—Sweeney thought—the fact that she was overdressed. Overdressed in a narrow, transparent bra of wide-mesh net, diaphanous as dew and confiding as air, that seemed to accentuate rather than conceal the beauty of her voluptuous breasts; and in a G-string which, in the slowly fading light, might not have been there at all, which needed to be taken on faith in the integrity of Chicago's vice squad; and one more garment: a six-inch strip of black adhesive tape, slightly slanting, across her white belly just below the navel. And somehow the contrast of that black on white made her seem even more naked than she had seemed when—two nights ago—Sweeney had seen her actually so.

The drumbeat faded slowly. Yolanda raised her arms—her breasts lifting with them—and spread her bare feet apart; the dog, from behind her, walked between her legs, halfway, and stood there with her astride him; his head raised to look out over the audience as though daring any man to approach that which he now guarded.

"Cerberus guarding the portals of Heaven," Sweeney whispered to Bline. Bline said, "Huh?"

The drumbeat faded, and the light faded and then went out and the stage was dark. When the lights went on, the stage was empty.

And the lights went on brightly all over the room, and the floor show was over. People applauded madly, but Yolanda Lang did not return, even to take a single bow.

Over the noise, Bline asked Sweeney, "How'd you like it?"

"It, or her?"

"It. The dance."

"Probably symbolic as hell, but symbolic of what, I don't know. I don't think the choreographer did, either. If there *was* a choreographer. My idea is that Doc Greene figured it out. It's just crazy enough—and just smart enough—for his fine Italian hand."

Bline said, "Greene's not Italian. I think he's mostly German."

Sweeney was spared answering because Guerney had turned around and Bline was looking at him balefully. He said, "You Goddam fool, for a plugged nickel I'd make you turn in your gun and go without one."

Guerney flushed and looked foolish. "I wasn't gonna shoot, Captain, unless—"

"Unless the dog jumped at her. And he did, twice. Good God, but that would have been a stink for the department."

Sweeney felt sorry for the squad-car copper. He said, "If you *had* shot that dog, Guerney, I'd have stuck up for you."

Bline said, "And a lot of good that would have done him, unless you could have got him a paper route carrying the *Blade.*"

Nick saved Guerney further embarrassment by appearing at their table. He said, "Another round of drinks is coming, gentlemen. How'd you like the show? Sure is a well-trained pooch she's got, ain't it?"

Sweeney said, "He showed more self-control, under the circumstances, than I would have."

"Me either," Guerney said. He started to grin, but caught Bline's eye and found he was still in disgrace. He said, "Gotta see a man about a—I mean, I gotta go to the can. Excuse me."

He threaded his way off between the tables. Nick slid into the vacated chair and said, "I'll stay a minute till he gets back. Did you notice anything during the show, Captain?"

Sweeney said, "Everything the G-string didn't cover. You know, some-time I'd like to see her without *anything* on."

Nick stared at him. "Huh? I thought, according to your story in the paper—"

Sweeney shook his head gloomily. "Gloves," he said. "She wore long, white gloves."

Bline snorted. He said, "This guy has a one-track mind, Nick. What did you mean, did I notice anything during the show?"

Nick leaned forward. "Only this; that part where she's posed there, still, facing the audience and front-stage-center, with the light fading out. Look, I shouldn't take a chance changing my own show—not that it matters; we could get a crowd here to listen to her sing Annie Laurie in a diving suit—but I been worried about that. I don't want her killed either, and if the Ripper should show here, that'd be his chance."

"Maybe, but how?".

"The audience is in the dark, almost dark anyway. And if he decided to throw that shiv of his, it'd be hard to tell just where it come from."

Bline looked thoughtful and then shook his head. "Sounds pretty remote, Nick. Unless he's already a knife-thrower, and it's a million to one against, it'd take him months of practice to learn. And I don't think he'd use a gun—guys like that stick to one weapon and one style of using it—and I don't think he'd try to kill her in a crowd anyway. I think the big danger point is on her way to and from here, or at her place at night. And we're taking care of that."

"For how long?"

"Until the Ripper's caught, Nick. At least as long as she'll be playing here, so *you* don't need to worry."

"You have someone go through her flat before she goes in when she goes home?"

Bline frowned. "Look, Nick, I'm not telling anybody *exactly* what precautions we're taking or not taking. Especially with a reporter sitting here who'd put it in the paper so the Ripper would be sure to know."

"Thanks," said Sweeney, "for demoting me from suspect to reporter. But that suggestion of going through her flat before she goes into it is good, if you aren't already doing it. If I were the Ripper and wanted to get her, I wouldn't try it on the street again; I'd be under her bed waiting for her. Say, does Devil sleep in the same room with her?"

Bline looked at him sharply. "That's not for publication. But yes."

"About that knife-throwing," Nick said. "What about if he can throw them?"

Sweeney said, "Here he comes. Ask him if he can."

CHAPTER 11

DOC GREENE was coming toward them, worming his way through the people who were leaving after the first floor show, a wide, satisfied grin on the bland, round face that Sweeney would have loved to slug.

Bline looked to see who was coming and then looked at Sweeney disgustedly. He said, "You and that damn hunch."

Maybe you feel disgusted with him too, and if so I hold no brief for him. It was just a hunch, and you know what a stubborn fool an Irishman with a hunch can be; if you didn't know when you started reading, you should know by now. Once a hunch gets into him, you almost have to blast to get it out; there wasn't much chance of blasting happening in the case of Sweeney. There was, of course, a much better chance, an excellent chance, of his finding out whether his hunch could leak out—along with other things—through the slit a knife or a razor could make across his abdomen. Yes, there was an excellent chance of that happening, and it almost did happen; but not just then. Doc Greene was carrying a foul, fat cigar, but no knife.

Nick stood up and said, "Hi, Doc. Well, I got to go. So long."

Doc nodded to him, and asked Bline how he liked the show.

Bline said, "Great. Sit down, Greene."

Guerney, coming back, hesitated as he saw his chair being taken. Bline motioned to him and then told him to take a break and get some fresh air outside. Guerney left.

Doc Greene grinned at Sweeney. Not a nice grin. He said, "Do I have to ask how you liked it?"

"No," Sweeney told him. "I hear you held Nick—or rather, Harry Yahn—up. For a thousand bucks."

"I wouldn't call it a holdup. Yolanda shouldn't be dancing so soon after what happened. It's taking a chance with her health. Naturally, she deserves something extra for that, if she does."

"Does she get it?"

"Naturally. Of course, as her manager, I get my cut."

"What per cent is that?"

"That's my business."

"And business is good," Sweeney said. "You know, Doc, there's something I'd like to ask you."

"I might even answer it."

"How come Yolanda is playing a place like this? It's peanuts to the bookings you could get her."

"You're telling me. But we're under contract here; I told you that. Yahn won't let us break the contract. Know what we're getting here? A lousy two hundred a week. I could get her a thousand a week damn easy, and we have to be tied down here for another month. And by that time—"

"You don't get me," Sweeney said. "What I mean is why *was* she working for a lousy two hundred a week? Even without the publicity, she ought to have been nearer to the big time than Clark Street."

Greene spread his hands. "Maybe you could do better for her. It's easy to say, Sweeney. Only you won't get a chance to try; I got her signed up under contract."

"For how long?"

"Again, my business."

Sweeney said, "I suggest you haven't wanted to get her better bookings, for reasons of your own."

"You're very suggestive. Would you like me to make a suggestion?"

"I could guess it in advance. But I can make another one." Sweeney glanced quickly to see that Bline was listening. He said, "How's this for a suggestion? Maybe the Ripper never attacked Yolanda at all. Maybe it was a publicity stunt. Nobody *saw* the Ripper slash at her. Maybe you cooked it up; she could have given herself that little cut with, say, a safety razor blade, and then she could have lain down on the floor till someone saw her through the glass."

"Having swallowed the razor blade?"

"Having possibly, dropped it in her mailbox slot. She was standing right by the mailboxes."

Bline said, "No, Sweeney. The hallway was searched, including the mailboxes. No weapon. And it wasn't in a shoe or in her dress, either. She was searched at the hospital. Don't think we didn't think of the possibility of it being a hoax."

Sweeney said stubbornly, "Doc could have been there and gone off with the blade, as easily as the Ripper could have been there and gone off with his weapon."

Greene bowed ironically. "Thank you, Sweeney. For implying for the first time that I'm not the Ripper."

"Don't mention it. And then, Cap, there's still another possibility. Maybe you've already thought of it. But that wound was pretty slight; not enough to incapacitate her. How do you know she got it in the hallway at all?

"I mean, she could have come home, gone up to her apartment, made that slit with a razor and washed the razor or whatever and put it away, then she could go back downstairs and lie In the hallway till somebody saw her."

Bline said, "We thought of that. Several little things against it, and one big one. Little things like the scratch marks on the back door. They could have been put there, sure, for the purpose of being found. And the fact that it would take a lot of nerve to give yourself a cut like that. *Could* be done, sure. Another little thing; it couldn't have been sure—unless you were in on it, Sweeney—that you'd be there to give it that write-up. Were you in on it?"

Sweeney grinned. "Sure. That's why I'm suggesting it now. Doc won't give me my cut, so I'm turning him in. But what's the one big thing that proves it wasn't a put-up job?"

"The shock, Sweeney. She got over it within twelve hours, yes, but she was really suffering from shock when she got to the hospital. Bad. And genuine. I talked to the doctors who treated her, and they're positive it couldn't have been acting—nor drugs, either, for that matter. It was bona fide shock and you can't fake it."

Sweeney said, "Okay. It was an idea while it lasted. I'm glad it was wrong. It would have made a prize sucker out of me for the story I wrote."

Greene said blandly, "I'll tell Yo what you thought and that you suggested it to the police. She'll like you better for it, no doubt."

Sweeney glared at him.

Greene smiled and leaned across the table. He said, "The thing I like about you, Sweeney, is that your reactions are so completely predictable, so primitive, so utterly lacking in subtlety. You should know that I would do no such foolish thing as to Inform Yolanda of your base insinuation."

"And why not?"

"Because I *am* subtle, and civilized. The last thing I would do is to make Yolanda angry at you, lest anger react. Women are subtle, too, whether civilized or not. But you wouldn't understand that. Even you, however, should have realized that if I were actually going to snitch to Yolanda, the last thing I would have done is to forewarn you that I would."

Bline was grinning at Sweeney. He said, "I'm liking this. It's your turn."

Sweeney said, "I'd rather discuss this outside."

"The animal plane," Greene said. "The three things for which the Irish are famous: drinking, fighting, and—well, the third, in Sweeney's case, is reduced to *voyeurism.* " He leaned still farther across the table and he no longer smiled. "And even for that, Sweeney, I hate your very guts."

"The mask slipped then," Sweeney said. "You really are a psychiatrist, Doc?"

"I really am."

"And you honestly do not recognize that you yourself are not sane? Look, I don't know your relations with Yolanda—and don't bother trying to tell me, because I wouldn't be able to believe you, either way. But, whichever, your attitude toward her is not sane and normal. As her manager, you let her get up in front of a crowd of creeps in a honky-tonk, strip for them, and get their tongues hanging out, and you tolerate it. Maybe you even like it; maybe you've got a case of inverted voyeurism. Or something. I wouldn't know what, but you ought to, if you're a psychiatrist."

Bline was looking from one to the other of them, chuckling. He said, "At it, boys; I'll referee. The first one to lose his temper to the extent of taking a poke at the other loses—and maybe goes to the hoosegow."

Neither Greene nor Sweeney even glanced at him.

Sweeney said, "Thousands of men must have wanted her and tried to get her. You couldn't have reacted to all of them as you've reacted to me; your adrenals wouldn't have stood the strain. So there's something different in my case. Know what it is, Doc?"

Greene was wary, his eyes hooded. You could have counted to ten, slowly, before he answered, and then it was only to say, "No, I don't." He sounded honestly puzzled.

"Then I'll tell *you*. It's because these other guys have only wanted, and tried. You know I'm going to succeed."

Bline must have been watching Greene's face, because he was on his feet and leaning over the table even as Greene started across it. Greene's chair went over backward, but he stopped as Bline caught his arms, although he paid no attention to Bline. He said softly, "I'm going to kill you, Sweeney."

Then he jerked loose from Bline's grip, turned and walked away.

Nick was suddenly there. "Anything wrong, gentlemen?" he asked.

"Everything is lovely," Sweeney told him.

Nick looked uncertainly from one to the other of them. He said, "Shall I send another drink?" Sweeney said, "Thanks, no, not for me," and Bline said, "I'll pass this one, too, Nick."

"There's not going to be any trouble?"

"No, Nick," Bline said. "But—yeah, I'll have a drink at that, if I can."

Nick nodded and left them. Bline relaxed in the chair and turned to Sweeney. "Just wanted to get rid of him. Sweeney, you'd better be careful."

"I guess maybe you're right, Cap. I honestly don't think he's completely sane. That's why I goaded him; I wanted to show you."

"Of course he didn't mean what he said about killing you; he wouldn't have said that in front of me if he really meant it. He was just trying to throw a scare into you; that's all."

Sweeney said, "I wish I was sure of that. If he's sane, yes. But—Ripper or no Ripper—I wouldn't bet on his being sane."

"How about yourself?"

Sweeney grinned. "I may be crazy, but I'm not insane." He stood up. "Maybe that's enough excitement for one evening. Guess I'll hit for home."

"Your door got a good lock?"

Sweeney frowned at him. "You should know," he said. "Unless I left it unlocked the other night when you borrowed my razor."

Bline stood up too. He said, "I'll walk with you a block or two; I can use some fresh air."

When they were outside, walking north on Clark, he said, "If your razor being missing really scared you, Sweeney, I'm sorry about it. Happened this way; I sent two of the boys around to bring you in for questioning Thursday night and told 'em to bring your arsenal too. I didn't tell them to bring the arsenal if you *weren't* there, and they overstepped a little. One of them—I won't say who—is pretty good on locks and loves a chance to show off how he can open them."

"I know who that would be. You needn't tell me."

"Don't be foolish, Sweeney. Lots of guys on the force are good at locks."

"But only one of them has been to my room before, and anybody else would have had to ask Mrs. Randall instead of going straight up. And with her there they couldn't have gone on in. So that makes it the guy I'm thinking about. And I thought he was a friend of mine."

"Forget it, Sweeney. God damn it, man, friendship doesn't count when you're looking for a killer. And I'd told him you were under strong suspicion. Sweeney, we've *got* to get that guy before he butchers any more dames."

"For the dames' sake, or so you don't lose your job?"

"Both, I guess, but it's not all on account of my job. I wasn't on the Lola Brent one two months ago, but they dumped it in my lap after the second case, when it began to look like there was a psycho loose. I looked at the B-girl, Gaylord, at the morgue for a starter, and I saw the steno, Dorothy Lee, before they moved her. They weren't nice to look at. Christ."

He turned to look at Sweeney. "You saw a job of his work—a botched one. It wouldn't be so funny to you if you'd seen the real McCoy."

"I don't think it's funny."

"Then I wish you and Doc Greene would lay off that Punch-and-Judy show of yours and quit messing things up trying to make each other out to be the Ripper. Yeah, he fooled me, Sweeney. It was after a talk with him Thursday evening that I sent the boys around for you and your cutlery. I didn't know then that he was using me as a cat's-paw because he hated you for personal reasons."

"And if I try to get you to suspect him, I guess you think it's for personal reasons, too."

"Isn't it? Mostly?"

Sweeney sighed. "That and a hunch."

"Well, play your hunch if you want to. But don't expect me to. Greene's couple of alibis may not be perfect, but they're good enough for me—especially because, like I told you, I figure that the killer either knew *all* the dames or none of them. One kind of nut might kill the woman he's crazy about, but it's another kind that follows strangers home and kills them. For my money—not that I'm a psychiatrist—the same kind of nut doesn't do both."

They were nearing the corner of Erie and Bline slowed down. He said, "You turn east here. Guess I'll go back to the madhouse. And look, stay away from Greene. I don't want to have to jug you both for mayhem, and it's going to be that or worse if you keep tangling."

He stuck out a hand. "Friends, Sweeney?"

"I'm not the Ripper? You're sure?"

"Reasonably sure."

Sweeney took his hand, and grinned. "And I'm getting to be reasonably sure you're not a son of a bitch, Cap. I sure had you pegged as one for a while."

"Can't say I blame you. Well, so long."

Sweeney stood for a moment on the corner. He saw Bline look around and then cut diagonally across the street, which took him out of his way if he was returning to El Madhouse. He understood when, a hundred yards down, Bline stopped to talk to a man who had been looking into the window of a hockshop, and then Bline and the man walked south together.

That meant—unless there'd been two of them, which he doubted—that Bline had pulled Sweeney's tail off the job. To make sure, he pretended to turn south at Erie and State and then waited in the doorway of a store next to the corner one to see if anyone would turn into State Street after him. No one did.

He whistled a little as he went back to Erie and on east to his room. There was no Ripper waiting for him. But there was Mimi.

Number SM-1 of the Ganslen Art Company of Louisville, Kentucky. Screaming Mimi.

He picked her up and held her gently, and she screamed at him, pushing toward him with tiny, fending hands; again that little chill went down his spine.

Somewhere in Chicago there was another Mimi just like this one, and *she* had something to scream about. The Ripper had her.

Call her Mimi number one. What if the Ripper knew that he, Sweeney, had Mimi number two?

But the Ripper couldn't know that. At least, not unless the Ripper was Raoul Reynarde, who'd sold him Mimi number two, after Lola Brent had sold Mimi number one to the Ripper and had tried to drag down the money on the sale. And if Raoul was the Ripper, then Raoul wouldn't have had any reason to tell him about Mimi and—Hell, if Raoul was the Ripper then the whole story about Lola having sold a Mimi might have been out of the whole cloth, to distract attention from himself. But then Raoul would have told the police about it. Well, of course,, Raoul had told the police the same story, but the police hadn't happened to follow through by looking at a duplicate of the statuette on which Lola had dragged down, and so they'd missed the point—the point that the man who'd bought the statuette had been the Ripper. Raoul himself had missed it. He, Sweeney, might have missed it except for the hunch that made him buy Mimi from Raoul—and then the remark of the counterman in the lunchroom.

He put Mimi down, very gently. He wished she'd stop screaming, but she never would. A silent scream can never be silenced.

No, definitely the police didn't know about Mimi; otherwise Bline would never have sat here in the same room with her without noticing or mentioning her. He'd looked right at her at least once.

And, of course, he'd mentioned Mimi to Doc Greene and Doc hadn't reacted. But—although he couldn't believe it—Doc might have been able to control his nerves enough not to let that sheet of paper move when "small black statuette" had been sprung on him. No, if Greene really was—despite alibis, despite everything—the Ripper, then maybe the whole Mimi lead was a blind alley; maybe the Ripper hadn't made that purchase from Lola Brent at the gift shop.

Sweeney, he told himself, you can't have your cake and eat it too; if Mimi is a legitimate lead to the Ripper, then Greene can't be the Ripper—as you damn well would like to have him be.

He sighed.

Then he sat down on the bed and started the job he'd come home to do—reading up on the third murder, the Dorothy Lee one. He felt that he knew Stella Gaylord and Lola Brent pretty well by now.

He picked up the *Blade of* August 1st.

That story, of course, he didn't have to look for; it was the third Ripper job, and it splashed page one banners the day it broke, in the biggest type size the *Blade* used short of a declaration of war or an armistice.

RIPPER SLAYS ANOTHER WOMAN

There was a three-column picture of Dorothy Lee, and Sweeney studied it. She was blonde—like Lola, like Stella, like Yolanda—and definitely pretty, if not beautiful. It was a good portrait photograph and—if it was taken recently—she was probably in her early twenties. Details were not too clear, as though it had been blown up from a small picture or—more likely, since it was a portrait—they'd had to make the halftone from a toned sepia print instead of a glossy. At any rate, Dorothy Lee had been at least attractive; she might have been beautiful.

The story said she was beautiful, but the story would have said that in any case, provided only that she was under forty and didn't have buck teeth or crossed eyes.

The story said that she was Dorothy Lee, 25, beautiful blonde private secretary of J. P. Andrews, sales manager of the Reiss Corporation at an address on Division Street that Sweeney recognized as being near Dearborn. Her home address, he noticed with surprise, was on East Erie Street, only a block from his own. Only a block from where he sat right now reading about it. Good Lord, he thought, why hadn't Bline mentioned that? Of course—Bline thought he already knew it, since he was working on the case.

And maybe that was another reason why Bline had suspected him.

Before reading on, he pictured mentally a map of Chicago and mentally marked the scenes of the four forays of the Ripper. Three had been quite near, on the Near North Side. One, the attempt on Yolanda, five blocks away; another, the murder of the B-girl, in the mouth of the alley off Huron between State and Dearborn, had been about four blocks; Dorothy Lee's murder, one block.

True, the very first murder, that of Lola Brent, had been on the South Side, miles away, but it had probably started on the Near North Side—when the killer had trailed her home from the gift shop on Division Street, only a dozen blocks north. As he might possibly have trailed Dorothy Lee home from the Reiss Corporation on that same street.

He fixed those imaginary x's on the imaginary map in his mind and then went back to the newspaper.

The body had been found a few minutes after five o'clock by Mrs. Rae Haley, divorcee, who lived in the apartment next to Miss Lee's. Returning home after an afternoon at the movies, Mrs. Haley noticed what seemed to be a stream of blood—and which, it later turned out, really was blood—coming from under the doorway of Dorothy Lee's apartment.

Of course it might have been that Dorothy—with whom Mrs. Haley was acquainted—had dropped and broken a jar of tomato juice or a bottle of ketchup. Nevertheless, this was the third Ripper case, and Mrs. Haley, along with most of the rest of Chicago, was Ripper-conscious. She had *not* knocked on Dorothy's door, perhaps to have it opened by someone she had no desire to meet. She had dashed into her own apartment and locked and chained the door; then she had phoned down to the janitor, telling him what she had seen.

David Wheeler, the janitor, had put an old service revolver In his pocket and climbed from the basement to the third floor—which contained five small apartments, Including those of Miss Lee and Mrs. Haley. With the gun ready in his hand, he had tried the doorbell first and then the door, which was locked. He then bent down to examine the little red rivulet and decided that it was quite probably blood; David Wheeler had once been a hospital orderly and knew what blood looked like.

He had rung the bell of Mrs. Haley's apartment and, when she opened it on the chain, told her that the police had better be sent for. Mrs. Haley had phoned them herself, being too frightened by that time to open her door wider than the length of the chain, even to admit Wheeler. Wheeler had stood guard in the hallway until the police arrived. They had broken down the door of the apartment and had found Dorothy Lee lying on the floor about three feet back from the locked door.

They had found that the chain of the door had not been fastened and that the lock was a snap type which would have locked automatically after the killer when he had closed the door after him. There seemed little reason to doubt that he had left by the door. Both of the windows of Dorothy Lee's apartment were open, but neither led to a fire escape and there was no way, short of dropping twenty feet to a concrete areaway, that he could have left by a window.

The police believed, from the position of the body, that the killer had barely entered the apartment. Miss Lee still wore her hat (it had been a hot day and she had worn no coat) and had obviously just returned to her room. Police believed the killer had followed her home and had rung the doorbell almost as soon as Miss Lee had closed the door.

When she had opened the door, he had stepped through and used his knife. Perhaps she had not had time to scream; if she had, no one had heard her.

Police were still canvassing tenants of the building to see which, if any, had been in their apartments at the time.

Having made the fatal cut, police reasoned, the Ripper had immediately backed out of the door, closing it and letting it lock after him. Aside from the body, there was no sign of his presence in the apartment, which was neat and in perfect order. Miss Lee's purse was on a small table near the door; it contained about fourteen dollars in bills and change. Neither her wrist watch nor an opal ring had been taken from the body.

She had left work at two forty-five, complaining of a toothache; the office manager had suggested that she visit a dentist and take the rest of the afternoon off. Her movements from that time on, until her death, had not yet been traced but police were canvassing dentists on the Near North Side and in the Loop to ascertain which one she had seen and when. The coroner's physician who had examined the body found evidence that she had really visited a dentist; there was a temporary packing in a tooth that appeared to be abscessed.

If the temporary packing hadn't stopped her toothache, the Ripper had. According to the physician who had examined the body at five-thirty, she had at that time been dead between one and two hours—between half-past three and half-past four. She had, then, probably been dead at least a half hour when Mrs. Haley, at five o'clock, had seen the blood which led to the discovery of the crime.

The story ended with statements by the Chief of Police and by Captain Bline, in charge of the special detail attempting to find the Ripper.

Sweeney took up the next paper and looked for further details.

The dentist had been found, a Dr. Krimmer, who had his office on Dearborn Street, a little over three blocks south of Division Street. Recognizing her picture in the *Blade,* he had come forward before the police canvass reached him.

Dorothy Lee had come to him at about three o'clock, suffering from a toothache. She had no appointment and was a new patient, but because she was obviously in distress, he had taken her out of turn, as soon as he finished work on the patient then in his chair. That would have been, he estimated, about ten minutes after three.

She had been in his chair only ten or fifteen minutes; he had been able to give her only a temporary treatment to relieve the pain. He had suggested an appointment for further work the next morning. She had asked if he could take her in the afternoon instead, explaining that she worked Saturday morning but was off in the afternoon and, with an afternoon appointment, she would not have to lose more tune from work.

He had given her an appointment at four o'clock, his first free time after noon, but told her that if the tooth became seriously painful earlier in the day she should come to him then and he would manage to take her out of turn to relieve the pain.

He had no record of the exact time she had left his office, but he thought it would hardly have been earlier than twenty minutes after three nor later than half-past.

Sweeney thought that through and saw that it did not change the situation concerning the time of the crime. She could have reached home as early as three-thirty if she had taken a taxi. Sweeney looked at his mental map again and estimated distances. If she had walked over to State from Dearborn and taken a State Street car south to Erie, then walked from State and Erie, she would have reached home about a quarter of four. Had she walked all the way—a total distance of about a dozen blocks—she would have reached home by four o'clock or a few minutes sooner. Assuming, of course, that she had not stopped over anywhere en route.

He skimmed through the few succeeding issues of the paper and found no new developments of importance.

He went back to the first one and studied the picture of Dorothy-Lee again. It looked vaguely familiar—which wasn't strange if she lived only a block away. Damn it, he'd probably passed her on the street half a dozen times. He looked at the picture again and wished that he had known her. Of course, if he had known her, he'd have found her just another uninterest- ing stenographer, stupid, vain and self-centered, who preferred Berlin to Bach and *Romantic Confessions* to Aldous Huxley. But now violent death had transfigured her and those things didn't seem to matter. Maybe, really, they didn't matter.

He jerked his mind back from the edge of maudlinness to the problem at hand.

The Ripper.

Bline had been right, then, about Doc Greene's alibi; it wasn't perfect, but it was good. If his alibi covered him—with the word of attorneys and a judge—until ten minutes after four, miles away, he *could* have taxied to the Near North Side in tune to pick up the trail of Dorothy Lee if, and only if, she had stopped over somewhere between the dentist's office and her home. But it didn't seem likely. To rush from court—

Damn Greene, he thought. If only he could positively eliminate Greene, maybe he could get some constructive thoughts in other directions.

He got up and began to pace back and forth, trying to think.

He glanced at his watch and saw that it wasn't yet quite midnight and the evening was a pup.

Maybe he could eliminate Greene, tonight. Maybe—better, if possible—he could implicate him, tonight.

A spot of burglary, suitably chaperoned, might accomplish either.

He grabbed for his suit coat and Panama.

CHAPTER 12

HE LOCKED the door on Mimi, leaving her alone and screaming in the dark. He stopped at the phone in the hallway and dialed the number of an inexpensive hotel on downtown Clark Street. He gave a room number; it was rung, and an annoyed voice answered.

Sweeney said, "Ehlers? This is Sweeney."

"The hell, Bill; I was just going to turn in. Tired. But since when you call me Ehlers instead of Jay?"

"Since last night."

"Huh?"

Sweeney said, very distinctly, "Since yesterday evening when you entered my room without a warrant."

"Huh? Listen, Sweeney, it was orders. And what was Bline's idea in telling you it was me?"

"Bline didn't tell me. And it wasn't orders." Ehlers said, "Oh—hell. All right, what you want me to do, get down on my knees and say I'm sorry?"

"No," Sweeney said. "Something harder than that—and more practical. Keep your clothes on till I get there. In about ten minutes; I'll take a cab."

He put the receiver back on the hook. Fifteen minutes later he knocked on the door of Jay Ehlers' room.

Ehlers opened it and said, "Come in, Sweeney." He looked faintly embarrassed and faintly belligerent. His coat and tie were off, but he hadn't undressed any farther than that.

Sweeney sat down on the bed, lighted a cigarette, and looked at Ehlers.

He said, "So you thought I might be the Ripper."

"That wasn't *my* idea, Sweeney. It was the captain's."

"Sure, and it was all right for him. Bline didn't know me; he hadn't been a friend of mine for ten years or more. And he sent you and your pal around to bring *me* in—and any cutlery you found around. I wasn't home and it was your bright idea to show how smart you are with locks and burgle my room. You didn't follow orders; you exceeded them. And how many drinks have we had together in ten or twelve years, how many games of cards, how much money have we borrowed from one another? And how about the time I—Hell, I won't remind you of that."

Ehlers' face was reddening. He said, "I remember the time you saved my job; you don't have to remind me. All right, so I should have thought twice. But is this leading to something or did you just come up here to get a bawling-out off your chest?"

"It's leading to something. I'm going to give you a chance to wash it out. I'm going to let you open a door for me, a I door to a man's office."

"You crazy, Sweeney? Whose?"

"Doc Greene's."

"Can't do it, Sweeney. You're crazy."

"Were you crazy when you opened the door of my place? You did that on your own hook, without a warrant and without orders."

"That's different, Sweeney. At least I had orders to exceed. I was told to get your razor and any knives you had, i for the lab. What are you looking for in Greene's office?"

"The same thing. Only I won't bother them unless they're bloodstained, and if we get anything on him you can have the credit."

"You don't think Greene really *is* the Ripper, do you?"

"I hope to find out, one way or the other."

"What if we get caught?"

"Then we get caught. We try to talk our way out of it." Ehlers stared at Sweeney and then shook his head. He I said, "I can't, Sweeney. I'd lose my job no matter how much I talking we did. And I got a chance to put in for lieutenant within a few months."

"To put in for it, but not to make it."

"What do you mean?"

Sweeney said, "It means we're not friends any more, Ehlers. It means you start off on the *Blade's* s.o.b. list, and go on from there. It means I'm going to spread the good word about you to every reporter I know. It means you wouldn't get your name in ink if you stopped a bank robbery single-handed, but we'll drown you in ink if you spit on the sidewalk. It means this is your chance to make up for the dirty trick you pulled on me and if you don't take it, by God, I'll pull every string I can get hold of—in the department itself as well as in print—to break you."

"Yeah? Goddam it, you can't—"

"I can try. I start off tomorrow morning by bringing suit against the police department for entering my room without a warrant, through a locked door, and for petty larceny." Ehlers tried to laugh. "You couldn't make it stick."

"Of course I couldn't. But don't you think the commissioners would start their own little investigation to see what it was really all about? They'd jump on Bline and Bline would tell them the truth. And they'd back you to save the department from paying damages, and let you lie out of it, and no, I couldn't prove my point and collect. But you'd sure rate highly with the commissioners after that. Lieutenancy hell; you'll be back in harness, pounding pavement so far out there wouldn't be any pavement."

"You wouldn't do that, Sweeney."

Sweeney said, "I thought you wouldn't burgle my room, and I was wrong. You think I wouldn't do that, and you're wrong."

"Where *is* Greene's office?" Ehlers was perspiring slightly; it may have been the heat.

"Goodman Block, not far from here. A few blocks, in fact. And I know the building and there won't be any trouble or any danger. I won't take over fifteen minutes inside."

He saw he'd won his point, and grinned. He said, "And I'll buy you a drink first. Dutch courage, if you're more afraid of Greene than you were of me."

"That was different, Sweeney."

"Sure it was different; I was a friend of yours. Greene isn't. Come on."

They caught a cab on Clark Street after Ehlers had turned down the Dutch courage in favor of a drink afterwards, and that was okay by Sweeney. They took the taxi only to within half a block.

The Goodman Block was an old ten-story office building, tenanted mostly by not-too-prosperous lawyers, agents, brokers and (Sweeney happened to know) headquarters of several bookies and at least one small numbers ring.

Sweeney had figured it would be the type of building that would be open twenty-four hours a day for those of its tenants who wanted to burn midnight oil, and saw that he was right. He and Ehlers walked past on the opposite side of the street and saw that lights still burned in several of the offices. And, through the entrance, they could see that an elevator man was on duty, reading a newspaper while he sat on a chair beside the open elevator door.

They kept on walking and Ehlers asked, "Going to take a chance on having him take us up? We can give him a song-and-dance, but even so, he'll remember us."

They crossed over. Sweeney said, "We'll try not to use him. We'll wait— a little while, anyway—outside the entrance and out of his sight; we'll be able to hear the bell ring and the elevator start if he gets a call from upstairs, and we can get through the lobby without his seeing us."

Ehlers nodded agreement, and they waited quietly outside until, luckily only ten minutes later, they heard the buzzer of the elevator and the clang of its door closing.

Sweeney picked Greene's room number 411, off the building directory as they went through the outer hall; they were on the stairway between the second and third floors when the elevator passed on its way down from whatever upper floor it had serviced.

They tiptoed quietly the rest of the way to the fourth floor and found 411. Fortunately no other office on that floor seemed to be occupied; Ehlers did not have to use particular caution in applying his picklocks. He got the door open in seven minutes.

Inside, they turned on the lights and closed the door. It was a little cubby-hole of an office. One desk, one cabinet, one file, one table, three chairs.

Sweeney shoved his hat back on his head as he looked around. He said, "This won't take long, Jay. Sit down and relax; you've done your share, unless I run across a locked drawer; there isn't any lock on that file."

The bottom drawer of the three-drawer file contained a pair of overshoes, a half-full bottle of whiskey and two dusty glasses. The middle drawer-was empty.

The top drawer contained correspondence—all incoming correspondence; apparently Greene didn't make carbons of his own letters. It disgusted Sweeney to find that the correspondence was filed only in approximately chronological order; that there was no separate section or folder for Yolanda; he'd hoped for some clue to what he thought was Doc's rather unusual way of handling her. But he didn't want to spend too much time on the file and glanced only at sample letters pulled out at random and put back when he'd looked at them. All he learned was that Greene really did business as a booking agent and did have other clients and get bookings for them. Not, as far as he could tell, on any big-time circuits or top clubs.

He left the file and tried the cabinet. Stationery supplies on the shelf, an old raincoat hanging on one of the hooks, and a portable typewriter case standing on the bottom. He looked in the raincoat's pockets and found nothing but a dirty handkerchief and a pair of month-old theater stubs. He opened the portable typewriter case to make sure that it contained a type-writer, and it did.

It looked pretty much like the one he himself had owned—up to the point on his recent bender when he'd taken it out to sell. It was the same make and model but when he looked at it closely he saw it wasn't the same type-writer, which would have been a fascinating discovery.

The drawer of the table contained nothing more fascinating than an old hectograph, two of the three chairs were empty and the third chair contained only Jay Ehlers, who was staring at him with a saturnine expression.

Jay asked, "Well, find anything?"

Sweeney grunted an answerless answer and turned to the desk. On top of it was a blotter pad, a pen set and a telephone. He looked under the blotter pad; there was nothing there. He tried the drawers. Only the left-hand top one was locked. He said, "Hey, pal. Your department."

That was the drawer that interested him. He went through the others hastily while Jay opened the locked one. There wasn't anything in any of the other drawers of particular interest to Sweeney, except, possibly, one full bottle of whiskey. And right now he wasn't interested in that.

Jay opened the drawer and glanced at his watch. He said, "Snap it up, Bill. You said fifteen minutes and we've been here twenty-three already."

Inside the locked drawer was a ledger and a thick brown envelope marked: "Current Contracts."

Sweeney looked at the ledger first, but it turned out to be a journal rather than a ledger, not indexed, and listing receipts and expenditures in chronological order. He thumbed through it rapidly but saw that he wasn't going to get anything from it—aside from the fact, which he didn't doubt anyway, that Greene had a legitimate business as a booking agent. Probably the figures wouldn't be too straight anyway, but were kept for income tax purposes.

He took up and opened the envelope marked "Current Contracts."

There were a dozen of them there, but only one interested Sweeney; that was the contract between El Madhouse, Nick Helmos signing, and Yolanda Lang. The contract called for two hundred dollars a week for the joint services of Yolanda Lang and Devil. But neither Yolanda nor the dog had signed it; the signature was Richard M. Greene.

Sweeney upped an eyebrow. He asked, "Can't she write?"

"Can't who write?"

Sweeney said, "I can understand why the dog didn't sign it."

"Look, I thought you were looking for a razor or a shiv."

Sweeney sighed. What he'd really been looking for most was a small black statuette. But if Doc had that, it was at his flat or hotel or wherever he lived, not at his office. And—even if he could find out, at this late hour, where Doc lived—he couldn't crowd Ms luck by burglarizing it tonight.

And, anyway, why couldn't he get Doc Greene off his mind so he could concentrate on other angles? A trip to Brampton, Wisconsin, for instance, to talk to the sculptor—what was his name? Chapman Wilson—who had made Mimi. There was a chance, an off chance, that might lead somewhere. He didn't see where or how. And maybe, getting back to Greene, damn him, a trip to New York to see whether Greene's alibi—his only solid one—was really one hundred per cent solid. The police there might or might not have dug under the surface fact that he was registered at a hotel. Sweeney doubted that they had.

Or, if he had a lot of money, he might save himself that trip by having a New York private detective do the job for him. But that would have to be on Sweeney; the *Blade* would never cover it.

Damn money! He still had a hundred dollars _or so out of the checks Wally Krieg had given him, but at the rate it was vanishing, he'd barely get by for the ten days before another check would be coming from the *Blade*. Let alone spending any money on the Ripper or on Yolanda.

He heard Jay Ehlers move restlessly, and looked back at the contract in his hand. He said, "Just a minute, Jay."

He read the contract through and frowned. He read one paragraph again to make sure it really said what he thought it said, and it did. He put the contract bade in the envelope with the others, put the envelope in the drawer, and told Jay to relock it.

Jay said, "Well, find what you were looking for?"

"No. Yes. I don't know what I was looking for, but I found something."

"What?"

"I'm damned if I know," Sweeney said. But he thought he did; he'd found some money if he was willing to take a chance.

Jay grunted as the lock clicked. He said, "Come on, then. Let's clear out of here. We'll argue about it over a drink."

Sweeney turned out the lights and waited in the hallway while Jay relocked the door of Room 411.

They walked very quietly down to the second floor and there Sweeney put his finger to his lips and then pressed the button of the elevator signal. As soon as they heard the door clang shut a floor below them, they started down the stairs and were on the first floor by the time the operator opened the door on the second. They were out of the building and two doors away by the time the elevator got back down to the first floor.

Ehlers said, "He'll know somebody pulled a fast one to get out of the building without being seen."

Sweeney said, "Sure he will, but he didn't see us. And he won't chase us."
He didn't.

They waited until they were out of sight around the corner before they
flagged a cab. Sweeney asked Jay where he wanted the drink and Jay suggested Hurt Meaghan's; it was only two blocks from his hotel and he could
walk back from there.

In Burt's place, Sweeney started toward the bar but Ehlers took
Sweeney's arm and pulled him toward a table instead. He said, "We got a
minute's talking, Bill, in private."

At the table, he glowered at Sweeney until their drinks had come and the
waiter had gone. Then he said, "Okay, Bill. I burgled your room and I
shouldn't have. But I burgled another place for you to make up, so we're
even. Right?"

"Right."

"We're friends?"

"Friends. All is forgiven."

Jay said, "All right, then, we start from there. We're friends now, but
we're not going to keep on being friends if you hold out on me. I want the
pitch; I want to know why you wanted into Greene's office and what you
got there, and didn't get I'm a cop, Sweeney, and I'm working on the
Ripper case. Just as a flunky under Bline, sure, but I'm still working on it.
I want to know what the score is. I can't *make* you tell me, because you got
me by the short hairs. I can't tell Bline or anyone else you were in Greene's
office because I'd lose my job for my part in it. You're safe as hell, but by
God, I write *you* off *my* books if you don't tell me."

Sweeney nodded. "Fair enough, Jay. So okay, I've had a strong suspicion
that Greene is the Ripper. No reason for it at all; just a dumb hunch,
because I hate the guy so much. Well, a little more than that: I think he fits
the role. Psychiatrist or not, I think he's psychopathic. A couple of hours
ago at El Madhouse, I got through his guard and he threatened to kill me.
Out loud and in front of the police. To be specific, in front of Cap Bline.
And another copper—hell, *two* coppers, guys named Ross and Swann, sitting right at the table. I got his goat on purpose to try him out."

"The hell. But what's that got to do with his office?"

Sweeney said, "I hoped I could find something there that would help me
make up my mind, pro or con, about Greene, gut—word of honor, Jay, I
didn't. I didn't find a damn thing to indicate Greene might be the Ripper. I
didn't find a damn thing to indicate he isn't, except the proof that he really is what he says he is, an agent and manager for night club talent."

"Keep on. What did you find?"

"Something that interested me personally, Jay. I found the contract for Yolanda and Devil versus El Madhouse. And there's something in it I think I can use. But illegally; you wouldn't want to know about it"

"Illegally how?"

"To pick up a piece of change that I need."

"Who from?"

"The guy who owns El Madhouse."

"You mean Nick Helmos or Harry Yahn?"

"Yahn. Nick's just a figurehead."

Jay Ehlers pursed his lips and stared into his glass for a moment. He said, "Careful, Bill. Harry Yahn's a tough mug."

"I know it. But I'm going to bite him. I'm going to make the bite small enough that it won't pay him to use his torpedoes on me. He's tough, but he's smart. He won't take a chance for peanuts."

"Me, I'd rather buck the Ripper, Bill."

Sweeney grinned. "Me too. But I'm going to buck Yahn for the dough to buck the Ripper with."

"You're crazy, Bill."

"I know it. Another drink?"

Ehlers said he'd better turn in, and left. Sweeney wandered over to the pinochle game and watched the play for a few minutes, then went to the bar for one more drink.

The few he'd had at El Madhouse had worn off completely and the one he'd had just now wasn't enough to feel. One more drink, even two, wouldn't hurt him.

He had two, and they didn't hurt him.

CHAPTER 13

THE TWO DRINKS didn't hurt him, but they didn't do him any good, either. He was cold sober when he went out of Meaghan's Bar into the night. The lonely, teeming night. I The warm, chilling night. The bright, dark night.

He was afraid, and it annoyed him that he should be afraid. He didn't mind being afraid of the Ripper; that was the Unknown, the Mysterious. But he didn't like being afraid of Harry Yahn. Harry Yahn was a mug. There wasn't anything mysterious about Harry Yahn; and the things that were unknown about him were strongly suspected by the police, whether they could-be proved or not. ~

Harry Yahn was a plenty tough mug, but still just a mug. Sweeney told himself that and told himself that he wasn't afraid, because the bite he was going to put on Yahn wasn't big enough to bother a man with an income like Yahn's.

The funny thing was that he'd had Yahn in mind as a possible source of revenue even before the trip to Greene's office tonight; there were some things that Sweeney knew about some things that Yahn had done, several years ago, that would have been worth money—to anyone desperate enough to try to collect it. But this new angle was better, and safer—a little safer, but a lot better.

It wasn't blackmail, exactly.

The neon sign said redly, "Tit-Tat-Toe Club." Sweeney took a deep breath and went in. It was an ordinary bar, only moderately swank, and not as large as Meaghan's place. It was populated at the moment by one bartender and half a dozen customers. It looked like the type of bar that might be a front for something else. It was.

Sweeney went to the bar and decorated it with a bill. The bartender lumbered over and Sweeney said, "Shot. Water chaser." And then before the bartender could turn away, "Is Harry here?"

"Harry who?"

"The name is Sweeney. Bill Sweeney. He knows me."

The bartender turned to the backbar for glass and bottle. As he poured the shot he said, "Knock on the back door there, around the corner from the John. If Willie knows you, you get in."

"Willie doesn't. But Harry does."

"Tell that to Willie. He can talk; he can ask Harry. If Harry's here."

"Okay," Sweeney said. "Have one with me."

"Sure."

"And wish me luck."

"Sure," said the bartender. "Luck."

"Thanks."

"For what?"

Sweeney laughed, and felt better. He went back around the corner from the John and knocked on a heavy door. It opened a few inches and a face looked out, the eyes—and they weren't nice eyes—well above the level of Sweeney's head.

Under the eyes was a broken nose, and under the nose was a pair of thick lips that said "Yeah?" and showed broken teeth between them.

Sweeney said, "Willie Harris. I didn't know the Willie on the door was Willie Harris."

"Yeah. What you want?"

"The hell, Willie. Don't you remember me? I covered three of your fights when I was doing Sports. Bill Sweeney. I was on the *Trib* then."

The door opened wider, eight inches instead of six. Willie said, "Yeah?"

Punchy, Sweeney thought. He said, "Okay, you don't remember all the reporters ever talked to you. Listen, Willie, I want to talk to Harry Yahn. On business. Not the games. He knows me. Tell him Bill Sweeney wants to talk to him. Bill Sweeney."

Short sentences like that, Willie would get. He said, "Sweeney. I'll see."

"Bill Sweeney. Hang on to it, Willie. Bill Sweeney."

The door closed.

Sweeney leaned against the wall and lighted a cigarette. When an —inch was gone from the length of the cigarette, the door opened again, wider.

Willie looked out to be sure nobody but Sweeney was there and said, "Okay. He'll talk to yah."

He led Sweeney along a short stretch of hallway and pointed to a door. "In there. Go ahead."

Sweeney went in. He said, "Hello, Harry," and Yahn said, "Hi, Sweeney. Sit down."

Harry Yahn, seated at a battered desk that looked as though it had been bought second hand for about ten dollars, looked like Santa Claus without his whiskers. He was fat and smiling; he looked both complacent and complaisant. Sweeney wasn't fooled. But he was glad, at least, that they were alone.

"Haven't seen you for a long time, Sweeney. Still on the *Blade?*"

Sweeney nodded. "Read that story about Yolanda?"

"Which one?"

"The eyewitness one, the scene in the hallway. In the *Blade.*"

"The hell; did you write that? I skimmed it, but I didn't happen to notice the by-line."

Sweeney didn't call him a liar. He merely said, "Yeah, I wrote it. And a damn fine job, if I say so myself—and why shouldn't I, since everybody else does?"

"Y'know, Sweeney, that story hasn't hurt business at El Madhouse a bit. Where you staying? I'm going to tell the boys to send a case of whiskey over for you."

"Thanks," Sweeney said, "but I'm on the wagon. Almost And I've got a better idea, Harry. How about letting me handle the publicity for you for the next four weeks—while Yolanda's playing there?"

Yahn pursed his lips and stared at Sweeney. He said, "That would have been a better idea before all this happened. We don't need it now, El

Madhouse is turning them away, Nick tells me, and what'd we do with more suckers? Hang 'em from the rafters? And we've got Yolanda under contract for only four more weeks, like you say, and it'll hold up that long."

He laughed. "You gave it away, Sweeney. Sure, I'd have paid you to get that story you wrote into print, but it *was in* print; it's a dead horse now. And look—there was plenty publicity outside of that. Just getting jumped by the Ripper, that's enough to pull them in to see Yolanda. Your eyewitness story just tied it up in cellophane. Nope, Sweeney, we got all the publicity we can make use of."

Sweeney shrugged. He said, "It was just an idea. I'll work on it from the other end, then."

"The other end?"

"Doc's end. A little more publicity—and I think I could swing it—and he could book Yolanda for real money in any one of several places with twenty times the take of El Madhouse. He could get two, maybe three thousand a week—instead of two hundred. Or instead of four hundred and fifty if you prorate over four weeks the thousand buck bonus she's getting for going back to work right away."

Harry Yahn's eyes were half closed, as though he was bored. He said, "It's an idea. If she can keep the publicity hot for four weeks more, she might still pull down that kind of money, or almost that kind."

Sweeney said, "She's worth it right now. I caught your first show at El Madhouse tonight, Harry, and did a little figuring. You ought to have capacity crowds for four weeks. Capacity's two hundred each show, three shows, six hundred a night. Let's be conservative as hell and say each mooch pays five bucks and that one buck out of that is clear profit. Six hundred bucks a night profit for a week is four thousand two hundred; times four weeks, sixteen thousand, eight hundred dollars."

Yahn said dryly, "We did some business before we had Yolanda."

"Sure, about half as much as you'll be doing for the next four weeks. And with half as much, the overhead is higher. Let's say having Yolanda for the next four weeks will bring in about ten thousand dollars profit that you wouldn't have otherwise. Fair enough?"

"Too high. But what are you leading up to?"

"All right, it's too high. Let's say it's worth seven thousand dollars. Is seven thousand conservative enough?"

Yahn's eyes were almost closed and he was smiling faintly; he looked now more like a sleeping Buddha than like Santa Claus. Sweeney wasn't fooled; Harry Yahn was neither sleeping nor contemplating nirvana. Not when money, in the thousands, was the subject of conversation.

Yahn said, "I hope you're leading somewhere." Sweeney stalled deliberately by taking out a cigarette and lighting it. Then he said, "If I do publicity for Greene and Yolanda instead of for El Madhouse, I would advise my friend Doc to book Yolanda elsewhere right away instead of waiting four weeks. But that would cost you seven thousand dollars, Harry, and I wouldn't like to do that, because I've always considered you a friend of mine."

"Yolanda is under contract for four more weeks." Sweeney smiled. He asked, "Have you read the contract?" Yahn's eyes opened fully halfway and he looked at Sweeney.

He asked, "Are you representing Greene on this? Did he send you to shake me down?"

"No. And nobody is trying to shake you down, Harry." Harry Yahn said a nasty word. He said, "It doesn't wash, Sweeney. If there was a hole in that contract that would let Greene book Yolanda elsewhere, he'd be in there pitching. For himself. Why would he tell you about it?"

Sweeney leaned back comfortably in his chair. He said, "He didn't tell me about it. He doesn't know about it, yet. He and I had a little bet about how much Yolanda and Devil were getting at El Madhouse and he showed me his copy of the contract—with—Nick's signature—to win his bet. And he won the bet. But while I had the contract in my hand I happened to read it. Have you?"

"What's the gimmick?"

"Sweet and simple. It must have been an El Madhouse contract, a standard one you give your talent there, because it's full of escape clauses for the party of the first part, which is El Madhouse. But there's also an escape clause for the party of the second part, only it's one that wouldn't be worth a damn in any ordinary case. But this isn't an ordinary case."

"And what is the clause?"

"One that wouldn't be worth the paper it's written on to anybody else, Harry. It provides that the contract may be canceled by the party of the second part by payment of the face amount of the contract—by refunding all moneys received under the contract and paying an amount equal to the balance still to be received under the contract.

"Yolanda's contract is for seven weeks, three down and four to go, at two hundred a week. Doc could buy her out of that for seven times two hundred—fourteen hundred dollars. And if he could book her elsewhere for two thousand a week for the next four weeks, he and Yolanda would be ahead six and a half thousand dollars. Maybe more; I think right now he could get more than two grand a week from her current publicity, even if I don't add to it."

Sweeney leaned forward and stubbed out his cigarette in the ash tray on Yahn's desk. He said, "The only bad thing about it is that Greene's gain would be your loss."

"Greene doesn't know that's in the contract?"

"Obviously not. He probably read the contract when it was signed, but a clause like that wouldn't have meant anything then. Only in case a performer's value suddenly increases ten times overnight would a clause like that really *be* an escape clause. And the odds are a thousand to one against his happening to reread the contract. He thinks he knows what's in it."

Sweeney stood up. He said, "Well, so long, Harry. Sorry we couldn't see eye to eye on my doing a little publicity for your club."

"Sit down, Sweeney."

Yahn jabbed a button on his desk and it seemed he had hardly lifted his finger off it before Willie Harris was in the doorway. He said, "Yeah, Boss?"

"Come in and close the door, Willie. And just stick around."

"Want me to take this guy apart for you?" Yahn said, "Not yet, Willie. Not if he sits down." Sweeney sat down. Willie stood, ready. If you looked at Willie's face you might have got the idea that Willie hadn't taken anybody apart for a long time and had been missing it badly. Anyway, that's the idea Sweeney got. He quit looking at Willie's face and got out another cigarette and lighted it, moving very slowly and carefully so as not to startle Willie. He wished that he felt as casual as he hoped he was acting. Yahn picked up the phone on his desk and dialed a number. He asked for Nick. He said, "Harry, Nick. You got the contract for Yolanda Lang in the safe there. Get it out and put it in your pocket and then call me back. Right away, and privately. Use that phone in the back office and be sure nobody's in hearing distance, see? And don't let anybody notice what you're taking out of the safe. . . . Okay."

He put the phone back on the hook and looked at Sweeney. Sweeney didn't say anything. Nobody said anything. In three minutes the phone rang.

Sweeney said, "Tell him the sixth paragraph, Harry. That'll save time."

Yahn talked briefly and then listened. He said, "Okay, Nick. Put it back. And don't mention this. . . . Yeah, that's why I had you read it to me. We'll talk it over tomorrow. How's business?" He listened a moment and then said "Okay," and hung up.

Sweeney asked, "How *is* business?"

Yahn didn't look at him for a moment. Then he did look at him. He said, "Well, what do you want?"

Sweeney said, "I figure handling publicity for you for the month in question ought to be worth nine hundred bucks."

Harry Yahn didn't look like either Santa Claus or Buddha. He asked, "And if Greene finds out anyway? Happens to reread that contract?"

Sweeney shrugged. "It could happen. There won't be any reason why he would."

Harry Yahn laced his fingers over his stomach and stared a moment at his knuckles. Without looking up, he said, "Willie, go tell Haywood to give you nine hundred. Bring it here." Willie went.

Harry Yahn asked, "How come nine hundred? How'd you hit on that odd amount?"

Sweeney grinned. Inside, the grin was a little shaky and he hoped the outside of it looked better. He said, "I figure you for a four-figure man, Harry. I cut just under. If I'd asked for a thousand—I might have got something else."

Harry laughed; he looked like Santa Claus again. He said, "You're a smart son of a bitch, Sweeney." He got up and slapped Sweeney on the back: Willie came in with money in his hand. He handed it to Yahn and Yahn handed it to Sweeney without counting it Sweeney didn't count it either; he put it in his pocket.

Yahn said, "Show him out, Willie. And let him in again any tune he comes." Willie opened the door and Sweeney went out to the hall; Willie started after and Yahn called him back for a moment. Then Willie came out and opened the door to the outer hallway.

As Sweeney started through it, Willie's hand, as big as both of Sweeney's put together would have been, grabbed his shoulder and spun him around. Willie's other hand, doubled into a fist the size of a football but harder and heavier, slammed into Sweeney's stomach. Willie let go of his shoulder and Sweeney fell, doubled up. He wasn't out, but he couldn't get his breath and he was sick at his stomach. And the pain was so great that he wished the blow *had* knocked him out, especially if there was more coming.

There wasn't.

Willie stepped back. He said, "Harry said to give you that, too." He added, as though explaining why Sweeney had got by so luckily, "He said just one, and easy." It was very obvious that Willie Harris would have preferred it to be more and harder.

He closed the door.

Within a minute Sweeney was able to get to his feet and, a bit doubled over, make it as far as the John. He was sick and after that he was able to stand almost straight. He bent over the wash bowl and rubbed cold water into his face, which the mirror showed him to be almost as white as the porcelain bowl.

But he was breathing almost regularly by now. His abdomen was almost too sore to touch and, very gingerly, he let his belt out two notches to take pressure off it.

He leaned back against the wall and took the money out of his pocket and counted it. It was nine hundred all right, and it was real. He'd got all he'd asked for, and only one thing more. He'd been lucky, plenty lucky.

He put the money into his wallet and walking as though on eggs, he went out through the bar of the Tit-Tat-Toe Club. He didn't look at the bartender or at anyone else on his way through.

He stood outside breathing the cool night air. Not in deep breaths; that would have been unbearably painful. He didn't look around to see if anyone came out after him; he knew no one would.

He'd been unbelievably lucky. Even that poke in the stomach was a good sign, in a way. Harry wouldn't have told Willie to do that if he'd intended to send some of the boys to work him over seriously, or to shoot him. He hadn't really thought there was much danger of being shot—not for nine hundred dollars. But a working-over had been a real possibility, a working-over that might have put him in the hospital for a week or a month and would have played hell with all his plans. Now he felt reasonably confident that he'd been paid in full, both ways. He was going to be plenty sore for a few days, and he was going to have to sleep on his back—and very gingerly at that. But there wasn't any permanent harm done. Worse things had happened to him—and for less.

A cab came cruising by and he hailed it. He walked to it as an old man walks and it hurt him to pull the door open.

He said, "Drive over to the lake and north along it for a while. A little sick; I can use some fresh air."

He got in. Closing the door jarred him.

The cabby peered back at him. He asked, "How sick, Mac? Not going to mess up my cab, are you?"

"Not sick that way. And I'm sober."

"Want me to take you to a sawbones?"

Sweeney said, "I had a poke in the guts, that's all."

The cabby said, "Oh," and started the cab. He drove east to Michigan Boulevard and north until they were on Lake Shore Drive. Sweeney leaned back in the cab and began to feel better, especially after they were on the Drive and a cool breeze off the lake came in the open windows.

The cab didn't jar him; the gentle motion seemed to help.

He felt pretty good with nine hundred bucks in his pocket and no worse price for it than this. A prizefighter took a hell of a lot worse and, except for the top few, for a hell of a lot less.

He wasn't angry at Willie. Willie was punchy to begin with, and had been carrying out orders—even though he'd enjoyed doing it and would have enjoyed doing more. But too many punches had addled Willie's brains, what few he had ever had.

He didn't blame Harry Yahn either. After all, it *had* been blackmail; Harry had let him off easy.

He saw they were passing Diversey Parkway and said, "Guess this is far enough; you can head back now."

"Okay, Mac. Feeling better?"

"Practically okay."

"Should I have seen the other guy?"

Sweeney said, "Yeah, you should have seen the other guy. He's about six feet three and weighs about two-twenty."

"The hell you say. Must have been Willie Harris. I picked you up in front of the Tit-Tat-Toe."

"Forget I said it," Sweeney told him. "I was kidding you."

"Okay, Mac. Where'll I drop you off?"

"Bughouse Square."

"Bughouse Square at this hour? What the hell you want to do there?"

Sweeney said, "I wish to commune with God."

The cabby didn't answer that. In fact, he didn't say another word until he announced the fare at Sweeney's destination.

CHAPTER 14

BUGHOUSE SQUARE stirred restlessly in the warm night as Sweeney walked into it. The benches were lined with human cargo; there were men sleeping on the grass, too. Shut off from the lake breeze by the buildings on Dearborn, the leaves of the trees hung dead still, the blades of grass did not ripple; the stirring was the restless moving of men who slept or tried to sleep because they had nothing else to do.

The fourth bench on the right on the northeast diagonal walk, that's where God would be if he was there. He was there, looking older and more dis- putable than when Sweeney had last seen him. But maybe that was part- contrast; Sweeney's own looks and dress were different tonight from what they were when he had last seen Godfrey. Unconsciously, one judges others by comparison with oneself; and two people both of whom have eaten onions cannot smell each other's breath.

But Sweeney didn't try to smell God's breath; he shook God's shoulder, gently and then harder, and God bunked and looked up. He said, "Whattahell?"

Sweeney grinned at him. He said, "Don't you know me?"

"No, I don't know you. Beat it before I call a cop."

"Want a drink, God? Badly enough?"

"Badly enough to what?"

Sweeney said, "To reach in your right-hand coat pocket."

Godfrey's hand reached into his pocket, clutched something, and stayed there. His voice was a little hoarse. He said, "Thanks, Sweeney. Haven't had a drink since afternoon; it'd have been a hell of a morning. What time is it?"

"About half past three."

God swung his feet off the bench. He said, "Good. How's it coming with you, Sweeney?"

"Good."

God pushed himself up off the bench. Sweeney said, "Look at the figure on the corner of that bill before you hand it over."

God pulled his fist out of his pocket and looked at a corner of the crumpled bill. He glared at Sweeney. He said, "A Goddam capitalist. Showing off."

He thrust his fist back into his pocket and got up off the bench. He walked away without looking back.

Sweeney, grinning, watched him until he'd reached the street—mostly to be sure that nobody had heard or seen and would follow. No one followed.

Sweeney went the opposite direction and caught a cab on Chicago Avenue. It was almost four o'clock when he got home, and he was tired. But before he went to his room he called the Northwestern Station from the phone in the hall.

Yes, they told him, Brampton, Wisconsin, was on the Northwestern Road; the next train that would take him there left at six o'clock, in a little over two hours. The train after that? None that went through Brampton before evening. What time did the 6:00 a. m. train get in? One-fifteen in the afternoon.

Sweeney said thanks and put the receiver back on the hook.

In his room he looked longingly at his bed, but he knew that if he lay down to try to get an hour's sleep before he started for the train, he'd never be able to get up when the alarm clock went off.

And if he waited until the evening train, he'd be losing a day's tune right when it mattered most. This was Saturday already and Monday morning he had to be back at the *Blade* ready for work and—even if Wally came through and assigned him to the Ripper case—Wally would never sanction a trip to Brampton on the paper's tune. Let alone sanction a trip to New York to check on Greene's alibi there. Well, unless something came up that would save him from having to do that, he could fly there and back next week end on his own tune. And his own money; that was no longer a worry.

An hour ago, with his own hundred, he'd had a thousand dollars. Now, after tithing with God, he still had nine hundred.

If he had any sense, he realized, he'd do something with part of it; he wouldn't carry that much money with him.

But he didn't have that much sense.

He looked again at the clock and sighed. He looked at Mimi and swore at her for being so important that he was losing sleep to trace down her origin and talk to her creator, little as that was likely to get him.

He went over and turned her around on top of the radio so her back was toward him and he couldn't hear her scream. But, even from the back, every line of her body showed terror.

He felt for her so strongly that, for a moment, he contemplated euthanasia. But even if he did break her there would be a gross minus one of her still screaming somewhere.

Wearily-r-and very gingerly because of his tender abdomen—he undressed. He bathed, shaved and put on clean clothes, decided he wouldn't have to take anything with him, and left for the station. He would be too early but he wanted to allow time for a couple of drinks. Not as drinks, but because with them he ought to be able to sleep on the train; otherwise he'd probably be too tired, after six, to sleep in a coach or chair car. He'd have paid double price for a Pullman but knew he couldn't get one; railroads have the strange idea that people should ride horizontally only at night.

He had to walk to State Street, through the gray still dawn, before he caught a cab. He took it to a place on West Madison within a block of the station which he knew would be open even at the late or early hour of five. He had his two drinks—and a third for the road. He considered, before he remembered that he was on the wagon, buying a bottle to take along on the train; but he remembered in time and didn't buy it. Besides, too much to drink would get him wide awake again.

He got to the station at a quarter to six, hoping that the train would be loading by then, and it was. Luckily there was a chair car on the train and the ticket agent sold him a ticket for it and said that he wouldn't need a reservation, that the chair car wouldn't be crowded.

It wasn't. He picked the most comfortable-looking seat in the car, sat down carefully, and put his ticket in the band of his hat so the conductor wouldn't have to wake him. He sprawled out his legs and put his hat, ticket side up, over the bruised portion of his anatomy. It was a lightweight Panama so it didn't hurt too much.

Or if it did, he didn't know it; he was asleep almost the minute he closed his eyes. He opened them briefly a couple of hours later and found the train pulling out of a station. It was Milwaukee, and it was raining. When he opened his eyes again it was a few minutes after noon, the train was in Rhinelander, and the sun was shining. And he was as hungry as a horse.

He found the diner and ate the biggest meal he'd eaten in weeks. And finished his second cup of coffee just in tune to get off at Brampton.

He went into the station and looked in the phone book; no Chapman Wilson was listed. Sweeney frowned and walked over to the ticket window. He asked, "You happen to know where in town Chapman Wilson lives?"

"Chapman Wilson?"

"Yes."

"Never heard of him."

"Thanks."

Sweeney left the station on the side opposite the tracks and took a look at Brampton. About five thousand population, he estimated. In a town that size, it shouldn't be too hard to locate someone, even if they didn't have a phone.

He was already, he found, on the main street; the business district, about four blocks long, started immediately to his left. He went into the first store he came to and asked about Chapman Wilson. He drew a blank. And in the second, the third, and the fourth. Not to mention the fifth and sixth.

The seventh place was a tavern and he ordered a drink before he asked his question. When the drink came, he asked. The drink was good but the answer wasn't.

Sweeney swore to himself as the bartender moved off. Could he have misunderstood the man he'd talked to at the Ganslen Art Company? No, he'd said it clearly enough: "Fellow by the name of Chapman Wilson, lives in Brampton, Wisconsin. He modeled it in clay."

At least he was sure of the Chapman Wilson. Could he have misunderstood the Brampton part?

He motioned the bartender over. He asked, "Is there any other town in Wisconsin that has a name that sounds like Brampton?"

"Huh? Oh, I see what you mean, let's see. There's Boylston, up near Duluth."

"Not close enough."

"Stoughton? Burlington? Appleton? And there's a Milton, but the full name is Milton Junction."

Sweeney shook his head sadly. He said, "You forgot Wisconsin Rapids and Stevens Point."

"They don't sound like Brampton."

"That's what I mean," Sweeney said. "Have a drink."

"Sure, thanks."

"But you've never heard of a Chapman Wilson?"

"No."

Sweeney took a meditative sip from his glass. He wondered if he could raise anyone by phone at the Ganslen Art Company in Louisville. Probably not, on a Saturday afternoon. He might possibly manage to locate the man he'd talked to there—Burke? Yes, Burke was the name. But it wasn't too good a chance.

Sweeney, the rest of his life, was never proud of it, but it was the bartender who saved the day. He asked, "What's this Chapman Wilson do?"

"Sculptor. Artist and sculptor."

For seconds nothing happened. Then the bartender said, "I'll be damned. You must mean *Charlie* Wilson."

Sweeney stared at him. He said, "Don't stop there, Esmeralda. Go on."

"Go on where?"

"To pour us another drink. And then tell me about Charlie Wilson. Does he model little statuettes?"

The bartender laughed. "That's the guy. Crazy Charlie."

Sweeney gripped the edge of the bar. He said, "What do you mean, Crazy Charlie? Crazy, as in *razor?*"

"Huh? Razor? Oh, you mean what *started* him. It was a knife, not a razor."

"A blonde," said Sweeney. "A beautiful blonde?"

"You mean the dame? Yeah, mister, she was both of those. Purtiest thing in town. Until she got attacked with that knife."

Sweeney closed his eyes and counted up to two slowly. It was too good to be true, and he had been about to leave town and go back to Chicago.

It had to be too good to be true; things didn't happen like this. He said, "You mean *attacked,* as in Ripper?"

"Yeah. Like that Chicago business on the radio."

"You are not referring, by any chance, to a small black statuette? You mean a real woman was attacked up here?"

"Sure. A blonde, like the radio said all the dames in Chicago were."

"When?"

"Three years ago. While I was sheriff."

"While you were sheriff?"

"Yeah. I was sheriff up to two years ago. Bought this place then and couldn't keep up both, so two years ago I didn't run."

"And you handled the Ripper case?"

"Yeah."

Sweeney said, "I am proud to meet you. My name is Bill Sweeney."

The bartender stuck a big paw across the bar. "Glad to know you. My name's Henderson."

Sweeney shook the hand. "Sweeney," he said, "of the Chicago *Blade.* You're just the man I was looking for, Sheriff."

"Ex-sheriff."

"Look, Sheriff, is there any way we can talk privately for a little while without you having to interrupt yourself?"

"Well—I don't know. Saturday afternoon and all that."

"I'll buy a bottle of the most expensive champagne you got, and we'll split it while we talk."

"Well—I guess I can get the frau to take over for ten or fifteen minutes. We live upstairs. Only let's split a pint of Haig and Haig instead; the champagne I got isn't very good and anyway it'd take time to ice it."

"Haig and Haig it is." Sweeney put a bill on the bar.

Henderson rang up money and gave Sweeney a little back. He took a bottle from the backbar, put it in his hip pocket, and said, "Come on; I'll get Ma."

He led the way to a door at the back that opened to a flight of stairs. He called up them. "Hey, Ma! Can you come down a few minutes?"

A voice called out, "Okay, Jake," and a few seconds later a tall, thin woman came down the stairs. Henderson said, "This is Mr. Sweeney, Ma, from Chicago. We want to talk a while, upstairs. Can you take over?"

"All right, Jake. But don't you get started drinking. This is Saturday, with Saturday night coming up."

"Won't touch a drop, Ma."

He led Sweeney up the stairs and into a kitchen. He said, "Guess we can talk best here, and glasses and everything are handy. Want anything to mix it with?"

"Haig and Haig? Don't be silly, Sheriff."

Henderson grinned. "Sit down. I'll get glasses and open this."

He came back with glasses and the opened bottle and poured a generous shot for each of them. Sweeney lifted his. "To crime."

"To crime," Henderson said. "How're things in Chicago?"

"Ripping," Sweeney said. "But let's get to Brampton. First, let's make sure this Chapman Wilson I'm talking about and your Crazy Charlie are one and the same person. Tell me something about him."

"His name is Charlie Wilson. He's an artist and a sculptor; guess what money he makes out of it is mostly from the stuff he models. He sells them to some companies that make statuettes and stuff. Arty little things. Guess he doesn't sell many paintings."

"That's the guy," Sweeney said. "Probably uses Chapman as a professional first name; Chapman Wilson sounds better than Charlie Wilson. But how crazy is he?"

"Not really. When he's sober, he's just—what you call it?—eccentric. He's pretty much of a lush, though, and when he gets tanked up—well, I've had to kick him out of my place half a dozen times. Mostly for trying to pick fights." Henderson grinned. "And he's about five feet two and weighs about a hundred and ten pounds soaking wet. Anybody take a real poke at him, they'd probably kill him, and yet he's always wanting to start a fight when he gets tanked. A real screwball."

"Does he make a good thing out of his work?"

"Hell, no. Doubt if he makes five hundred bucks in a year. He lives in a little shack out at the edge of town that nobody else'd live in; gets it for a few bucks a month. And proud as hell; thinks he's a great artist."

"Maybe he is."

"Then why doesn't he make some money out of it?"

Sweeney opened his mouth to mention Van Gogh and Modigliani and a few others who'd been great artists and had made less than five hundred bucks a year out of it; then he remembered his audience and that time was flying.

He asked, instead, "And Charlie Wilson is now running around loose? In Brampton?"

"Sure. Why not? He's harmless."

"Well, this Ripper business. How does Charlie Wilson tie in with that?"

"He shot him."

"You mean Charlie shot the Ripper or the Ripper shot Charlie?"

"Charlie shot the Ripper."

Sweeney took a deep breath. "But the Ripper got away?"

"Hell, no. Killed him dead as hell. Charlie got him with a shotgun from about two yards away. Blew a hole through him you could stick your head through. Only good thing Charlie ever did in his life. He was kind of a hero around town for a while."

"Oh," said Sweeney. He felt disappointed. A dead ripper wasn't going to be much help to him. He took another sip of the Scotch. "Let's start it from the other end. Who was the Ripper?"

"His name was Pell, Howard Pell. A homicidal maniac who broke out of the county insane asylum—that's about twenty miles from here. Let's see, it was four years ago; I told you wrong when I said three because it was in the first year of my second two-year term and that would've been at least four years ago, maybe a few months more than that even. Yeah, a few months more because it was in spring, I remember, and it's August now. Think it was in May."

"And what happened?"

"Well, this Pell broke out of the asylum. Killed two guards with his bare hands; he was a big guy, built like an ox. Bigger than I am. Outside, the siren hadn't gone off yet and he flagged a car and the damn fool driver stopped to pick him up. Guy named Rogers. Pell got in the car and killed Rogers. Strangled him."

"Didn't he use a knife at all?"

"Didn't have one yet. But he got one all right, then and there. This Rogers was a canvasser selling a line of aluminum kitchenware.. But he had some sidelines and one of them was a carving set. The knife in it was a beauty, ten inches long and an inch wide, sharp as hell. Don't know exactly what he was searching the car for, but he found that. And liked it. He tried it out on Rogers, even though Rogers was already dead. Want the details on that?"

"Not right now," Sweeney said. "But I could use another drink. A short one."

"Sorry." Henderson poured it. "Well, he operated on Rogers and threw his body out of the car into the ditch. Not all at once, y'understand."

Sweeney shuddered slightly and took a quick sip of the Scotch. He said, "I'd just as soon not understand too thoroughly. Go on."

"Well, this was about eight o'clock in the evening, just after dark. Anyway, that's when they found the two guards dead and Pell gone from the asylum. They called me quick—along with sheriffs of other counties around, and local police officers and everybody and meanwhile what guards they could spare fanned outward from the asylum in cars to start the search.

"Well, right off they found what was left of this guy Rogers, and the car tracks showed 'em what'd happened, so they knew Pell had a car. They cut back to the asylum and phoned me and everybody that Pell would be in a car and to set up roadblocks and get him.

"We got the roadblocks up quick, but he fooled us. He did head toward Brampton all right, but a little outside of town he turned the car into a side road and left it there. And he came in across the fields on foot so he got through us. Even though between us, me and the police chief here in Brampton, we had every road guarded by that time. Within fifteen minutes of the time we got the call from the asylum."

"Fast work," Sweeney said, approvingly.

"Goddam tooting it was fast work, but it didn't do any good, because he got through us on foot. The next day we could trace back exactly the way he went from the car because he had so much blood on him. Y'see he cut up Rogers right in the driver's seat of the car and then had to get there himself to drive the car, and he was kind of covered with blood all over. God, he even had it in-'his hair and on his face and his shoes were soaked with it. And looking like that, and with the bloody knife in his hand, was how he come across Bessie taking a shower."

"Who is Bessie?"

"Who *was* Bessie. Bessie Wilson, Charlie's younger sister. She was about eighteen, then, maybe nineteen. She was staying with him then because she was sick. She didn't live in Brampton; she had a job in St. Louis, hatcheck girl in a night club or something, but she got sick and broke and came back to stay with Charlie; their parents had been dead ten years or so.

"Guess she didn't know, when she came back, how broke he was or she wouldn't't've come, but she probably, through the letters he'd written her, thought he was doing pretty good. Anyway she was sick and needed help, and what happened to her here in Brampton didn't help her any, I guess. Maybe it'd been better if she'd been killed right out."

"This Pell attacked her?"

"Well, yeah and no. He didn't actually lay a hand on her, but it drove her nuts and she died later. It was this way. That shack *of* Charlie's is just one fair-sized room that he uses to live in and work in both and that's where they lived. But there's another littler shack, sort of like a tool shed, out in back of it on the lot. The can's in there, and Charlie fixed up a shower in there, too. In one corner, just a makeshift kind of shower.

"Anyway, this would've been about half-past eight, the kid sister, Bessie, decides to take a shower and goes out of the shack and along the path to the shed, in a bathrobe and slippers, see? And that must've been just about the time Pell is coming to their yard, cutting into town and keeping off the streets and the road, so he sees her go into the shed.

"And with the carving knife in his hand, he goes up and yanks the shed door open."

"Wouldn't there be a catch on it?"

"I told you—he was big as an ox; he just yanks it open so hard the hook pulls off. And Bessie is standing there naked under the shower getting ready to reach up and turn it on. And he takes a step inside toward her, waving the knife. How's about another drink?"

"An inspiration," said Sweeney.

Henderson poured two.

He said, "You can't blame her for going nuts, can you? Sick to begin with, and seeing *that*. Guy over six feet, two-twenty pounds, in a nuthouse uniform that started out being gray but that ended up being red, with blood in his hair and on his face, and coming at her with a ten-inch carving knife. God."

Sweeney could picture it. He'd seen Mimi.

He took a sip of Scotch. He asked, "What happened?"

CHAPTER 15

HENDERSON SAID, "Well, I was two blocks away and I heard her scream and keep on screaming. It was maybe five minutes before I got there—and of course it was all over long before that—but she was still screaming then.

"What happened was that the first scream she let out, Charlie grabbed for his shotgun—he's got one because he does a lot of hunting, not so much for fun like most of us but because he gets some of his eating that way. And he ran out the back door of the shack and saw the guy with the knife in the doorway of the shed and past him he could see Bessie back in the corner under the shower that wasn't turned on yet, screaming her head off.

"So he runs toward the door; it's only about ten feet from the shack to the shed, and runs a little to one side so he can shoot Pell without shooting Bessie too, and from right outside the door he lets go with the shotgun and, like I said, puts a hole through Pell that you could stick your head through."

"But *must* I?" Sweeney asked. At the blank look on the ex-sheriff's face, he changed his question. "And Bessie Wilson went crazy?"

"Yeah, and died about six-seven months later. Crazy as a bedbug. No, not in the asylum near here; that's for incurables. And for a while they thought they could cure Bessie. It was in some little private sanitarium downstate near Beloit. There was a lot of publicity on the case and one of the doctors down there got interested. He had a new treatment and thought he could cure Bessie and took her on as a charity case. But it didn't work; she died six-seven months later."

Sweeney asked, "And Charlie? Did he go off the beam then, or was he crazy before that?"

"Like I told you, he isn't really crazy. But he was off the beam before that, and I guess that didn't make him any worse. He's an artist. That's crazy to begin with, isn't it?"

Sweeney said, "I guess it is. Where is this shack of his?"

"On Cuyahoga Street; that's eight blocks west of here, almost at the edge of town in that direction. I dunno the number, if there's a number on it, but it's a block and a half north of Main Street—that's the street you're on now—and there are only a few houses in that block and his is the only one-room shack and it's painted green; you can't miss it. Another drink? There's still a couple left in here."

Sweeney said, "Why not?"

There didn't seem to be any reason why not, so Henderson poured them and they killed the bottle.

Sweeney stared moodily into his. This had looked so good, less than half an hour ago. He'd found a Ripper. Only the Ripper was dead, four and a quarter years dead, with a hole in him that Sweeney could stick his head through if he wanted to, only he didn't want to, especially with the Ripper four and a quarter years dead.

Sweeney took a sip of his drink and glared at Henderson as though it was Henderson's fault.

Then he thought of a new angle. It didn't seem likely. He asked, "This Charlie. Wilson. He ever out of town?"

"Charlie? Not that I know of. Why?"

"Just wondering if he ever got to Chicago."

"Naw, he couldn't afford train fare to Chicago. And besides, he didn't."

"Didn't what?"

"Didn't commit your three Ripper murders. Our new sheriff—Lanny Pedersen—was talking about them the other night downstairs. Naturally, we thought of the coincidence of our having had a Ripper here, even if he was dead, and I asked Lanny what about Charlie, if maybe Charlie could have—uh—sort of got the idea from what he saw, or something, and he said he'd thought of that and that he hadn't thought so or anything but that he'd checked with Charlie's next-door neighbors out on Cuyahoga Street, and Charlie hadn't been out of town at all. They see him every day and most of the day because he does most of his painting or sculpting outdoors in his yard."

Sweeney took another sip. "And this Pell," he asked. "There's no doubt but that it was Pell that Charlie shot? I mean, the shotgun didn't mess him up so he couldn't be recognized or anything?"

"Nope, didn't touch his face. No doubt about identification at all, even if he didn't have the bloody uniform on and everything. Shotgun blast bit him in the chest; guess he must have heard Charlie at the door and turned around. Blew a hole in his chest that you could put your head through."

Sweeney said, "Thanks just the same," and stood up. "I guess it was a bust, Sheriff. I had an idea I could tie your Ripper case up with ours, but it doesn't look like it can be done with Charlie alibied and everybody else concerned dead. And anyway, you thought of it before I did. Well, thanks anyway."

He waited while Henderson washed out the glasses they'd used and hid the empty bottle at the bottom of the garbage pail, and then went downstairs with him and Henderson relieved his wife at the bar. She glared at him before she went back upstairs and he had a feeling that Henderson's precautions with the glasses and the bottle had been futile. Even if she didn't find the bottle, she'd know that there had been one.

There were only four customers in the bar and Sweeney unhappily set up a drink around for them before he went out He had only a short beer for himself.

He trudged back to the railroad station and asked what time the next train left for Chicago.

"Eleven-fifteen," the agent told him.

Sweeney glanced up at the clock and saw it was only half past four. He asked, "Is there an airport around where I can get a plane for Chi?"

"A plane for Chicago? Guess the nearest place is Rhinelander. You can get one there."

"How do I get to Rhinelander?"

"By train," the agent said. "The eleven-fifteen. That's the next train headed that way."

Sweeney swore. He bought a ticket for Chicago on the eleven-fifteen and had the agent wire to reserve him a lower berth. Any way, he'd get to Chicago early Sunday morning with a good night's sleep under his belt.

He sat down on a bench in the station and wondered how he'd ever manage to kill over seven and a half hours without drinking too damn much if he drank at all. And if he did that, he'd probably miss the eleven-fifteen and that would ruin tomorrow, which was his last day on his own before he had to go back to the *Blade.*

He sighed, and decided that he might as well see this Charlie-Chapman Wilson while he was here anyway and had to do something to kill the time.

But he'd lost all enthusiasm for it now. It had sounded so beautiful when the ex-sheriff had opened up about a Crazy Charlie named Wilson and a blonde being attacked by a Ripper. It had sounded so good that the anticlimax made nun wish he'd never heard of Brampton, Wisconsin.

Well, he still had Mimi as a lead, but he'd have to trace her the other way, forward instead of backward, and find the Ripper who had a copy of her. Tracing her back here had led only to a coincidence—but a coincidence that was a beautiful confirmation of the idea that Mimi would appeal strongly to a Ripper: she'd been born, in a sense, through contact with a Ripper. Only, alas, not the one who was now operating in Chicago.

Well, he'd still talk to this Chapman Wilson. And if Wilson was a lush, a bottle would be the best way to get him to talk. He bought a bottle, a fifth this time, at a liquor store on his way down Main Street to Cuyahoga. He found Cuyahoga and the small green shack with a shed behind it. But there wasn't any answer to his knock at the door.

He tried the door of the shed, but there wasn't any answer there either. The door of the shed was unlocked; it was fixed to lock only from the inside. Sweeney pushed it open and looked in. Inside, one corner had been partitioned off with beaverboard and was obviously a toilet. In the opposite back corner, sans curtains or partition, was the crude shower the ex-sheriff had described.

A string hanging beside the door operated to turn on the light, a bare bulb in the middle of the ceiling. Sweeney turned it on, and he could see in the far wall, between the shower and the toilet, the place where the charge of the shotgun must have hit, and gone through; there was a square of beaverboard nailed over it now.

He looked back at the shower corner and shivered a little, picturing a full-scale model of his Screaming Mimi—only in soft white instead of hard glossy black—standing there screaming, her slender, rounded arms thrust out in ineffable terror, warding off—Sweeney turned out the light and pulled the door shut. He didn't like his mental picture of *what* she had been warding off. No wonder the poor girl had gone fatally mad.

He went back to the front of the shack and knocked again. Then he went to the house next door and knocked. A man with handlebar mustaches answered the door and Sweeney asked if he knew whether Charlie Wilson was gone for the day or would be home soon.

"Oughta be home soon, I guess. Saw him walk toward town couple hours ago. He always gets home in time to fix his own supper; he wouldn't be eatin' downtown."

Sweeney thanked him and went back to the front of the shack. It was five o'clock and already beginning to be dusk; he might just as well wait here as do anything else he could think of.

He sat down on the wooden step and put his package—the bottle—down on the grass beside the step, resisting an impulse to open it before Charlie came home.

It was six o'clock, arid twilight, when he saw Charlie coming. He recognized him easily from Henderson's description—five foot two, a hundred ten pounds dripping wet. He looked even lighter than that, possibly because he wasn't dripping wet, not on the outside, anyway. From the way he walked, he was not suffering from an internal drought.

He could have been, Sweeney decided as he turned in the gate and came closer, anywhere between twenty-five and forty-five. He had straw-colored, uncombed hair and wore no hat; his clothes were rumpled and he hadn't shaved for at least two days. His eyes were glassy.

Sweeney stood up. "Mr. Wilson?"

"Yeah." The top of his head was just level with Sweeney's chin.

Sweeney stuck out a hand. He said, "Sweeney. Like to talk to you about a certain statuette you made. Ganslen's number SM-1, a girl screaming—"

Charlie Wilson's hand came out, too, but it passed Sweeney's instead of shaking it. And the hand was doubled up into a fist that landed in Sweeney's sore stomach. Sweeney's stomach screamed silently and tried to crawl through his backbone.

Sweeney himself said something inarticulate and bent almost double, which put his chin in handy reach for an opponent Charlie Wilson's height. Charlie's fist hit his chin and knocked him off balance, but didn't straighten him up. Nothing would have persuaded Sweeney to straighten up, just then. Nothing at all. He didn't really feel the poke on his chin at all because the pain in his stomach was too intense. You don't feel a mosquito bite when you've got your leg in a bear-trap.

Sweeney staggered back, still doubled up, and sat down on the doorstep again, his hands protectively clasped over his stomach. He didn't care if

Charlie Wilson kicked him in the face, as long as he didn't touch his stomach again. He didn't care about anything in the world except protecting his stomach. Still with his hands over it, he leaned sideways and started to retch.

When he recovered sufficient interest to look up, Charlie Wilson, arms akimbo, was staring down at him with an utterly amazed expression on his face. His voice matched his expression. He said, "I'll be damned. I licked you."

Sweeney groaned. "Thanks," he said.

"Didn't really hurt you, did I?"

Sweeney said, "It feels lovely. Everything's lovely. Everything's wonderful." He retched again.

"Didn't mean to hurt you, really. But hell, I always get licked whenever I take a poke at anybody, so I try to take as good a poke or two as I can get in before it happens. Hey, want a drink? I've got some gin inside. Inside the hovel, I mean; not inside me. That's whiskey."

"What's whiskey?"

"Inside me. Want a shot of gin?"

Sweeney picked up the wrapped fifth of whiskey beside the step. "If you can open that—"

Wilson got it open by using the rough edge of a key on the celluloid and turning the cap with his teeth. He handed the bottle to Sweeney and Sweeney took a long drink. Sweeney handed back the bottle. "You might as well have one too. To the start of a beautiful friendship. And just what *did* start it?"

"I hate reporters."

"Oh," said Sweeney. He thought back. "And just what gave you the idea I'm a reporter?"

"You're the third in a week. And who else would—?" He broke off, a puzzled look coming into his eyes.

Sweeney said, "Who else indeed? But let's start over again, and differently. You're Chapman Wilson?"

"Yes."

"My name is Sweeney. Mortimer Sweeney. I'm with the Ganslen Art Company. Of Louisville."

Charlie Wilson put a hand to his forehead. He said, "Oh, my God."

"You may well say it."

"I'm sorry as hell. Look, can you stand up yet? So I can get the door open. Don't; I've got a better idea. I'll go around back and open it from inside and then I can help you in."

He went around the side of the shack, looking considerably more sober than when he'd first come up the walk. Sweeney heard a back door being opened and then the front door. It nudged his back.

Wilson's voice said, "Sorry, I forgot it opens out. You'll have to stand up anyway to let me get it open. Can you?"

Sweeney stood up. Not all the way up, but far enough for him to move to one side and then go in when the door opened. He made it to the nearest seat, which was a camp stool without a back; that didn't matter because he didn't feel inclined to lean back anyway.

The light was on, a single overhead bulb as in the shed back of the shack. Wilson was washing two glasses at the sink in one corner. The sink was piled high with dishes but there weren't any on the shelves above the sink; obviously Wilson washed dishes when and as he needed them for use rather than the more orthodox system of washing them and putting them away each tune after they'd been used.

He poured a generous slug from Sweeney's bottle into each of the glasses and came over with one of them for Sweeney.

Sweeney took a sip and looked around him. The walls, every available inch of them, were hung with unframed canvases. There were landscapes vaguely in the manner of Cezanne that Sweeney rather liked, and there were abstractions that looked interesting; Sweeney wasn't enough of an expert to know how good they were, but he could tell that they weren't bad. There didn't seem to be any portraits or figure work.

At one side of the room a sculptor's stand held a partially finished twelve-inch statuette of what appeared to be a gladiator.

Wilson had followed Sweeney's gaze. He said, "Don't look at that. It isn't finished, and it's horrible anyway." He walked across the room and threw a cloth across the clay figure, then sat down on the edge of the cot across from Sweeney.

Sweeney had begun to feel better. He said, "It's not bad—the gladiator, I mean. But I'd say oil is your real medium and that the statuettes are pot-boilers. Right?"

"Not exactly, Mr. Sweeney. Of course if you weren't from Ganslen I'd say you were exactly right. By the way, what is your job there?"

Sweeney had been thinking about that. He didn't know anything about the set-up of the Louisville art firm and, more important, he didn't know how much Wilson knew; Wilson might even have visited there and be pretty familiar with the officers. Besides, he didn't want to do any buying or rejecting. He said, "I'm just a salesman for them. But when the boss heard

I was passing through Brampton on this trip, he told me to stop off and see you."

"I'm sorry as hell, Mr. Sweeney, that I—uh—"

"That's all right," Sweeney lied. "But first, what's this business about two other reporters—I mean, two reporters having__ been here to see you? From what papers, and why?"

"From St. Paul papers. Or maybe one was from Minneapolis. It was about that statuette you mentioned, your SM-1. That's why I thought you were another reporter, I guess. What was it *you* wanted to ask about that?"

Sweeney said, "Let's get it straight first about what these oth—these reporters wanted to know about SM-1."

Wilson frowned. "On account of these Ripper murders *in* Chicago they wanted to do a rehash of my shooting of the maniac I had to shoot here about four or five years ago. Both of them knew about the statuette I made of Bessie, so I guess they must have talked to Sheriff Pedersen before they came out here."

Sweeney took a thoughtful sip of whiskey. "Had either of them seen it, or a photo of it?"

"I guess not. What they wanted to know mostly was what company I'd sold it to. If they'd seen one, they could have found what company made it. They stamp their name under the base."

"Then the sheriff here knew you'd made such a statuette but didn't know what company you sold it to?"

"That's right. And he never saw it. I got a crying jag about it one night when he jugged me for disorderly conduct."

Sweeney nodded and felt relieved. Then the St. Paul-Minneapolis papers didn't have the important part of the story about Screaming Mimi. They had the inconsequential part—the part he'd learned today from the ex-sheriff—but they didn't know the important, the art-important, fact that Chicago's Ripper had a copy. And they didn't have even a photo of the statuette. All they had was a rehash of an old local story; it would make their own papers but wouldn't go out on the AP and UP wires to spoil Sweeney's angle.

Wilson leaned back against the wall behind the cot he was sitting on and crossed his legs. He said, "But what is it Ganslen sent you to talk to me about, Mr. Sweeney?"

"Something that I'm afraid won't work, if you don't like the idea of publicity for the statuette and how it-originated. You see, we're taking a loss on that particular number, as things stand. We made a gross of them to try them out—and we'd have lost money *if* the whole gross had sold, but it sold too slowly to justify our making it in quantity. But it's even worse than that. We're stuck with about a hundred out of the original gross; it just turned out not to have any general appeal at all."

Wilson nodded. "I told Mr. Burke that when he took it. It's one of those things; you like it a lot or else you don't like it at all."

"How did you feel about it, as an artist? How did it strike you?"

"I—I don't know, Mr. Sweeney. I should never have done it, and I should never have sold it. It's too—personal, Jesus God, the way Bessie looked standing there screaming, the way I saw her through the doorway past that—Well, the picture just stuck in my mind until I finally had to do it to get it *off* my mind. It was haunting me up to last year. I had to either paint it or model it and I'm not good at figure work with the brush so I modeled it. And once I did that, I should have destroyed it.

"But I'd just finished it when Mr. Burke stopped in on one of his buying trips, and he liked it. I didn't want to sell it to him, but he insisted, and I needed the money so badly I couldn't turn it down. Hell, it was like selling my own sister; it *was,* in a way. I felt so lousy about it I stayed drunk a week, so the money didn't do me any good anyway."

Sweeney said, "I can see how you must have felt about it."

"But I told Mr. Burke then I didn't want any publicity about it and he promised he wouldn't give the story of it to anybody to try to sell more of them. So why does he send you now to open the subject again?"

Sweeney cleared his throat. "Well—he thought that, under new circumstances, you might change your mind. But I can see you still feel pretty strongly about it, so I won't even try to persuade you."

"Thanks, Mr. Sweeney. But what new circumstances do you mean?"

"The same thing those St. Paul reporters meant. You see, right now, there's a Ripper actively operating in Chicago, and it's a big story—not just local, but a coast-to-coast big crime story, about the biggest thing since Dillinger. Right now, while the iron's hot, we could sell a flock of them if we could cash in on *that* publicity, advertising them—and honestly—as a statuette of a woman being attacked by a Ripper, and from life. From the memory of a sculptor who'd actually seen the attack—and prevented it. But we'd have to release the whole story to do that."

"I see what you mean. And it would mean a little extra, I guess, in royalties to me. But—no, I guess not. As I said, I'm sorry I told it at all and to drag poor Bessie before the public again—How's about another drink? It's your whiskey."

"Ours," said Sweeney. "You know, Charlie, I like you. Not that I thought I would after the way you greeted me.'"

Wilson poured refills. He said, "I'm really sorry as hell about that. Honestly. I thought you were another of those Goddam reporters like the first two, and I'd made up my mind I wasn't going to *take* another one of them."

He sat down again, glass in hand. "What I like about you best is your not trying to talk me into letting Ganslen release publicity on it. I might weaken if you did. God knows I need money—and God knows it wouldn't do me any good if I got it that way.

"Even with the God-awful prices you get for your statuettes, you might sell thousands of them with a story like that back of them. And with that much money—"

Sweeney asked curiously, "How much money? I mean, Burke didn't happen to mention exactly what the arrangements with you were on the deal."

"The usual. Usual for me, anyway; I don't know what kind of a contract they give their other sculptors, but on all the statuettes they buy from me, it's a hundred bucks down and that covers all they sell up to a thousand copies—that's the point, Burke says, where they start to break even on a number and over that they show a profit. Is that right?"

"Close enough," Sweeney said.

"So if they would sell two or three thousand copies, I'd have one or two thousand coming in royalties—and that hasn't happened yet. And God help me if it did—in this case. I told you I stayed drunk for a week on the hundred bucks I got out of selling that figure of Bessie the first tune. Well, if I cashed in a thousand or two out of the story of it getting dragged through the papers again—after she's dead, at that—well, I'd go on such a Goddamn drunk I probably wouldn't live through it. Even if I did, the money wouldn't. I'd be broke and broken, and hate myself the rest of my life."

Sweeney found he could stand up, not too certainly. He stuck his hand across the space between them. He said, "Shake, Charlie. I like you."

"Thanks. I like you, Sweeney. Another drink? Of your whiskey?"

"Our whiskey. Sure, Charlie. Say, which *is* your first name, Charlie or Chapman?"

"Charlie. Chapman Wilson was Bessie's idea. Thought it sounded more like an artist She was a swell gal, Sweeney. A little screwy sometimes."

"Aren't we all?"

"I guess I am. They call me Crazy Charlie around here."

"Around Chicago they probably call me Crazy Sweeney." He picked up his glass. "Shall we drink to craziness?"

Charlie looked at him somberly for a moment. He said, "Make it to our kind of craziness, Sweeney."

"What oth—Oh. To our kind of craziness, Charlie." They touched glasses and drank, and Sweeney sat back down.

Charlie stared into his empty glass. He said, *"Real* craziness is something horrible, Sweeney. That homicidal maniac, covered with blood and the carving knife in his hand. I still get nightmares about his face as he turned away from Bessie and looked at me as he heard me coming.

"And Bessie—she was such a swell girl. And to see her go to pieces— well, you can hardly call it going to pieces; that implies something gradual. And she went wild-crazy all at once from that horrible experience. Why, we had to hold her down to get clothes on her; she was stark naked when—But you know that, of course; you've seen that statuette. I—I think it's a good thing that she died, Sweeney. *I'd* rather be dead than insane, really insane. Like she was." He dropped his head into his hands. Sweeney said, "Tough. And she was only nineteen."

"Twenty, then. She was twenty-one when she died in the asylum almost four years ago. And she was swell. Oh, she wasn't any angel. She was kind of wild. Our parents died ten years ago when I was twenty-four and Bessie was fifteen. An aunt of ours tried to take her but she ran off to St. Louis. But she kept in touch with me.

"And when she got in trouble five years later, it was me that she came to. She was—Well, that business with the maniac gave her a miscarriage and took care of that." He looked up. "Well, maybe she's better off—Life can be a hell of a mess." Sweeney got up and patted Charlie on the shoulder. He said, "Quit thinking about it, kid." He poured them each a drink and put Charlie's glass into Charlie's hand.

And once he was up he wandered around the room looking at the canvases on the wall, studying them more closely. They weren't bad; they weren't bad at all.

Charlie said, "We were really close, a hell of a lot closer than brother and sister usually are. We never lied to each other about anything. She told me everything she did in St. Louis, every man she'd had anything to do with. She was a waitress first, and then a pony in a chorus line in a cheap burlesque; that's what she was doing when she found she was pregnant and came here. And then that escaped loonie—"

"Quit talking about it," Sweeney ordered gruffly. "He died too quickly. If I'd've shot his legs off instead of shooting at his chest, I could have taken that carving knife and—Oh, hell, I wouldn't have, anyway." He shook his head slowly.

"Anyway, at that range," he said, "it put a hell of a big hole in him. Big enough you could stick your head through it."

Sweeney sighed and sat down. He said, "Look, Charlie, forget it. Let's talk about painting."

Charlie nodded slowly. They talked about painting, got off onto music, got back to painting again. Sweeney's bottle emptied itself and they started on Charlie's gin. It was pretty horrible gin. After a while Sweeney found difficulty focusing his eyes on paintings they were discussing but his mind stayed clear. Clear enough anyway to know that he was enjoying the evening and having some of the best conversation he'd had in a long time. He wasn't sorry any more that he'd come to Brampton. He liked Charlie; Charlie was his own breed of cat. And Charlie could hold his liquor, too, remarkably well. His tongue got thickish, but he talked sense.

So, for that matter, did Sweeney. And he had sense enough to keep an eye on his watch. When it was ten-fifteen, an hour before his train tune, he told Charlie he'd better leave.

"Driving?"

"No. Got a reservation on the eleven-fifteen. But it's quite a hike to the station. I've had a swell evening."

"You won't have to hike. There's a bus runs back and forth the length of Main Street. You can catch it on the corner a block and a half down. I'll walk down with you."

The cool night air felt good and began to sober him up.

He liked Charlie and wanted to do something for him. More than that, he suddenly saw *how* he could do something for nun. He said, "Charlie, I got an idea how I can get you those royalties on the Scream—on SM-1, without that publicity you don't want. It'll be publicity for the statuette itself, but it won't have to bring either you or your sister into the picture at all."

"Well, if you can do that—"

They were at the corner and Charlie was waiting with him until the bus came along.

"Sure, I can do it. Just on the Chicago angle. Look, Charlie, I know something nobody else knows—and it'll give you a flock of publicity for that statuette in its own right, apart from the way it was conceived and executed. Your name or your sister's won't have to come in it at all."

"If you can keep Bessie out of it—"

"Sure, easy. That isn't even the real story, as far as the story I'm going to break is concerned. It's frosting, but we can leave it off the cake. And for your sake I'll send Ganslen a telegram and tell them to start making more SM-1's right away to cash in on the boom. And listen, Charlie, do you ever get to Chicago?"

"Haven't for a couple of years. Why?"

"Well, look, when you get some of these royalties, drop down, and we'll have an evening together; I'll show you the town. We'll hang one on. If you get in town in the daytime, phone me at the *Blade,* city room. If you get in after dark, phone—"

"City room? *Blade?* You a reporter?"

Sweeney said despairingly, "Oh, Lord." He shouldn't have; he should have put his hands over his stomach right away, quick. But he didn't.

Charlie's fist went in it, up to Charlie's wrist, and Sweeney folded like a jackknife, just in time for Charlie's other fist to meet his chin coming down. But, as before, he didn't even feel the punch on his chin.

He heard Charlie say, "You lousy, double-crossing son of a bitch. I wish you'd get up and fight."

Nothing was farther from Sweeney's mind, or rather, from what was left of Sweeney's mind. He couldn't even talk. If he'd opened his mouth something might have come out, but it wouldn't have been words.

He heard Charlie walk away.

CHAPTER 16

THERE'S no need to describe how Sweeney felt; that was the third time he'd been hit in the stomach and it didn't feel any different, except in degree, from the first two tunes. To go into detail would be sadistic, not to say redundant. And it's bad enough that *he* had to go through it a third time; you and I do not.

After a few minutes he managed to get to the curb and sit there doubled up until, after about ten more minutes, he heard and saw the bus coming and managed to get to his feet, if not quite erect, and boarded it.

He sat doubled up in the bus, he sat doubled up In the station, and then on the train he lay doubled up in his lower berth. He didn't get to sleep, soundly, until early dawn, just as the train got into Chicago.

By the time he got to his room, though, the worst was over, and he slept. It was well into the afternoon—thirteen minutes after two, if you wish exactitude—when he awoke. But by then the worst was over and he could walk without being bent over.

And it was Sunday and the last day of his vacation, and three o'clock by the time he was bathed and dressed.

He went outside and looked east and west along Erie Street with a jaundiced eye and finally made up his mind to go east and see if he could find any angle on the Dorothy Lee murder that the police had missed. He didn't think he would. He didn't.

Luck was with him in finding both the janitor and Mrs. Rae Haley, the woman who had phoned the police, in. But luck was against him in finding Out from either of them anything significant that he didn't already know. He ran out of questions to ask after fifteen minutes with the janitor, who had not known Miss Lee personally at all. It took him an hour and a half to listen to everything Mrs. Haley thought of to tell him, and at the end of that hour and a half he knew a lot more that he had known about Dorothy Lee—nearly all of it favorable—but none of it in the slightest degree helpful, unless negatively.

Rae-Haley, a buxom wench with hennaed hair and just a touch too much make-up for a Sunday afternoon at home, turned out to be an ad-taker for a rival newspaper, but seemed nonetheless eager to talk to the *Blade*—or to Sweeney.

She had known Dorothy Lee fairly well and had liked her; Dorothy was "nice and quiet." Yes, she'd been in Dorothy's apartment often. They had eaten together frequently, taking turns, each in her own apartment, in doing the cooking, and that way avoiding each having to cook a separate meal. Not all the time, of course, but several times a week. So she knew Dorothy's apartment pretty thoroughly and, as he had suspected, Sweeney found that "small black statuette" drew a blank. The apartment was rented furnished and Dorothy hadn't gone in for buying pictures or bric-a-brac of her own. She did, though, have a nice table-top phonograph and some nice records, mostly "sweet swing." Sweeney concealed a shudder.

Yes, Dorothy had had boy friends; at one time or another she'd gone out with four or five of them, but none had been "serious." Mrs. Haley had met each of them and knew their names; she'd given the names of all of them to the police. Not because there was any possibility that any of them had been concerned in the horrible thing that had happened to Dorothy, but because the police had asked for the names and had insisted. But apparently the police had found all of them to be all right, because if they had arrested one of them it would have been in the papers, wouldn't it? Sweeney assured her that it would have been. She said that they were all nice boys, very nice boys, and when one of them had brought her home he'd always said goodnight at the door and hadn't come in. Dorothy had been a nice girl.

The walls of these apartments were almost paper-thin and she, Mrs. Haley, would have known if. She carried the sentence only that far and stopped delicately.

The poor kid, Sweeney thought, and wondered if she had died a virgin. He hoped that she hadn't, but not aloud. It's fine, he mused while Mrs.

Haley talked on, for a girl to save herself for Mr. Right, but it's damn tough on her if Mr. Wrong comes along with a carving knife first. Even the prototype of Screaming Mimi, poor Bessie Wilson, hadn't been handed that tough a break.

Sweeney thought, for no particular reason, that he would have liked Bessie Wilson; he rather wished that he had known her. And damn it, he liked Charlie Wilson in spite of what Charlie had done to him. A cocky little guy but quite likeable when he wasn't punching one in the stomach.

He decided that he'd keep his promise to Charlie anyway and send that telegram to the general manager of Ganslen. He was planning how to word it when he remembered where he was and realized that Mrs. Haley was still talking and that he hadn't been listening at all. He listened for long enough to find out that he hadn't been missing a thing, and made his getaway, turning down an invitation to stay for dinner.

He walked downtown to the Loop and found a Western Union office open. He sat down with a pencil and pad of blanks and tore up two tries before he evolved a telegram that came even close. Then he read that one over again, saw several things missing in it, and gave up. He tore that one up too and walked to a telephone exchange where he asked to see, and was given, a Louisville telephone directory. Luckily Sweeney had a good memory for names and he recalled, from his previous call to Ganslen Art Company, the first name as well as the last name of the general manager. He found a home telephone listed.

He got a handful of change and went into a booth. A few minutes later he was talking to the general manager and buyer of Ganslen.

He said, "This is Sweeney of the Chicago *Blade,* Mr. Burke. I talked to you a few days ago about one of your statuettes, the SM-1. You were kind enough to tell me who modeled it."

"Yes, I remember."

"To return the favor, I want to tip you off to something that will make some money for you and for Chapman Wilson. Only I'm going to ask you to keep this confidential until the *Blade* breaks the story tomorrow. You'll agree to that?"

"Uh—exactly what am I agreeing to, Mr. Sweeney?"

"Merely that you don't tell anyone at all what I'm going to tell you now until after tomorrow noon. You can go ahead meanwhile and act on the information; you can start getting ready to cash in."

"That sounds fair enough."

"Okay, here's the dope. You sold two SM-1's in Chicago. Well, I've got one of them and the Ripper's got the other one. You've heard of our Ripper murders, haven't you?"

"Of course. Good Lord! You mean—"

"Yeah. Tomorrow the *Blade* will print a picture of Screaming Mimi— about four columns wide on page one, if I judge rightly—and break the story. Probably the Ripper will be caught. A friend or his landlady or some-one will have seen it in his room and phone the police. He can hardly have had it for two months without *someone* having seen it.

"But whether he's caught through it or not, it's a nationwide big story. You're likely to be swamped for weeks with orders for Mimi. I'd suggest you put her in production immediately—work a night shift tonight if you can get anybody down to your factory or workshop or whatever it is. And if I were you I wouldn't sell those hundred-odd copies you have; I'd get them to dealers quickly to use as samples to take orders. Get them to Chicago dealers, in particular, as fast as you can. Start one of your sales-men up this way tonight with a trunk full of them."

"Thank you, Mr. Sweeney. I can't say how much I appreciate your giving me this much notice on—"

"Wait," said Sweeney. "I'm not through yet. One thing I want you to do. Put a special mark somewhere on each one you sell from now on, so it can be told from the one the Ripper's got. Keep the mark secret so he can't duplicate it, and let the police know what the mark is when they come to you—as they will after that story breaks. Otherwise, they'll be on my neck for tipping you off to flood the Chicago market with them, see? But they'll see that, in the long run, we're doing them a favor. If there are more Mimis coming, the Ripper may keep his, whereas if he knows his is going to keep on being the only other one in Chicago, he'll get rid of it quick. And he won't know about the secret mark all the others will have. Listen, make the secret mark a tiny chip out of the bottom of the base in the right front cor-ner—so it'll look accidental if anyone looks at just *one* of them."

"Fine. That will be simple."

"I'll do it on mine. And you've got a record, I hope, of just where the forty or so that you actually sold throughout the country went, haven't you?"

"Our books would show that."

"Good, then if an unmarked Mimi shows up, it can be traced back to prove it's not the one the Ripper bought. And one more thing—"

"Yes?"

"I'm not going to drag in the origin of Mimi. Charlie—Chapman Wilson's pretty sensitive about what happened to his sister, and this is a big enough story without using that After all, that's past history and our Ripper is very much current. He said you promised not to use that for publicity—so stick to your promise to him."

"Of course, Mr. Sweeney. And thanks again, tremendously.'"

After he hung up, Sweeney dropped another nickel But Yolanda's phone wasn't answered so he got it back. It was too early for her to be at the night club; she was probably out eating somewhere. Well, maybe he'd better skip trying to talk to her until after tomorrow when he'd broken the Screaming Mimi story in the *Blade*. And maybe by then the Ripper would be caught and she wouldn't have an escort of cops everywhere she moved.

Or course he could watch her dance tonight. Or could he?

He looked up the number of the Tit-Tat-Toe Club and called it. A bit of argument and the use of his name got him Harry Yahn. Harry's voice boomed cheerfully over the phone. "Hello, Sweeney. How're things?"

"Going fine, Harry. I'm going to break a big story on the Ripper tomorrow. Extra publicity for Yolanda."

"That's great. Does it—uh—concern anyone I know?"

"Not unless you know the Ripper. Do you?"

"Not by that name. Well, what about it? You don't want any more money, I hope."

"My God, no," said Sweeney. "Look, Harry, that's a dead issue. What I want to know is, are we still friends?"

"Why, sure, Sweeney. Did you have any reason for thinking we weren't?"

"Yes," said Sweeney. "But did that wash it out? Specifically, am I going to be *persona non gra*—I mean, if I show up at El Madhouse or the Tit-Tat-Toe, do I get in and out again safely? Or do I wear a suit of armor?"

Harry Yahn laughed. "You're welcome any time, Sweeney. Seriously. As you said, it's a dead issue."

"Swell," said Sweeney. "I just wanted to be sure."

"Uh—did Willie use discretion?"

"For Willie, I imagine it was. I just wanted to be sure you hadn't passed the good word on to Nick. I'll probably, otherwise, go around to El Madhouse tonight."

"Fine. Nick's due to phone me soon and I'll tell him to hold a chair for you, and not to take your money. No kidding, Sweeney, I like you. No hard feelings?"

"Very tender feelings," Sweeney said. "And the worst of it is, they've been worked on twice since then. That's just why I wanted to be sure before I went to El Madhouse tonight. Since it's okay, thanks for everything."

"Don't mention it, Sweeney. Take care of yourself."

After he'd hung up, Sweeney took a deep breath and—although it hurt his stomach a little—he felt better.

He went back for another handful of change, an even bigger handful this tune. A nickel of it got him the long distance operator again. He let the New York operator do the looking up this time for he felt pretty sure Ray Land would have a home telephone in his own name. Ray Land had been a Chicago homicide cop once; now he was running a small agency of his own in New York.

Ray was home.

Sweeney said, "This is Sweeney. Remember me?"

"Sure. So?"

"Want you to investigate an alibi for me. In New York." He gave the details, Greene's name and hotel and the exact date. "I know he was registered at the hotel on that day and the day before and the day after. The police checked that. What I want to find out—for sure, not a probability—is whether he was really there that night, the 27th."

"Can try. It's almost two weeks ago. How far do you want me to go?"

"As far as you can. Talk to everybody at the hotel who might have seen him come in or go out, the maid who'd have made up his room in the morning, everything like that. Listen, the crucial time is 3 o'clock in the morning. If you can definitely locate him six hours or less either side of that, I'll settle."

"Twelve hours isn't so bad. Maybe I can do it How much you want me to spend?"

"Spend all you want provided you do it right away. Within reason, that is. I'll wire you a hundred cash for a retainer. If you go a little over it, even double it, okay."

"That ought to cover it, Sweeney. It'll cover two days' time and since it's right on Manhattan there won't be any expenses to speak of. If I can't get anything in two days, I probably can't at all. Why the six hour leeway?"

"I want to convince myself that he wasn't in Chicago at 3 a.m. Counting time to and from airports on either end, getting a plane and everything, that's the least he could have done it in. Maybe five hours would be safer. If you can prove he was at the hotel as late as ten in the evening or as early as eight the next morning, I'll be convinced. And, just in case it could have been a ringer, someone else there using his name, here's a description." Sweeney gave it. He added, "If you can't alibi him, you might try that description at the airport. Or if it comes down to that, I'll try to get you a photo. Check with me after you've got everything you can get at the hotel. Good enough?"

"Good enough. I'll get around there this evening. It'll be the night shift I'll mostly want, to talk to."

Outside the telephone exchange, Sweeney found that it was getting dark and that he was getting hungry. He remembered he hadn't seen a Sunday paper and might have missed something; he found copies of two of them still left on a newsstand and very early editions, still sticky with ink, of two Monday morning papers. He bought all four and took them into a restaurant with him.

Reading while he ate, he found out that nothing new had happened or transpired. All the papers were keeping the story alive—it was too big a story to let an issue pass without *something*—but the somethings added up or canceled out to nothing.

He stretched the eating and the reading until it was almost ten o'clock and then left. He remembered the retainer and stopped in at the Western Union office again to send it to Ray Land.

That still left him over seven hundred dollars and he wished there was some way he could spend some of it on Yolanda. Well, there'd be tune for that after the cops quit watching her. Meanwhile, there was one sighting shot he could take. He found a flower shop in a hotel still open and ordered two dozen red roses sent to her at El Madhouse as soon as they could get a messenger to take them there. He tried writing on, and tore up, three cards. On the fourth, he wrote "Sweeney" and let it go at that.

He caught a taxi and directed it to El Madhouse; it would get him there just in time for Yo's first performance of the evening.

It did, and Nick was still saving a place for him.

After the floor show (you wouldn't want me to describe it again, would you?) he wandered out to the bar and managed to get a place at it But it was ten minutes before he could get a drink.

He sipped it and brooded.

Unless breaking the story that the Ripper had bought and now presumably still owned a copy of Ganslen's SM-1 brought results, it looked as though he was stymied. That was the only real lead he'd found: the fact that the killer of Lola Brent, two months ago, had undoubtedly been the same person who had purchased from her the statuette whose purchase price she had dragged down. Sweeney didn't doubt that for a second; it fitted too perfectly to be a coincidence. It *had* to be.

But for the rest he had nothing. The trip to Brampton had been completely a blind alley—an alley populated with little men who kept pounding on his sore stomach, before and after getting drunk with him. And almost worse than those punches had been the anticlimax of learning—after he'd heard first of a Ripper, a blonde, and a crazy artist—that the Ripper and the blonde were dead long since and the crazy artist was well alibied. And even if Charlie Wilson hadn't been alibied, Sweeney couldn't picture him as the Ripper. He had a hair-trigger temper, but he wasn't the type that ran to carving knives.

Well, tomorrow would tell the tale. If a four-column picture of SM-1 splashed on the front page of the *Blade* didn't make something happen—

He sighed and took another sip of his drink.

Someone tapped him on the shoulder.

CHAPTER 17

SWEENEY turned and found himself staring full into the thick glasses that magnified Greene's eyes and made them so frightening.

Sweeney grinned and said, "Hi, Doc. What'll you have?"

"I've got a drink, over at a table. And Nick's holding my chair and another. Come on over."

Sweeney picked up his drink and followed Greene to a corner table. Nick, standing beside it, said, "Hi, Mr. Sweeney," and then hurried off about his business. Sweeney and Greene sat down.

"Getting anywhere?" Greene asked.

"Maybe. I don't know. I'm breaking a big story tomorrow; the biggest one to date."

"Outside of the actual murders."

"Maybe bigger," Sweeney said.

"It would be useless for me to ask what it is, I suppose."

"You've got something there, Doc. But cheer up; it'll be on the streets in twelve hours."

"I'll watch for it. I'm still worried about something happening to Yo. So I hope you have really got something." He took off his glasses and polished them. Sweeney, studying him, saw that he looked quite different without them. He looked tired, genuinely worried. Stranger, though, he looked human. Sweeney almost wished he had back the hundred dollars he'd just wired to New York. Almost, not quite.

Doc Greene put the glasses back on and looked at Sweeney through them, and his eyes were enormous again. Sweeney thought the hundred dollars was well spent.

Greene said, "Meanwhile, Sweeney, take good care of yourself."

"I will. Any special reason?"

Greene chuckled. "Yes, for *my* sake. Since I lost my temper the other night and shot off my mouth, Captain Bline has had me on the carpet. Everything but a rubber hose. It seems he took my little threat seriously."

"And was he right?"

"Well—yes and no. You did, that one time, get under my skin and I think I meant it when I said it. Of course, after cool deliberation I realized I'd been silly. By saying that, I did the one thing that made you completely safe—from me. If you ever want to kill a man, Sweeney, don't make the announcement before the police and hope to get away with it."

"Then why the warning to take good care of myself?"

"As I said, for *my* sake. Bline told me—*promised* me—that if anything happens to you after my threat, my silly threat, he'd arrest me and rubber-hose me to hell and back. Even if I had an alibi, he'd figure that I hired the job done. I'm going to be a dead duck, Sweeney, if anything happens to you."

Sweeney smiled. "Doc, you almost tempt me to commit suicide, without leaving a note."

"Don't, please. Not that I think you would, bub you worry me talking about breaking a big story tomorrow. You might say that to someone who wouldn't want a big story to break for fear of what it might be. You see what I mean."

"I see what you mean. But you're the first person in Chicago whom I've told. The only other one is hundreds of miles from here. Of course, you could pass it on."

"Perish the thought, Sweeney. Your safety has become a matter of importance to me. I've told you why." He shook his head slowly. "I am amazed-at myself for having said such a foolish thing—in such company. I, a trained psychiatrist—Have you had any psychiatric training, Sweeney? From the skillful way you maneuvered me into loss of control—Well, there's no harm done if nothing happens to you. But until this mess is over, I'll chip in half the cost if you want to hire a bodyguard. Willie, maybe? Have you met Willie Harris?"

"Willie is wonderful," Sweeney said. "But I doubt if Harry Yahn would care to part with him. No, thanks, Doc, whether you're serious or not I'll take my chances without a bodyguard. Or if I should hire one, I won't tell you about it"

Greene sighed. "You still don't trust me, Sweeney. Well, I've got to run along. To see a client at another club. Take care of yourself."

Sweeney went back to the bar and had his drink replenished. He drank it very slowly and thought about how he was going to write the story for tomorrow's *Blade,* and thus managed to kill time until the second floor show went on.

He saw it; it was different in one very minor but very important detail. Yolanda Lang wore a red rose pinned to the waist of her black dress. Sweeney's roses had arrived, then, after the first show but before the second.

And she'd worn one. That was all he wanted to know. He thought, but wasn't sure, that her eyes met his in the instant after the dog had reared up behind her. But that wasn't important; she *had* worn one of the roses he'd sent.

After the show—wondering whether he was being as astute a psychiatrist as Doc Greene had credited him with being—he didn't try to see her or speak to her. There'd be cops—and Doc—around if he did. Maybe, just possibly, by tomorrow night the cops wouldn't have to be guarding Yolanda. And Doc—well, he'd worry about Greene when the time came.

At least, he didn't have anything to fear from Greene for the moment; he did believe him that far. Doc had pulled his own stinger by making that open threat on Sweeney's life.

He didn't wait for the third show. Tomorrow might turn out to be a big day, and it was after midnight already. He went home and-to bed, read a while and got to sleep by two o'clock. His alarm-woke him at half-past seven, and it was Monday.

It was Monday, and it was a bright, cheerful day; the sun was bright but not unduly hot for August the eleventh. No clouds in the sky, but a cooling breeze off the lake. Not bad at all.

He had a good breakfast and got to the *Blade* promptly at nine.

He hung up his coat and hat and then, before the city editor could catch him, he headed right for Wally Krieg's office. The package containing SM-1 was under his arm.

Wally looked up as he came in. He said, "Hi, Sweeney. Reported to Crawley yet?"

"Nope. Want to show you something first." He started to unwrap the package.

"All right, but after that report to Crawley. Somebody took a jewelry salesman for his samples last night and we want to get on it quick. Over at—"

"Hush," said Sweeney. He got the package unwrapped and set Mimi on the desk, facing the managing editor. "Mimi, meet Wally Krieg. Wally, meet Mimi. Screaming Mimi."

"Charmed. Now take that thing out of here and—"

"Hush," said Sweeney. "She's got a sister. *One* sister, in all of Chicago."

"Sweeney, what are you getting at?"

'The Ripper," said Sweeney. "He's got Mimi's sister. We got Mimi—and don't think she doesn't go on the expense account for the full purchase price. That is, if you want to send her up to the photo department and run a pic of her on page one today."

"You say the Ripper's got one like her? Are you sure?"

"Reasonably sure. There were two in Chicago; the Ripper bought the other one from Lola Brent just before he followed her home and killed her. It's probably what set him off. Look at it!"

"And his is the only other one in Chicago?"

"Yes," said Sweeney. "Well, if you're not interested I'll go stick it in my desk drawer and then look up Crawley." He picked up Mimi and started out the door. Wally said "Hey!" and he waited.

"Wally," he said, "I'm getting fed up on this Ripper business. Maybe you'd better keep me off it. Of course I could get the whole thing for the first edition today, but you can have Mimi anyway, if you want her, and one of the other boys can check her pedigree—with Raoul Reynarde—and trace her back like I did, and give you the story for tomorrow or part of it for a late edition today. But I'd just as soon not—"

"Sweeney, quit blithering. Shut the door."

"Sure, Wally. From which side?"

Wally just glared at him and Sweeney decided that enough was enough and shut it from the inside. Wally was getting the city ed on the phone. He barked that someone else should go on the jewelry case and that Sweeney was on special assignment. He jiggled the receiver and got the photo department and apparently was satisfied with whoever answered the phone for he told him to come down right away.

Then he swung on Sweeney. He said, "Put that thing down, carefully, before you drop it and break it."

Sweeney put Mimi back down on the desk. Wally stared at her. Then up at Sweeney.

He said, "What the hell are you waiting for? A kiss? Go ahead and write the story. Wait a minute; don't start yet. Lots of tune before first edition; sit down and tell me about it first. Maybe there are angles somebody else can be doing while you're batting it out"

Sweeney sat down and told most of it. As much, at least, as he intended to put into the story itself. There was an interruption while a photographer came in and Wally gave him Mimi with instructions—and with threats of almost unbelievable things that would happen to him if Mimi were dropped and broken before the photograph had been taken. The photographer left, walking carefully and holding Mimi as though she were made of eggshell. Sweeney resumed, and finished.

Wally said, "Good. Go ahead and write it. Only you didn't do the story any good phoning Ganslen and telling them to cash in while it's hot The police aren't going to like that They'll want there to be only *one* Mimi in Chicago for as long a time as possible. And I mean *one;* I'm going to order this one broken to pieces as soon as I see a good photo of it. Put that in the story. It narrows things down. Plenty. What the hell did you want to phone that art company for, to tip them off?"

Sweeney felt uncomfortable. It *had* been a boner, and he didn't want to explain about Charlie Wilson and his real reason for the call. He said, weakly, "Thought I ought to pay 'em back for the favor they did me on the first call, Wally. Telling me only two had been sold in Chicago. Without that—"

Wally said, "Well, I'll phone them and head them off while you write the story. Look, mention that the statuette was made by Ganslen Art Company, Louisville, and they won't *have* to send any salesmen or samples to Chicago or anywhere in this area. They'll be swamped with orders by telephone, just from that information and the photo in the paper. Every dealer in the area will be calling them.

"I'll phone and tell them that Who'd you talk to?"

"General manager. Burke."

"Okay, I'll talk to Burke and tell him to go ahead and take all the orders he wants from this area but to stall as long as he can on shipping and not to send any samples right away. And I'll make sure he's taking your suggestion on putting a special mark on each of them. Don't mention *that,* though, in the story. And bring it here when you've finished; I want to pass on it personally."

Sweeney nodded and stood up. Wally said, "And one other thing I'm going to do, and that's phone Bline. If we break this story without tipping him off first, we'll be number one on the department's s.o.b. list. I'm going to give him the story first and tell him we're breaking it today but we're giving him advance notice."

"What if he crosses you by giving it to the other papers?"

"I don't think he will. If he does, they still won't have Mimi or a pic of her. The story itself isn't worth much without the pic, and I'm going to splash that smack in the middle of the front page. Four columns by about fifteen inches."

"Shall I mention that we're running the pic in full color—black?"

"Get the hell out of here."

Sweeney got the hell out and sat down at his desk. He realized, as he pulled paper into the ancient Underwood, that both of Wally's ideas had been good; it wouldn't hurt the story to give the cops a couple of hours' notice, and it wouldn't hurt Ganslen's sales (or Charlie's royalties) if they didn't fill orders from Chicago for a week or so. The story would stay good—and would turn better if it actually led to the capture of the Ripper.

He looked at his wrist watch, saw that he had an hour to go, and started typing. His phone rang and it was Wally. Wally asked, "Going to have plenty of tune? Or would you rather dictate it to a fast rewrite man?"

"I can do it."

"Okay. Send it to me as it comes out of the mill, a page at a time. I'll have a boy waiting at your desk. Slug it MIMI."

Sweeney slugged it MIMI and kept typing. A minute later a copy boy was breathing down his neck, but Sweeney was used to that and it didn't bother him. He sent the last page in ten minutes before the first edition deadline.

After that he lighted a cigarette and pretended to be busy so Crawley wouldn't think of anything else for him to do right away, until deadline was past and he figured Wally would be free again, and then he wandered into Wally's office again. "How's Mimi?" he asked.

"A broken woman. Look in my wastebasket if you don't believe me."

"I'd rather not," Sweeney said.

A boy came in with papers fresh off the press and put three of them on Wally's desk. Sweeney picked one up and glanced at the page one layout. There was Mimi, all right, slightly larger than actual size. She had the banner head, two columns of story, four columns of picture. And Wally had by-lined the story for him.

Sweeney said, "Nice layout," and Wally grunted, reading. . Sweeney said, "Nice story, too. Thanks for telling me so." Wally grunted again.

Sweeney said, "How about the rest of the day off?" This time Wally didn't grunt; he put down the paper and got ready to explode. "Are you *crazy?* You've been off two weeks, come back to work for two hours and—"

"Relax, Wally. Don't break a blood vessel. Where do you think that story came from? Out of the air? I've been working twenty hours a day on it, more or less, for three days. On my own time. I came in with that story ready to write up. And brought Mimi with me for company. And why? Because I worked till four o'clock this morning and got two hours sleep, that's why. Dragged myself out of bed half-awake to come in and write the biggest story of the year for you and then you—"

"Shut up. All right, get the hell out of here. Of all the Goddam gold-bricks—"

"Thank you. Seriously, Wally, I *am* going home. I'll be in my room to rest, but I won't get undressed—and if anything breaks on this story call me quick. I'll be on it just as fast as I would if I were waiting around here. Okay?"

"Okay, Sweeney. If anything breaks, you're on it. And listen, Sweeney—win, lose or draw, it's a swell story."

'Thanks," Sweeney said. "And thanks to hell and back for carrying me while I was—gone."

"This makes up for it. You know, Sweeney, there are damn few real reporters left. And you're—"

"Hold it," said Sweeney. "Pretty soon we'll be crying into our beer, and we haven't got any beer to cry into. I'm going to beat it."

He beat it.

He took one of Wally's papers with him so he wouldn't have to hunt one up elsewhere or wait for one on the street, and went home. He took a cab, partly because he still had more money than he knew what to do with, and partly—because—temporarily—he really did feel tired as hell. It was part-ly the letdown, but mostly the fact that, for a while now, there was nothing intelligent to do but to wait.

Either the story of Mimi would lead to a big break in the story of the Ripper or it wouldn't. If it did, it would probably happen this afternoon or this evening. Or possibly tonight.

If it didn't—well, then it didn't. He'd be back at work at nine o'clock tomorrow morning and he didn't think, now, that Wally would keep him off the Ripper case. He'd just have to forget Mimi and try to dig up another angle, somewhere. Probably by going over again, and more thoroughly, a lot of the ground he had already covered.

At home, he made himself comfortable and read the story through, leisurely and carefully. Wally had added to it, splicing in some recapitula-tion on the stories of the other three women who had been attacked (for the Mimi story had concerned directly only Lola Brent, who had sold Mimi to the Ripper), but he had changed hardly a word of what Sweeney had writ-ten.

This time he even read the continuation on an inside page; then he fold-ed the paper together and put it with the others that covered the various Ripper murders.

He sat down and tried to relax, but couldn't. He went over to the phono-graph—it seemed naked now without the naked statuette atop it—and played the Brahms Fourth. That helped a little, although he couldn't really concentrate on it.

By two o'clock he was hungry, but he didn't want to risk missing a phone call so he went downstairs to Mrs. Randall's rooms and got her to fry some bacon for a sandwich.

By that time he'd decided he didn't give a damn if the phone rang or not. Then it rang, and he almost choked swallowing the big bite of sandwich he'd just taken and almost fell getting up the stairs to answer the phone in the second floor hallway. The call was for another roomer, who wasn't in.

He went back downstairs and finished the sandwich. He went back upstairs to his room, put the records of a De Falla album on the phonograph and, while they played, tried to reread the short stories in a Damon Runyan collection. He didn't do too well with either the reading or the listening.

The phone rang. He got there in nothing flat, slamming the door of his own room to shut off part of the sound of the phonograph—which was about one second quicker than stopping to shut off the phonograph itself would have been.

It was Wally. He said, "Okay, Sweeney. Get over to State Street. You know the address."

"What's up?"

"They got the Ripper. Now listen, we got a headline and a bulletin going in the Final—it's going to press now—and we're not holding it for details. We got the main facts, and the full story will have to go in tomorrow. It's an even break; we'll beat the morning papers on the bulletin and the main facts, but they'll beat us on getting a detailed story.

"So there's no rush. Get over there and get the full dope, but you can write it up when you get in tomorrow."

"Wally, what happened? Did he make another try at Yolanda Lang? Is she all right?"

"I guess so. Yeah, he made another try and this time the dog got him, like it almost did last time except that last time he slammed the door on the dog—"

"I *know* what happened last time. What happened *this* time?"

"I told you, dammit. They *got* him. He's still alive but probably won't be long. Took him to a hospital, but don't waste time; they won't let you talk to him. He went out a window. At the dame's place, I mean. Good work, Sweeney; that Mimi story of yours broke it He not only had the statuette, but had it *with* him."

"Who? I mean, have they got his name?"

"Name? Sure, we got his name. It's Greene, James J. Greene. Captain Bline says he's suspected him all along. Now quit pumping *me;* get over there and get the story."

The receiver banged in Sweeney's ear, but he stared into the black mouthpiece of the wall phone for seconds before he put his own receiver back on the hook.

CHAPTER 18

IT WASN'T quite believable somehow. He'd thought it all along, and yet the reality was hard to swallow. For one thing, one simple thing, he couldn't think of Doc Greene as being dead. But Horlick—who was already there when Sweeney got there—was saying that he was.

"Yeah," he said. "Bline got a call from the hospital; he sent two of the boys with Greene to try to get a detailed confession and get it signed, but I guess they didn't make it, and that he couldn't have signed it anyway what with both arms broken, among other things. And he wasn't very coherent, what I heard of him. I got here before they took him away."

"How come so quick, Wayne?"

"Bull luck. I was already on my way here. For part of the follow-up tomorrow on that Mimi story you broke today, Wally sent me to interview Yolanda Lang, to ask her if she'd ever seen such a statuette. And if not, and it probably would have been not, I was to get a story anyway by asking her what her reaction was to a picture of it—whether it looked like she felt when the Ripper was coming at her in the hallway. That kind of crap. And I got here about the time the police ambulance did."

"And Yolanda isn't up there?"

"Nope, she ran out with the dog, just after it happened. Shock again, or fright. She's probably having the meamies somewhere but she'll show up. I'm going In with what I got; you go on upstairs and see if you can get more if you want to. Bline's up there."

He went his way, south on State Street, and Sweeney pushed his way through the knot of people who were standing around the doorway of the apartment building on State just south of Chicago Avenue, the same doorway through which Sweeney had stared only a few nights ago and had seen a woman and a dog. This time the crowd was bigger, although there was nothing to be seen through the glass. Sweeney pushed through to a policeman guarding the door. His press card got him inside and he ran up the stairs to the third floor.

Yolanda Lang's apartment was the rear north one of four on the third floor. There wasn't any need checking the number on the door because the door was open and the place was full of cops. At least it looked full of cops; when Sweeney got in, he saw there were only two besides Bline.

Bline came over to him. "Sweeney, if I wasn't so happy, I'd break your neck. How long did you have that Goddam statuette?"

"Don't remember exactly, Cap."

'That's what I mean. But—well, we got the Ripper, and without another ripping, although that must've been a pretty close thing. And I'll settle for that. I'm even ready to buy you a drink. Guess I'm through here; I'll leave one of the boys to wait for the Lang dame to be sure she's all right when she comes back."

"Is there any doubt that she isn't?"

"Physically, sure. He didn't touch her with the knife at all this time; the pooch got in ahead. But she's probably In a mental tizzy, worse than last time. Hell, not that I blame her."

"Did Devil kill Greene?"

"Well, he chewed him up a bit but didn't kill him; Doc must've managed to keep an arm over his throat. But he went out that window and that killed him all right. Must've backed up against it and a lunge of the dog knocked him out backwards."

Bline had gestured to a wide-open window and Sweeney went over to it and looked out. Two stories below was a small cement courtyard. It was pretty well littered with junk people had thrown out of windows.

Sweeney asked, "Where's the statuette?"

"Down there in the courtyard, most of it. We found enough pieces of it to identify it. Doc must still have had hold of it when he went out the window. Probably trying to club off the dog with it. The knife was there, too; he must've had the statuette in one hand and the knife in the other—it's a wonder the dog managed not to get hurt. But I guess Doc had to keep one arm to cover his throat and wasn't fast enough with the other. A dog like that is hell on wheels in a fight."

Sweeney looked down into the courtyard and shivered a little.

He said, "I'll take that drink, Cap. And I'll buy back. Let's get out of here."

They went to the corner of State and Chicago, the tavern from which the phone call had been made the night of the first attack on Yolanda. Bline bought.

Sweeney said, "I know everything except what happened. Can you put it in order for me?"

"The whole thing? Or just this afternoon?"

"Just this afternoon."

Bline said, "Yolanda was alone in her apartment—as of a few minutes after three o'clock. We know that because I had a guy stationed to watch the place, from across the hall. We'd sublet the flat across from hers for that purpose, and there was a man stationed there at all times, except of course when she was working at the club. He had a peephole rigged so he could watch the door to her place.

"He saw Doc Greene come up with a shoebox under his arm and knock on her door, see? Well, that was all right; Doc had called there before and I'd said it was okay to let him in. If it had been a stranger, Garry—that's the guy who was on duty—would have had his door open and a gun ready."

Sweeney asked, "Did Doc call on business? I mean, when he'd been there before?"

Bline shrugged. "Don't know and didn't care. We're not the vice squad; we were just hunting the Ripper. And I'd thought, from Greene's alibis, that he was in the clear. Well, I was wrong. Did you really suspect him, Sweeney, or did you keep needling him just because you didn't like him?"

"I don't really know, Cap. But what happened?"

"Well, Yolanda answered the door and let him hi. He was in there about five minutes when things started to happen. Garry heard Yolanda scream and the dog growl and Greene yell, almost all at once, and he yanked his own door open, and started across the hallway. He yanked at Yolanda's door, but it was locked—a snap lock—and he was just about to put a bullet through the lock when the door opened.

"He says Yolanda had opened it and she pushed past him into the hallway, her face as white as a sheet and looking like something pretty horrible had happened. But there wasn't any blood on her; she wasn't hurt. Garry tried to grab her with his free hand—he had his gun in the other—but the dog jumped at him and he had to let go to cover his throat. The dog took a piece out of his sleeve but didn't happen to get hold of his arm.

"By that time Yolanda was past him and starting down the stairs and the dog wheeled and followed her. So he didn't have to shoot the dog. And as long as Yolanda seemed all right, he ran into Yolanda's apartment to see what went on there. There didn't seem to be anyone in there and he wondered what happened to Greene; then he heard a groan from the courtyard and looked out the open window—it's a pretty big one, the kind that swings out instead of raising—and there was Doe Greene lying in the courtyard.

"So he phones for me and the ambulance and we get here. Greene was still alive, but dying and not very coherent. He could just say a few words, but they were enough."

Sweeney asked, "What do you figure sent Greene around there?"

"How do you figure how a homicidal maniac reasons, Sweeney? How the hell do I know? But I think it was your story about that statuette that set him off. He had it, and maybe Yolanda knew that he had it and the jig would be up as soon as she happened to see your front page. Why he took it along in a shoebox when he went to kill her, I don't know.

"But he had it out of the box, in one hand, and the knife in the other hand—when the dog saved her by getting him. Chewed him up pretty bad; maybe he even jumped out of the window to get away from the dog, but I think it's more likely he got backed up against it and went out accidentally when the dog jumped for him again."

"What do you figure happened to Yolanda?"

"Shock again, of course. She's probably wandering around in a daze, but she's well protected. She'll snap out of it by herself, probably, and come back. If not, she can't be hard to find—a dame like that with a dog like that. Well, I got to get in and report. So long, Sweeney."

Bline left and Sweeney ordered another drink. And another and then one more. It was getting dark when he left the tavern and went back to Yolanda's flat. There was still a policeman at the door. Sweeney asked him if Yolanda had come back, and she hadn't.

He strolled over to Clark Street, stopped in at Ireland's and ordered a lobster. While it was cooking he went to the phone booth and called Ray Land, the private detective he'd hired in New York.

He said, "This is Sweeney, Ray. You can call it off."

"That's what I figured, Sweeney. Heard on the radio while I was eating dinner that your Chicago Ripper was caught and his name was familiar. So I figured you wouldn't want me to keep on. Well, I put in a day on it, so you got fifty bucks coming back. I'll send you a check."

"Get anywhere on it?"

"Hadn't yet. It was tough going, what with it being two weeks ago. Best bet I had was a maid who managed to remember that one morning his bed hadn't been slept in, but she couldn't remember which morning it was. I was going to see her again after she'd had time to think it over. Shall I send you that check care of the *Blade?*"

"Sure. And thanks, Ray."

He called Captain Bline at headquarters and asked, "Any reports on Yolanda yet?"

"Yeah, Sweeney. A funny one." Bline's voice sounded puzzled. "She turned up at El Madhouse some time ago. Just half an hour after Greene had tried to attack her. She got some money from Nick and left again. And no report on her since."

"The hell," said Sweeney. "How did she act?"

"A little funny, Nick said, but not too bad. He said she was pale and a little jittery, but he didn't think anything of it; he hadn't heard about what happened to Doc yet, and she didn't say anything about it. Just wanted some money—gave him a song-and-dance about being able to buy something she wanted for a hell of a bargain if she did it right away for cash. Nick said he figured somebody had offered her a stolen mink coat or something for a few hundred bucks and she wanted it but was a little afraid of the deal and that was why she was nervous."

"How much did he give her?"

"A week's salary. She had it coming as of tomorrow night anyway so he figured he might as well give it to her a day sooner."

"That's funny."

"Yeah, but I think I can figure it. I'd guess it that she just wanted to hide out for a day or two. It was shock, but temporary, that sent her chasing out of the building after Greene tried to attack her a second time; but she must've got over the worst of it quick if she could talk normally to Nick within a half hour. Only I'd guess she just didn't feel up to facing us and all the reporters and everything. But she'll show up in a few days when she gets her balance back. She won't miss cashing In on her contract and all the publicity and everything."

"Could be. You hunting for her?"

Bline said, "No. Why should we? We could find her easily enough, just checking hotels. But from what Nick says, she's all right, so it isn't our business. If I thought she was wandering around in a daze from shock or something—"

"She didn't go back home to get any clothes or anything?"

"No; our man's still there and he's to phone me if she shows back there. Guess that's partly what she wanted money for, so she wouldn't have to go back there and face the music."

"Okay, Cap," Sweeney said. "Thanks a lot."

He got back to his table just as the lobster arrived.

He ate it thoughtfully. He didn't know exactly what he was being thoughtful about until the lobster had been reduced to a shell.

And then, suddenly, he knew what he had been thinking and it scared hell out of him.

CHAPTER 19

HE didn't hurry. His coffee came and he drank it slowly, still horrifying himself by what he was thinking. And then it got worse, for he found he wasn't thinking it any more; he *knew* it. A lot of it was guesswork, but each guess dropped into place like a piece in a jigsaw puzzle that will fit nowhere else and at no other angle.

He paid the check and walked south to El Madhouse. Nick saw him the moment he went in and came to meet him. He said, "Hi, Sweeney. I'm worried; know anything about where Yo is, or if she's coming tonight?"

Sweeney said, "I'm worried, too. Listen, Nick, did you happen to notice when Yolanda left here whether she took a taxi?"

"No. She walked north."

"How was she dressed?"

"In green, what they call a daytime dress. No coat or hat And the dog was along, but not on a leash. Sometimes she has him on a leash, sometimes not. Say, it's hell about Doc, isn't it?"

"Yeah," said Sweeney.

"And he threatened to kill you. You're lucky, Sweeney."

"Yeah," said Sweeney.

He went outside and wondered how lucky he was going to be. It had been about five hours ago that Yolanda had left here. It was a break that she'd walked north, away from the Loop. In the Loop, it would have been impossible to trace her.

He was lucky. A block north, and thirty questions later, he found a newsboy who'd been at his stand all afternoon, and he'd seen Yolanda Lang; sure, he knew her. By sight, he explained. She'd passed him and turned west on Ohio Street.

Sweeney turned west on Ohio Street.

It wasn't too difficult. A gorgeous blonde in bright green, with a dog that looked like a fugitive from a James Oliver Curwood story. Within two blocks he found two people who had seen them.

In the third block, without turning off Ohio Street, he hit the jackpot. A tobacconist had not only seen girl and dog, he had seen them enter a building across the street—"the one right there, with the sign 'Furnished Rooms.'"

Sweeney entered the building with the sign that said "Furnished Rooms."

Just inside the door was a bell and a sign that said "Ring for Landlady." Sweeney rang for landlady.

She was big and slovenly; she had a mean eye. Sweet reasonableness wasn't going to work, and she didn't look as though she'd scare. Sweeney pulled out his wallet.

He took a twenty-dollar bill out of it, she could see the figure in the corner. He said, "I'd like to talk to the girl who took a room late this afternoon. The one with the dog."

She didn't even hesitate in reaching for the bill. It disappeared into the neckline of her dress, Into a bosom so redundant that Sweeney wondered if she'd be able to find a bill without searching. She said, "She took a room on the second floor—the door right opposite the head of the stairs."

Sweeney said, "Thanks." He took another bill, of the same denomination, from his wallet. She reached for that one, too, but he didn't give it to her. He said, "I'm rather curious to know the circumstances; what she told you and what she's done since she came here."

"What do you want with her? Who are you?"

Sweeney said, "Okay, it doesn't matter. I'll just go up and talk to her." He started to put the second twenty back into his wallet.

She said, very quickly, "She came here late this afternoon and wanted a room. I said we didn't take dogs and she said she'd pay extra if I did and that the dog was well behaved, so I gave her the room. She didn't have any baggage. Not even a coat or hat."

"How long did she say she'd be staying?"

"She didn't know. But she said she'd pay for a full week no matter how short a time she stayed."

"How much *did* she pay you?"

She hesitated. 'Twenty dollars."

Sweeney looked at her. He thought, *you bitch. And you sell her out for another twenty.* Aloud, he asked, "And since then?"

"She went out and left the dog in her room. She came back with a lot of packages. Then she took the dog down for a walk, on a leash; she hadn't had one on him before. And she was disguised; she had on a black wig and shell-rimmed glasses and a different dress. You'd have hardly knowed her."

"Was it a wig or a dye job?"

"A dye job couldn't have dried that quick."

"Anything else you can tell me about her?"

She thought for a moment, but shook her head. Sweeney held out the second bill, holding it carefully so his hand wouldn't be touched by hers. He watched its course into her capacious bosom and thought that for forty dollars he wouldn't reach down there to take his two twenties back.

Something In his expression made her take a step backwards.

And that was fine; Sweeney didn't want to have to brush against her as he went by and up the stairs. Halfway up, he heard her door slam. For forty dollars, she didn't care what he wanted with her new guest. Sweeney wished he hadn't given her any money; he could have got most of that information out of her anyway. He felt ashamed of himself for having taken the easy way.

And then he stood in front of the door on the second floor at the head of the stairs, and he quit thinking about the landlady who'd directed him there.

He tapped gently at the door.

There was a rustle of movement within, and it opened a few niches. Wide eyes stared at him through shell-rimmed glasses, under black hair. But the eyes themselves he'd seen before, and often. They'd stared at him blankly through the glass of a door on State Street on a night that seemed many years ago. They'd looked at him across a table at El Madhouse. They'd looked at him from the El Madhouse stage.

And they'd looked at him from the face of a small black statuette that screamed as silently as its model had screamed noisily.

Sweeney said, "Hello, Bessie Wilson."

Her eyes widened and she gasped. But she stepped back and Sweeney walked in.

It was a small room, and dingy. It contained a bed, a dresser and a chair, but Sweeney didn't notice them. To Sweeney, the room seemed full of dog. Even though the landlady had talked about the dog, even though he himself had been thinking about it and had traced Yolanda through it, he had somehow managed to overlook the fact that Devil would be here.

But Devil was. He crouched, ready to spring at Sweeney's throat. The sound that came from deep in Devil's chest was that ominous buzzsaw sound that Sweeney had heard once before.

Yolanda said, "Quiet, Devil. Guard him." She had closed the door.

Sweeney felt something wet on his forehead. He felt something cold crawling down his back. It came to him now that he had been so interested in solving a problem that he had completely forgotten the personal danger its solution would place him in.

He stared at Yolanda Lang—at Bessie Wilson. Even with the black wig, with the glasses, she was incredibly beautiful. Her only visible garment was a house-coat; under it, her feet were bare. The housecoat had a long zipper down the front.

,Sweeney wondered if—and then realized he didn't have time to wonder. He'd better say something, anything.

He said, "I finally figured it out, Bessie, except a few details. The doctor or psychiatrist from the sanitarium near Beloit, the one who took an interest in your case after—after what happened to you at Brampton. That must have been Doc Greene—wasn't it?"

He'd have felt better if she'd answered—even to say, uselessly, that she didn't know what he was talking about—but she didn't speak.

She took off the glasses and the wig and put them on the dresser beside the door. She shook her head and her blonde hair fell again into the pageboy bob. She regarded him gravely —but silently.

Sweeney's throat felt dry. He had to clear it before he could talk. He said, "It *must* have been Greene, whether he was using that name then or not. And he fell madly in love with you. Literally madly—so insanely that he ran out on his career to be with you. Or did he get into some trouble that made him have to leave his profession anyway?

"Did you know that he sent your brother a letter telling him that you had died? He did; Charlie thinks you're dead. But Greene must have signed papers to get you out, and then quit his Job to bring you to Chicago.

"He must have thought he'd cured you as nearly as you could be cured. He must have known that you'd never be fully sane, but figured that, as a psychiatrist, he could handle you and control you. And he could and did, I guess—until something that he didn't know about set you off. He was a pretty brilliant guy, Yolanda. I'll bet he did the choreography for that dance you and the dog do. And it's good, damned good. I wondered for a while why he didn't get you better bookings—but it must have been because he didn't dare risk letting you become really famous, under the circumstances. He kept you in the small time deliberately—as deliberately as he covered his real relationship to you, as doctor and patient, by becoming a bona fide agent and getting other clients." Sweeney cleared his throat again, hoping she'd say something.

She didn't She just looked at him. And the dog looked at him yellowly, ready to spring at the slightest word or signal from its mistress—or at the slightest move from Sweeney.

He said, "And you were all right until that day, two months ago, when you happened to go into Raoul's gift shop and bought that statuette from Lola Brent. Did you recognize that statuette, Yolanda?"

He thought she might answer that. She didn't.

He took a deep breath and the dog began to growl because his shoulders had moved. Sweeney stood very still and the dog quit growling.

He said, "Your brother Charlie made that statuette, Bessie. You were the model for it. It expressed, pretty perfectly, what you felt when—when the thing that drove you insane happened. Whether you recognized yourself in *the* statuette and knew that it was Charlie's work, I don't know. But seeing that statuette undid everything Doc Greene had done for you.

"Only there was a *transference*. Seeing yourself—in that statuette—as a *victim*, seeing yourself in that state from the outside, you became, in your mind, the attacker. The killer with the knife.

"And the woman from whom you bought the statuette was a beautiful blonde, and your mania fixed on her. You went out and bought a knife and waited, with it in your purse, until she left to go home. And because she was fired, it wasn't a long wait. You followed her home and killed, her—as the ripper in Brampton would have killed you if Charlie hadn't shot him. So—"

There wasn't anywhere to go from the "So—" and it hung there. When it got tired of hanging there, Sweeney said, "You took the statuette home and—did you make a fetish of it, Yolanda? It must have been something like that. Did you worship it, with a ritual that involved a knife? Or what?"

No answer yet, and he thought her eyes were starting to glaze a little, staring at him. He went on talking because he was afraid of what would happen when he stopped.

"And you killed twice more. Each time, a beautiful blonde. Each had passed your place on State Street just before she was killed. I'd guess that each time was just after some mystical ritual with the statuette after which you went down to the street and followed—and killed—the first woman who went by and who was blonde and beautiful, who fitted your fixation.

"And it wasn't until after that third killing that Doc Greene suddenly found out, or suddenly realized, that it was *you* who'd been doing them. He didn't know about the statuette then, but somehow he learned or realized who the Ripper was. And it scared him stiff. He would have been in a beautiful mess if the truth came out. They'd merely put you in an institution again, but Doc—I don't know exactly what grounds they'd get him on, but they'd get him plenty; they'd throw the book at him. So he tried something pretty desperate. Did you know it was he who attacked you that night, Yolanda?"

If she'd only answer—

He said, "Doc tried a really heroic cure. Shock treatment. He thought being attacked again might reverse your fixation—at least put you back into the type of insanity you had before. And *anything* would be better than having you homicidal. He probably figured he could handle anything short of homicidal insanity.

"So he attacked you that night in the hallway. Of course he wouldn't have used an ordinary knife or razor—because he didn't want to hurt you physically. What he used would have been a piece of wood, say, with a razor blade projecting out only an eighth of an inch or less, so it would make just a surface cut. And unorthodox as his psychiatry was, it worked —up to a point. If he'd known, then, about the statuette and had hunted it up in your apartment while you were in the hospital, you might not have gone haywire again.

"But he didn't know about the statuette until after I broke the story in today's paper. He must have had a hunch all along that I was going to crack this thing, though, because he kept in touch with me, pretending he was interested in getting the Ripper caught so *you'd* be safe from another attack. We had a lot of fun, Doc and I. I'm sorry he's—"

Sweeney took a deep breath. He said, "But when Doc read today's paper, he learned about the statuette and saw that it was what had set you off. So he decided to get it away from you right away. He went up to your flat this afternoon with an *empty* box that would hold it. He didn't want to-tie seen carrying a package *out* that he hadn't brought *in;* he didn't want anyone who might be watching your place to wonder what was in the package. He was still gambling his life to save you, and this time he lost.

"He found the statuette—in your dresser or closet or wherever you kept it—and the knife with it. He had both of them in his hands, and the sight of him touching your fetish threw you into—well, you sicked Devil on him, and Devil killed him."

Sweeney glanced down at Devil, and wished he hadn't.

He looked back at Bessie Wilson. He said, "You didn't know for sure whether he was dead or not, down there in the courtyard, and didn't know what he'd tell the police if he wasn't, so you ran. But he didn't tell on you, Yolanda. In-stead—because he knew he was dying—the damn fool took the rap for you; he said *he* was the Ripper. He must have thought, or at least hoped, that once the statuette was broken and you didn't have it any more, you'd be all right again, even without him."

He stared at her and opened his mouth to ask the sixty-five dollar question—*Are you? Are you all right now?*

But he didn't have to ask it, because the answer was there, in her eyes. Madness.

Her right hand fumbled for the tab of the zipper of her housecoat, found it, zipped downward. It fell down in a circle about her bare feet. Sweeney caught his breath a little, just as he had that night when he had looked through the glass into the hallway.

Reaching behind her, she opened the top left drawer of the dresser, felt inside it. Her hand came out holding a knife, a brand-new eight-inch carving knife.

A nude high priestess holding the sacrificial knife.

Sweeney sweated. He started to raise his hands and the dog growled and crouched before he'd moved them an inch. He quit moving them.

He made his voice quiet and steady. "Don't, Yolanda. I'm not the one you want to kill. I'm not blonde or beautiful. I'm not a prototype of Bessie Wilson who was attacked by a maniac—"

He was watching her eyes and it came to him that she didn't understand a word he was saying by now, that the connection had broken, just when he did not know. Yet she had started a step forward when he had stopped speaking and had stood still, the knife in her hand and ready—but words, the sound of his voice, had arrested her in midstep. Words, not what he said, but the fact that he was talking—

Her foot was moving again, the knife coming up. Again Sweeney took the mere ghost of a backward step, and again the dog growled and crouched to spring at his throat.

"Four score and seven years ago," Sweeney said, "our fathers brought forth on this continent a new nation, conceived in liberty and dedicated to the proposition that all men are created equal. . . ."

Yolanda stood still again, an almost cataleptic stillness.

Sweat was running down Sweeney's sides, from his armpits. He said, "Now we are engaged in a great civil war, testing whether—uh—that nation—That's all I remember. Mary had a little lamb; its fleece was white as snow. . . ."

He finished Mary and the lamb, hit high spots of the *Rubaiyat,* Hamlet's soliloquy. After a while he remembered that he could repeat himself, and after another while he found that—if he did it a sixteenth of an inch at a time—he could ease his way back toward the wall behind him and, finally, lean against it.

But he couldn't move, even a sixteenth of an inch, toward the door or toward Yolanda. He couldn't raise his hands.

And after a tune—a long time—his voice was so tired he couldn't talk any more. But he kept on talking anyway. If he stopped talking for as much as ten seconds he was going to die.

Sweeney, could tell from the one small window of the room, on the side opposite from the wall he leaned against that it was dark outside. Years later a clock somewhere tolled midnight. Centuries after that, the window began to get light again.

". . . Beneath a spreading chestnut tree," said Sweeney hoarsely, "the village smithy stands. The smith, a mighty man is he, beneath the spreading chestnut tree. A rose by any other name would waste its fragrance on the desert air, and all our yesterdays have lighted fools the way to dusty death. And when the pie was opened, they all began to sing. . . ."

Every muscle of his body ached. He marveled, with what was left of his mind, at how Yolanda could stand there—incredibly beautiful, incredibly naked—and not move at all. Catalepsy, of course, hypnosis, whatever you called it, it was hard to believe—

". . . Alas, poor Yorick!" said Sweeney. "I knew him, Horatio: a fellow of infinite jest, of most excellent—uh—The owl and the pussycat went to sea, in a beautiful pea green boat . . ."

It got lighter, slowly. It was nine o'clock in the morning before there was a knock at the door. An authoritative knock.

Sweeney raised his voice, with as much effort as it would have taken him to raise a piano. It was a hoarse croak. "Bline? Come in with your gun ready. The dog will, jump one of us."

The dog, growling, had moved to a position where he could watch both Sweeney and the knocked-on door. But the door moved and Sweeney didn't, and the dog jumped at Bline, in the doorway. But Bline had been warned; his coat was wrapped around his forearm, and as the dog leaped and closed its jaws on the coat, the barrel of Bline's pistol tapped the dog's skull.

"The mouse ran up the clock," Sweeney was saying in r, voice that wasn't much above a hoarse whisper; "the clock struck one—Thank Heaven you finally came, Cap. I knew you'd see holes in Doc's story when you had time to think it out and that you'd come looking for Yolanda and get to her the same way I did. Listen, Cap, I have to keep on talking and I can't stop. She isn't even looking at you and doesn't know what's going on except that if I stop talking—Walk up on her from that side and get the knife—"

Bline got the knife. Sweeney, still mumbling hoarsely, slid slowly down the wall.

And then it was late evening. Godfrey was there on the park bench and Sweeney sat down beside him. "Thought you were working," God said.

"I was. But I broke such a big story Wally let me talk him into getting off a while without pay. A week, two weeks, or whenever I get back."

"You sound hoarse, Sweeney. Did you spend a night with that dame you were raving about?"

"That's why I'm hoarse," said Sweeney. "Listen, God, this time I left money, quite a bit of money, with my landlady. But I held out three hundred. Do you think we can get drunk on three hundred bucks?"

God turned his shaggy head to look at Sweeney. "If we want to badly enough. If you want something badly enough, you can get anything you want, Sweeney. Like spending a night with that dame. I told you you could."

Sweeney shuddered. He pulled two flat pint bottles out of the side pockets of his coat and handed one of them to God. . . .